SANGRE DE CRISTO

A Novel

SANGRE DE CRISTO

A Novel

For Donna,
Merry Christmas
2004

Leonard Davies

To order additional copies of this book, contact:
Xlibris Corporation
1-888-795-4274
www.Xlibris.com
Orders@Xlibris.com
23675

For Olivia, Emlyn, and Harrison.

CHAPTER 1

Sam Curran stood on the balcony of his hacienda looking over the valley that was the Sangre de Cristo land grant. It had been in the Curran family for over a hundred years. His grandfather had come to the southwest after the war with Mexico in 1846 and seized it from the Mexicans who had been given it by the king of Spain. When he got control it was 6000 square miles of flat, semi-desert land. Now it was the richest agricultural land in seven states.

On the far horizon, nearly fifty miles away, rose the peaks of the Fremont Mountains, still snowcapped in early June. At their foot sat the Sand Dunes, the wind-blown hills of mocha colored sand that mimicked in their shape the granite mountains that towered above them. All that grew on the dunes was yucca, a mean, prickly plant also called Spanish Bayonet. The Sand Dunes were the remains of the once great inland sea that had covered this valley, which was now as flat as the lake had been in prehistoric times.

Curran had built the hacienda to resemble an Indian pueblo. It was strategically placed high in the foothills of the mountains that bordered the east side of the valley halfway between the north and south boundary lines of the grant. Behind it was the range of mountains that gave the Sangre de Cristo its name.

The sun had dropped behind the mountains. The late afternoon light made the entire valley vibrate with the colors of the growing fields. It was early summer and the fields, planted in round patterns for the sprinkler systems, were brilliant green. The non-irrigated land was light brown earth and grass.

Today the prehistoric lake was a hundred feet under the surface, one of the largest underground bodies of water in the country. Pumping water from the lake beneath watered every inch of ground that was used for growing. The barren land was covered with dirt roads or buildings.

The Curran family had fought bitterly, sometimes ruthlessly, to make it into a rich feudal empire of almost four million acres. The family owned it all. They owned the fields; the packinghouses and canneries; the ten towns in the valley; even the people who in every aspect of their lives owed their existence to the Currans. Someone was always trying to take it from them, of course, or change it. The workers wanted more money; the cities in the region wanted the water; the locals wanted to own their own land; the politicians wanted more power. So far, in every instance, the Currans had gotten their way.

Sam Curran's grandfather had obtained ownership of the entire valley in 1854, after the war with Mexico. His son used the land to build a vast empire that was now one of the biggest in the nation. When Sam took over in the thirties he began to use sprinkler systems to pump water from the great underwater lake to irrigate crops. With canning, then freezing and refrigeration he was able to turn the valley into the country's biggest supplier of summer vegetables.

Now Sam Curran wondered if it could continue that way for the next hundred years. He was eighty-three and knew that his time was short. The pressures for change had increased over the past few years. Legislation in congress proposed new laws for migrant workers. The burgeoning cities had increased their demands for the valley's water. The residents were beginning to chafe under the feudal way of life. Crime was increasing and reports of corruption in the local government agencies came with more frequency. These were the reasons he wanted Alfred to come back to the valley.

It had been fifteen years since Alfred had lived there. He'd gone to the east to attend prep school, college and then law school. After he got his law license he decided to stay in New York and practice securities law. He met his socialite wife Patricia a few years later. As far as Curran could tell Alfred was happy with the social life New York offered.

Sam had married late in life. There were fifty-two years difference between him and his son. Alfred's mother had died when he was two years old. Sam wasn't up to raising him and had turned that job over to Isabella and Eduardo Romero the hacienda's cook and valet. They had been with him over thirty-five years. Sam and Alfred had more of a business relationship than one of father and son.

Sam sighed with some regret but accepted the past for what it was and forced himself to concentrate on the future. His years were limited and he intended to do everything he could in his remaining time to ensure that the land grant would continue exactly as it was for generations to come. His only hope was Alfred. He wasn't convinced Alfred was up to it, but he knew he had to try. Alfred and Patricia had arrived that morning to attend a weekend party to celebrate Sam's 84th birthday. During the time they were there, he hoped to convince Alfred to return to the valley and take over its operation.

The crepuscular light behind the mountains was fading into night, the way Sam's time to save the valley was. He had a meeting with Alfred in a few minutes and before turning to go into the library he scanned the land he so loved one more time. He knew his next few days would determine the valley's future and Alfred's future. He knew that if Alfred agreed to return he would face some difficult times. In his wildest dreams Sam Curran couldn't have guessed just how difficult those times would be.

CHAPTER 2

When Sam went back into the library he found Eduardo Romero putting a decanter of water on the desk. Eduardo looked up as Sam came in.

"Sam," Eduardo said. "When you had this room made soundproof they did a great job. Today when the man was here installing the equipment in the desk I couldn't hear his electric drill even when I stood just outside the closed doors."

"I'd forgotten he was coming today" Sam replied. "How does it work?"

"It's very simple. He showed me everything. It's what they call voice activated. In other words, it turns on automatically when it hears voices and stops when the voices stop."

"Did you learn how to change the tape?"

"Yes, but that won't happen very soon. He said the tape would record sixty hours of conversations before a change is necessary. That will take a long time."

While Eduardo was explaining everything Sam had walked around the large oak desk. "I can't see anything," he said. "He did a good job. Where are the microphones?" Eduardo took him to each side of the desk and pointed out a microphone recessed out of sight in the overhang of the top.

"Does anyone else know about the recorder?" Sam asked.

"No, just the man who installed them and the two of us. He's from Denver, and he probably won't have another job in the valley the rest of his life. In fact he'd never been to the valley before this."

Eduardo left the library and closed the heavy doors behind him. Unlike the rest of the hacienda, which had many windows, the library had only the sliding glass doors onto the balconies on the east and west sides. All the other walls were covered with bookshelves with the exception of the heavy oak doors leading into the library from the house. It was Sam Curran's sanctuary and war room. Its heavy beams, its massive thick walls and doors let no sound enter or leave, giving the room an almost vault-like feeling. He'd made sure that everything said there was private.

There was a knock on the door. Sam opened it to find his son Alfred. Sam greeted him warmly. "Alfred," he said shaking his hand. "You look terrific. I'm sorry I wasn't here to meet the plane. I had some business with the city council in El Centro."

"Think nothing of it, father," Alfred responded. "We were a little tired from the flight and it was nice to rest for awhile." Sam was pleased to see his son. It had been two years since their last visit. During that time Alfred had continued to put on weight. The tuxedo he was wearing for the party that night, as beautifully tailored as it was, couldn't hide the fact that he was fifty pounds overweight.

Alfred's blue eyes came from his father but his olive skin and black hair was from his mother. His good looks were diminished considerably by the fact of his being overweight. His appearance was of one who didn't work or workout and who led an indulgent lifestyle. At thirty-two he was too young to have given himself over to the physique of a much older man.

"How was the flight?" Sam asked as he led Alfred to a couch and chairs at one end of the room.

"Uneventful," Alfred said sitting down in one of the chairs. "Of course that is the way I like all my flights to be. The charter from Denver was particularly beautiful. I asked the pilot to fly us along the west side of the valley, then rather low along the Sangre de Cristos on this side. Patricia isn't the best flyer but she was very impressed by the scenery."

"How is Patricia?" Sam thought he saw just a flicker of concern cross Alfred's face before he answered.

"She's a little tired from the trip and is lying down."

"Good. I can't wait to see her. Does she need anything? I can have Eduardo take something to her."

"No, thank you. She's fine." Both men paused lost momentarily in their own thoughts, and then Sam spoke again.

"Alfred, I'm glad the two of you could come back for this party. There are a lot of people coming that I'd like you to meet. But I'm also glad because I think it's time we talked about the Sangre de Cristo. I know in the past you've expressed your desire to live in New York and practice securities law. I admit the valley doesn't hold the glamour the East Coast does. But I don't have a great many years left and I don't have as much energy as I used to have. I have to think about the future as it might be without me."

"Father," Alfred interjected, "you look awfully fit to me. I'm sure you have many productive years before you."

"That's nice of you to say, Alfred, but I'm afraid your observation may be colored by more affection than fact. It may very well be that I have many years to go, but the reality is that I must plan for the alternative." Alfred didn't respond.

Sam continued. "I've always regretted that I married so late. Now as I reach the end of my life I know we haven't had as much time together as I would like."

Alfred began to speak. "No," Sam held up his hand. "Let me finish. It has been even more difficult because your mother died when you were so young, and I think my grief prevented me from being as close to you as I should have been. But we can't change the past or control the future. We must deal the cards we have." Sam poured Alfred and himself some water from a crystal decanter.

"It's my greatest dream that you come back here and live, and that we have what years remain to me to make up for some of the lost time. It's also my dream that you be able to save the Sangre and keep it in the family for many generations to come."

Alfred sat forward in his chair and looked at his hands. "Father, I've always felt that the life I wanted to lead is in New York. I love the opera, the symphony, and the art museums. Everything I want is there and not here. There's nothing I want more than to be closer to you, but if I came here just to make you feel better and made myself miserable it would be self defeating. It wouldn't work."

"I know your feelings," Sam responded, "and I respect them, but please don't give me a final answer now. I want you to think about it and I want you to know a little more about the situation before deciding."

"All right," said Alfred. "What did you mean when you said your dream was that I could save the Sangre? That sounds rather ominous."

"Ever since your great-grandfather got title to this land there have been attempts to take it away. There have been lawsuits that claim he got it illegally. Several groups have sued to have the land returned to the people who were named in the original land grant. Some firebrand in New Mexico even declared that one of the grants was a separate country. Caused quite a stir, even shot up the Tierra Amarilla courthouse. Of course he didn't get anywhere, but now that the states realize we're sitting on enough water to serve their needs for a hundred years they are taking a different look at these cases."

"Also there is the migrant labor problem. Every year the labor organizers get louder and get more people to sign up. I don't know how long we can hold the line. Today I was told there's a vigilante group running an extortion racket. The list goes on. Every time I turn around there seems to be another problem. Let's face it, Alfred, in some parts of the world we own what amounts to a small country. There are a lot of people that would like to have all or part of it."

"Can't we hire lawyers to fight?"

"For some of the things, yes. But there are other problems that need someone here. I'm afraid if you try to be an absentee landlord we'll eventually lose." Sam looked at his watch. "I lost track of the time," he said. "I'd better go and change for the party. We'll have more time to talk about these things. In fact tonight I've asked Senator McNamara to discuss some of them with us." He got up and started for the door. "Will Patricia feel well enough to attend the party?" he asked.

"Yes," Alfred replied. "In fact I'm due to meet her in the small salon now."

CHAPTER 3

When Alfred opened the door to the small salon, Patricia was sitting on a white couch directly across the room. There were chairs on either side of the couch and a small table in front. A Folwell landscape of the Sangre de Cristo valley was above the couch. The light that illuminated the painting reflected onto her hair. The picture of her sitting there took his breath away. For the moment any thoughts and concerns he had about their relationship were pushed aside, and he reveled in her beauty.

The royal blue taffeta gown she was wearing framed her head and shoulders. The gown was cut low enough to expose the upper swell of her bosom just enough to let the observer know that what was shown was merely a delicious hint of what was covered. Her skin had tanned to the color of a polished light wood. At her throat was the diamond and sapphire necklace he'd given her as a wedding present. Her long neck led to a finely yet softly sculpted face. Her sensual lips suggested a passion that Alfred knew wasn't there.

"Patricia you look lovely," Alfred said as he closed the door. Patricia only patted the small armchair across from her and indicated she wanted him to sit there. If he'd been a stranger telling her how nice she looked, she would have responded graciously to the compliment. She knew she looked lovely and took the statement from Alfred as her due.

Alfred had married Patricia shortly after his graduation from law school. They met through mutual friends, and she was everything he thought he wanted in a wife. She'd gone to all the proper finishing schools and had learned all the ways to charm members of the opposite sex. It was only after the honeymoon that Alfred realized it was a triumph of form over substance. Her beauty and charm never translated into passion. Her intellectual curiosity never went beyond the inanities of New York society.

Patricia spent all her days concerned with introductions into new and better social circles while maintaining her position in those which she felt were inferior. Each night they went to some social function designed, so far as Alfred could see, for gossiping, networking and social climbing. There was never time for the deep development of a personal relationship between them so their love life was infrequent and unimaginative.

In the beginning Alfred had enjoyed the nonstop socializing as much as Patricia, but it was beginning to wear thin. He felt their life was merely a facade surrounding a hollow core. And the constant partying was a drain on the energy he would rather expend on his law practice and his interests in the arts.

Patricia had come to realize that their life wasn't fulfilling but couldn't articulate why. She enjoyed being involved with all the power brokers her socializing brought her in contact with but she realized she was only an observer and didn't have the power base to be taken seriously. Out of frustration, she found herself turning to alcohol and pills to help her through the days.

As so often happens in unhappy marriages, the communication had broken down-if it ever really existed-and each attributed to the other thoughts and feelings that were the opposite of the truth. Alfred's feeling that Patricia would rebel at any suggestion of moving back to the valley was wrong. Alfred assumed that life in the valley away from her social connections would drive Patricia crazy. He couldn't conceive that she would agree to live there. Patricia, on the other hand, had a growing resentment for what she saw in Alfred as weakness and lack of ambition. The more she found out about the Sangre, the more she realized that being in control of it would provide the power she craved.

She'd done her homework about what the Sangre was worth. The valley was an opportunity to rule an area as big as a state. It would be a state where Alfred would be king and she would be his queen. It would be power that would allow her to do everything she wished. Senators, mayors, governors and giants of industry would pay court to them. The money from the valley was endless. The treatment they would receive in New York as owners and operators of the Sangre would be far greater than it was now.

"Tell me something about tonight," she said as Alfred sat down. She took a glass from the table next to her and drank from it. He noticed a slight tremble in her hand. Alfred knew from experience that it was her drink of choice. Straight scotch.

"I thought you knew everything about it," he answered. "It's father's birthday and a chance to introduce you to our friends."

"Alfred, don't be stupid." Patricia's voice took on the condescending note that often crept into their conversations. "I know the social reason we're having it, but what is the real reason? What is the agenda? Who are we trying to win over or get something from? People like your father don't have lavish affairs like this unless he needs something. I want to know what he's trying to accomplish."

"There are several reasons," answered Alfred, a little surprised at her curiosity. "There's a bill in congress called the Migrant Workers Relief Act that will make it much more expensive to hire the migrant workers who work here. I know father is opposed to that. Several of the guests are politically well placed. I'm sure he wants to convince them that their interests are in defeating the bill."

"Is there anything else?"

"There's a lot of pressure from many of the cities in this area to buy the water in the valley and have it piped to them."

"What water?" Patricia asked. "There hasn't been a cloud in the sky since I've been here. There is no river in the valley. What water are they talking about?"

Alfred smiled. Patricia was right. To the casual observer of the valley it would seem more like a desert than rich agricultural land. There were no rivers and very little rainfall.

"Thousand of years ago this valley was a great inland sea over a hundred miles long and almost as wide. Over the ages the water has dropped below the surface to become a massive underground reservoir. We have no idea how deep it's. Along with the Ogalalla aquifer in Kansas and Nebraska it's the largest underground reservoir in the country. The world for all I know. We pump it into those irrigation sprinklers to water the crops, but we only use a small amount and most of it returns to the lake."

"What is it worth?"

"Hundreds of millions of dollars. Maybe billions, depending on how much there is."

"Wouldn't it be easier to sell the water than manage all these farms and everything that goes with it?"

"It might be easier, but the one thing father and I are in complete agreement on is that we will not sell the water. We don't know what would happen to the land if we begin to move the water. The valley is important as a flyway for birds, and we protect them. There are many people here who live off the land. We just don't think it makes sense to pump the water to cities that will deplete it forever."

"But the money," Patricia began. Alfred shut her off.

"We have enough money," he said.

Patricia looked at him for a moment. "Alfred, I simply don't understand you sometimes. You don't want to manage the valley. You would rather be in New York going to the symphony or art museum. You would rather read Marcus Cicero . . ."

"Marcus Aurelius."

"Whatever, than care about the profit and loss of this valley. And yet you get all teary eyed over a bunch of birds and the people and their land. It doesn't make much sense"

"It really does make sense Patricia. And we're not going to sell the water. Believe me. Not while father is alive and not while I'm alive.

Patricia changed the subject. "Whom should I pay particular attention to tonight?"

"Well everyone invited is a friend, so just being charming will be enough for most. Senator McNamara is very important. He's the chairman of the Senate subcommittee that's holding hearings on the migrant workers bill and we are counting on him to defeat it."

"Will he?"

"Of course. He'll do what father wants, besides the migrants don't vote or deliver votes. Father delivers votes and large amounts of money, so he'll get his way. This will also be your first meeting with my special friend Father Augustine Romero. Augustine is now a priest and has just returned to the valley. His mother is Isabella and his father is Eduardo, my father's aide.

Patricia was quiet for a moment then she said, "Whoever runs this valley has an awful lot of power. Don't you think it may be a mistake not to come back?"

"I don't want the power, Patricia. I want the money to do what I want to do. I want to travel and enjoy all the centers of civilization in the world. I want to meet all the people who run the world. I want to live and practice law in New York. That's what I want to do."

"Aren't you afraid someone will take this from you?"

"I don't think that is a possibility. They'd have to kill me to do it, and I don't think there is anyone who would do that. There's no reason."

There was a knock on the door and one of the servants came in. "Mr. Curran sends his regrets," he said. "He won't have time to join you here before the guests arrive. He'd like you to join him in the receiving line."

CHAPTER 4

Father Augustine, the son of Isabella and Eduardo Romero, could see the luminarios of the hacienda from several miles away as he drove the bishop past the planted fields of the flat valley. The driveway leading from the gates and all the walls, roofs and balconies had been decorated with the traditional candles in paper sacks. There was still enough light in the sky to give outline to the massive peaks that served as a backdrop to the estate.

The hacienda was located fifteen miles from the town of El Centro, where Augustine's church was located, and the route was flat until it made a short climb through the foothills.

Before the use of efficient irrigation, the land in the valley would be under water in the spring when the snow from the adjacent mountains melted. Now the water was harnessed and delivered evenly to the land. Each 160 acres was irrigated by large center pivot sprinkler systems that rotated slowly and delivered a steady even mist of water to the crops. It was an indication of how valuable this land had become when one realized that each of these watering systems cost over $50,000.

"Augustine," said the bishop. "Tell me about this wonderful rich land and the people that live here and own it. I recall from your records that you were born here."

"Yes. And my father before me and his father and his father's father, and his father's father. How many is that? Well, no matter, we have been here over three hundred and fifty years. The Romero family was one of the first families to settle here. We came to the valley when it was part of Spain. After we arrived all the families petitioned the king of Spain to give us the land for our use. When Mexico became independent from Spain it honored all the grants. The families held all this land jointly. After the war with Mexico in 1848 all the land that is now the southwest was taken by the United States."

"When did the Currans become the owners?" the bishop asked.

"I believe it was about 1854," Augustine answered. "The land had been guaranteed to the native owners by the treaty of Guadalupe Hidalgo. Soon all the grants were seized by enterprising Americans who got the congress to ignore the treaty."

"What are the boundaries of the grant?"

"You see the mountains in front of us," said Augustine. "They are the eastern boundary. As you know they are also called the Sangre de Cristo. The mountains behind us are called the Fremont Mountains. The entire grant lies between the two ranges. It's more long than wide. In fact you can think of it as a cross. At the north is the town of Del Norte. At the south is the town of Linda Vista. On the west, about where the end of the cross bar would be, is the town of La Garita and on the east the village of Arboles. El Centro, where I live, is just where the two bars of the cross intersect."

"And using this description we are reminded of our lord," said the bishop "Where is the hacienda?"

"Just there in front of us in the foothills of the mountains. Mr. Curran tried to build it as close as possible to the center between north and south. You will see when we get there it has a wonderful view of the entire grant."

The bishop was silent for a moment. Then he said, "let's talk of the present," he said. "You're very fortunate to have this parish, Augustine. It's much richer than any of its neighbors. You have two very good schools as part of the parish and, unlike some of your colleagues outside the valley, you will be able to do many good things here."

"Yes," said Augustine, "I'm very lucky. But there are problems."

"Really?" asked the Bishop in a surprised tone. "Everything seems so good. What problems are you talking about?"

"There are two problems that I believe are related" Augustine answered. "The first and most obvious is the plight of the migrant workers. They are badly exploited. They work hard for meager wages and poor living conditions. They are caught up in a cycle of despair. They can never make enough money to permit their children to get out of the fields and get an education. The result is that each generation is no better off than the previous one."

"This surprises me," said the bishop. "I've heard that Mr. Curran is very generous in his payment of the workers."

"That's the problem," Augustine replied. "The money paid by the Currans is generous. But it doesn't all stay with the workers. After they receive it they must pay extortion to gang bosses for the work. And they must pay kickbacks to others for their housing. I'm sure the Currans are not even aware of it."

"If it's not the Curran's that are responsible then who is?"

"To appreciate that you must first know a little history. In this part of the country, among the Hispanic population, there has always been a secret society called *La Mano Negra*. The Black Hand. Sometimes the Anglos refer to it as the Mexican mafia. This society can be benevolent or evil, depending on its leaders. Here it's very bad. Since its members are secret I don't know whether they are outsiders or people here in the valley. Whoever they are they make everyone pay. If people don't pay they are beaten."

"Do you have any suspicions about who they are?"

"Not about individuals. I believe it's people who live in the valley all the time."

"Why do you believe that?"

"Because they are never caught. I think they are close to the law enforcement or part of it. Also because almost all the exploitation is of the migrant workers. Only rarely are permanent residents bothered and that is only when they have spoken out on behalf of the migrants."

"What happens then?"

"So far they have only been beaten. But each time it gets worse."

"Are you frightened for yourself?"

"Yes, but I must continue the fight to gain rights for the workers. Will the archbishop support me?"

"I don't see that as a problem, Augustine," the Bishop responded. "Just follow the procedures for requesting expenditures for projects and I'll give them my personal attention."

"I'm afraid it's more than money. I believe it will take the moral authority of the church to change the way they are treated."

"This may be more difficult," the bishop answered. "We mustn't offend the very people that contribute so much to the treasury. We need their support to do the good things we do. Let's try to cure the problem with money first. In the meantime I'll expect a report from you on what you wish to do with our moral authority, and I'll discuss it with the archbishop."

Before Augustine could go any further with the conversation they arrived at the hacienda.

CHAPTER 5

Anthony Marquez stood before the mirror in the bedroom of his home in El Centro and tied his black bow tie. He took pride in the fact that he would be one of the few at the Curran party that tied his own tie. Most of the others would have ties that were tied when they bought them and then clipped around the neck. When he was first invited to the formal parties at the hacienda he'd struggled to learn how to make the tie look like a perfect bow. Now he always looked forward to the end of the evening when things were more relaxed and he could untie the bow and let each end hang down the front of his shirt. He considered it a challenge to the *gringos* around him. It was a silent way of saying to them that, for all their self-sense of superiority, here was a challenge on their own turf from a working Mexican.

It was small victories like these and others that helped Anthony deal with his anger. All of his 70 years he felt he'd been treated as a second-rate person by the Currans and their power broker friends who attended the parties. For all his years Anthony had dealt with his anger in a variety of ways. A small act of perceived superiority such as the bow tie was one way. There were other more important ways, which included wielding power and using force.

The ancestors of Anthony Marquez had been one of the original families to be named in the Sangre de Cristo land grant. Only his family, the Romero family, and the Martinez families had remained on the land. The others had all drifted away.

In those days the land was marginal. It had no water except artesian wells that rose to the surface in scattered locations around the valley. The land was mostly sagebrush and some wild grass. It was hot in the summer and bitterly cold in the winter. Because the land wasn't productive and making a living was difficult, most of the families who lived there ultimately moved to more hospitable land. Some of them went to Santa Fe. Others moved to more prosperous farm and ranch land, such as the Tierra Amarilla grant in northern New Mexico.

Only the Marquez, Romero, and Martinez families believed that by staying on the land it would be theirs forever. Then, in the 1850's, when the gringos came to the territories after the war with Mexico, there weren't many locals to fight for the land. Men like the Currans found it easy to take ownership of it.

Anthony's grandfather had hired a lawyer in Santa Fe to fight to preserve the rights of the original grant holders. But Santa Fe was two hundred miles away. There wasn't much he could do. Anthony had always been told that the lawyer in Santa Fe was bought off. The bottom line was that the treaties that guaranteed the rights of families such as the Marquezes were swept away, and the Currans were declared the owners of the Sangre de Cristo.

Under the Currans, the Marquez family silently accepted the loss of the land they believed was theirs. Instead of fighting the situation, they had gone to work for the Currans. They were ambitious and resourceful and with each generation they became more powerful.

By the time Anthony's father died, all the operations in the valley were controlled in one way or another by the Marquez family. Curran had the vision and the great profits, but the Marquez family quietly built its own fiefdom within the larger one. Now, next to Sam Curran, Anthony and his son Richard were the most powerful men in the valley.

In fact, Anthony and Richard managed the entire civic and economic well being of the valley. The Currans took all the profits. But the amount skimmed by the Marquezes before the profits was enormous. They decided who got the jobs in the valley, they controlled the votes in the valley and they hired all the law enforcement. They decided who would be the district attorney and who would be the judges. And when Richard returned from law school two years ago they made him district attorney.

Anthony had worked too hard and too long to get where he was. He felt he'd recovered the grant for his family in everything but name. He wasn't going to let it slip away. But maintaining the control became more difficult each year. Outsiders put constant pressure on the valley for change. Civil rights groups questioned whether corruption existed in the small towns and in the courts. Each year there were attempts to organize the migrant workers. This year the organizers seemed more articulate and determined than ever.

He'd just finished adjusting his bow tie when the door opened and his son, Richard, came in.

"Richard" he said. "You aren't dressed yet. We have to leave soon."

"I want you to go without me," Richard replied. "I'll join you later."

"Why not come now?" His father asked.

"The migrant workers union is having a meeting to organize the workers at Linda Vista. I understand that Michael Chacon will be there. This might be a good time to make him understand that it's best for him to leave the valley."

"Is this the Chacon that's having so much success organizing the workers?"

"Yes," Richard replied. "He and his friend Alberto Falcon are very good. They're by far the best ones the union has ever sent."

Anthony considered this for a moment. "Richard, we must do something about him. Once the union gets the workers organized our position will be threatened. Much of our profits are based on the kickbacks we get from the workers. With the union representing them it will be over."

"That's why I'm not going to the party with you. I think it's time Chacon was given a more physical reason why he should leave the valley. I'm sending some members of the Black Hand to the meeting. By the time I get there they'll have Chacon tied-up and ready for the whip. After tonight he may want to be somewhere else."

"Wouldn't it be best if you left it to someone else?" Anthony asked. "What if you are recognized? Now that you're district attorney it will be difficult to explain being involved."

"Don't worry I'll wear the hood. Besides I won't be there long. When I'm finished I'll come here and change and go to the hacienda. I'm sure I'll be there in plenty of time."

Anthony thought for a moment. "Richard," Anthony asked, "do things get more difficult each year or am I just growing old? Each year there seems to be a new group or agency coming to inspect the valley. I feel it's becoming more difficult to maintain control."

"Papa," said Richard, "you've worked very hard for many years. You've deserved a rest. Perhaps compared to years past it's more difficult. Because of your hard work I've returned with the new power of being a lawyer. As long as we control the courts, the police, and the workers, we will run the valley."

"What about Alfred Curran? What if he returns to run the business? Won't that make it more difficult?" Anthony asked.

"My sources say it's unlikely he'll return. He likes the social life in New York too much. Believe me he and that socialite wife won't want to live here no matter how nice the hacienda is. It's too isolated. Really father, the future looks better than the past. Soon John Taylor will retire and I've already arranged for his successor as lawyer for the corporation. It's someone who sees things our way and understands the economics of the situation. After we send Chacon and Falcon packing we'll be right where we want to be. It'll be no problem to keep Alfred Curran in the dark so long as we send him enough money to support his life style." Richard got up to leave.

"I hope you're right," said Anthony. "But what if the old man convinces Alfred to come back and run the operation. What then?"

"Then we may have to arrange an early retirement for him," said Richard.

CHAPTER 6

The main patio of the hacienda had been lavishly decorated for the party.

At one end a bar had been set up. At the other, ten round tables were tastefully set for dinner. The patio was decorated with lanterns and luminarios that gave a soft vespertine glow to the adobe walls. Potted plants gave color and perfume to the warm night air.

When Patricia and Alfred joined Sam Curran on the patio of the hacienda, several of the guests had arrived and were congregated near the bar enjoying cocktails. One of the guests that Sam introduced them to was Senator McNamara. The Senator owned a ranch that adjoined the land grant, and his eighteen years in the United States Senate was largely due to Sam Curran. It was a mutually beneficial relationship. McNamara got to be the Senator he'd always longed to be and Sam had a vote he could always count on. The Senator had flown in from Washington for the party.

Shortly after the exchange of pleasantries Alfred saw Augustine Romero come through the open French doors from the house onto the patio.

"Would you excuse us?" he said to his father and the others. "I see an old friend I would like to say hello to and introduce him to Patricia." There were murmurs of assent from the group, and he and Patricia intercepted Augustine near the doors.

"Alfred!" exclaimed Augustine as the two threw their arms around each other in an *abrazo*. "It's been too long. Let me look at you." Augustine stood back from Alfred. "Ah," he said. "No more the slender youth, but you look wonderful."

"And you," said Alfred, "still slender but no longer a youth." He turned to Patricia. "Augustine, I want you to meet my wife Patricia."

Augustine extended his hand. "I've heard a great deal about you," he said. "But nothing I've heard prepared me for how beautiful you are. This is a real pleasure."

"Thank you," Patricia replied. Augustine then presented the bishop to both of them and after an exchange of pleasantries Patricia volunteered to introduce the bishop to other guests and left Alfred and Augustine alone.

Augustine was surprised at the change in his friend. When they had last been together Alfred was an athletic, slim man who exuded fitness. Now he was fat and out of condition. "Alfred, I don't know whether the city life agrees with you or not. You obviously do not have the same opportunities to exercise." Alfred laughed.

"No," he said, "my law practice and the social whirl don't seem to leave much time."

"Perhaps you should come back here," said Augustine finding the opening he sought to raise the question.

"My father tells me the same thing," Alfred responded. "I don't think it's in the cards, but tell me the reasons you think I should return?"

"There's much in the valley that's not right," Augustine replied. "People are taken advantage of and the workers are mistreated."

"By whom?" Alfred asked. "Are you suggesting my father does this?" Alfred's voice had an edge to it.

"No, of course not," Augustine protested. "That's part of the problem. Your father and John Taylor have earned the chance to enjoy these years and retirement. They can't keep up with everything. What's happening is without their knowledge, I'm sure of that. That's why it's important that you return. We need a Curran here who is young and able to spend the energy solving the problems." Before Alfred could respond he heard a voice from behind him.

"Padre, are you preaching your socialism again?" Alfred turned and faced Richard Marquez who had just arrived. Richard didn't wait for an answer. He extended his hand to Alfred. "I'm Richard Marquez," he said. "I don't think we've seen each other for twenty years."

"Has it been that long?" Alfred asked shaking the outstretched hand.

"Surely it hasn't been that long!" Augustine exclaimed. Then he thought for a moment as if counting the years. "I suppose that's right. Alfred left for school in the east when he was twelve and we were left to make do."

As the three men spoke Patricia excused herself and started toward them. When Richard Marquez stepped through the doors leading onto the terrace from the house Patricia had been looking in that direction. She was fascinated by what she saw. The tuxedo Richard was wearing for the party fit his athletic frame perfectly. Instead of the traditional black bow tie he wore a bolo tie, a woven black leather cord around the neck drawn together at the throat by a large turquoise stone inlaid in beautifully worked silver.

He was over six feet but his wide shoulders and narrow hips made him seem shorter. His eyes were a turquoise color, which showed even more brilliant against the olive color of his skin.

The deep black color of his hair and his skin, like highly polished wood, gave him the dark brooding good looks of an Aztec god. His looks, while darkly handsome, were more dark than handsome. His quick smile, which showed white, even teeth, served him well in breaking down barriers with strangers. But it was a smile that never seemed to work its way into his eyes. The overall effect was a strange combination of warm friendliness and something sinister.

As she walked toward them Patricia noted the difference between Richard and Augustine. It was as much in appearance as in fact. Augustine was as frail as Richard was strong. Richard's appearance had an aura of strength and domination, while Augustine's was one of frailty and vulnerability. Augustine's posture always seemed halfway between standing upright and the genuflection that was so much a part of his priestly life.

The contrast between Richard and Alfred was equally pronounced. Between them she saw the contrast of an oak and a willow. Richard was the oak; strong, decisive, and domineering. Alfred the willow; flaccid, uncertain, and undecided.

Alfred saw her approaching and turned to greet her. "Patricia," he said. "Let me introduce you to Richard Marquez. He's the son of Anthony Marquez, whom you met earlier with the Senator." Patricia extended her hand to Richard. He grasped it in both of his, and as he bent to kiss it she noticed that the knuckles of the left hand were covered with a bandage.

"It's a pleasure to meet you," he said. "Tell me, have you had a chance to see the Sangre de Cristo since you have been here?"

"Only from the plane," she responded. "What I've seen I like very much. Can you tell me why it's called Sangre de Cristo?"

"Yes. When the sun sets the light that is cast on the mountains reminded the early explorers of the blood of Christ. That's what the words Sangre de Cristo mean; the blood of Christ. My ancestors were among those explorers. In fact they were one of the original families that owned the grant. Unfortunately it was stolen from them after the war with Mexico."

Alfred interjected. "Richard, please, I thought these recriminations about our ownership of the grant had long been settled. You know very well that the Currans gained ownership because your family and the others abandoned it."

"So I've always been told, Alfred. Since my law school education I'm not so sure." He paused for a moment and his look caused Patricia to feel a slight chill. He seemed to gain control of his emotions and went on. "Of course, even God cannot change the past and we must live with what now exists. Do you agree, padre?" he asked, turning to Augustine.

"Do you mean that even God cannot change the past or that we must live with what now exists?" Augustine replied. "The first is too deep a question of theology for my small skills. But the second I disagree with. In fact there are things that must be changed if the valley is to continue to exist." He turned to Patricia and continued. "There are many in the valley who now believe that the name Sangre de Cristo means the blood of the migrants that is spilled each year for the benefit of others"

Patricia looked at Richard. "Is this true?"

Richard made a motion with his hand dismissing what Augustine had said. "This is the talk of rabble rousers. The migrants are treated very well in the valley. There are always those who would destroy the house to make it more luxurious. Unfortunately Father Augustine has adopted his predecessors' point of view without first learning all the facts."

There was an uncomfortable silence. Then Alfred changed the subject. "Patricia," he said. "In a way I think both Richard and Augustine are correct about the workers. Augustine is correct when he says some of the migrants are unhappy. And why not? Theirs isn't a happy lot. On the other hand, Richard is right when he says they are treated fairly."

"Augustine and his group are really communists," said Richard. "He believes that in our capitalist society man exploits man."

"Yes," said Alfred. "And I believe that in communism it's the other way around. Come now this is a reunion. Let's not spoil it with politics." Just as he finished, dinner was announced. Patricia turned to go to the table and stumbled. She fell against Richard and he realized she was slightly drunk. He steadied her with one had around her waist and the other on her arm. The pressure he used was more than necessary and Patricia felt a sense of domination and comfort. Alfred quickly came to her aid and took her in the direction of their table. Augustine watched as Patricia pushed Alfred away from her and stopped at the bar for a fresh drink.

CHAPTER 7

Isabella had outdone herself in preparing the dinner. A salad of hearts of palm and avocado dressed with a vinaigrette of sesame seed and vinegar and oil was followed by a cold green-chili soup. The main course was a specialty of Isabella's that she'd created for a dinner in honor of the Mexican ambassador. She called it Filete Bandera. It was three thinly cut filets, each garnished with a different sauce. The sauces were the colors of the Mexican flag, red, green and white. The red sauce was a tomato base flavored with ripened red chilies. The green was made from the tomatillo flavored with cumin. The white was a simple sour cream sauce. The appearance and mix of flavors made it a unique dish. The dessert of flan was so light it seemed to float from the plate to the mouth. Shortly after coffee was served John Taylor approached the table and whispered something to Sam who then turned to the others.

"Excuse me for interrupting," he said. "I need to borrow Alfred and the Senator for a few minutes." He turned to Augustine who was seated at the next table. "Would you mind telling your father to hold off on the fireworks until I send word?" he asked. "I need to spend a short time with Senator McNamara since he's leaving immediately after the party." Augustine said of course and left. Sam turned to Patricia as Alfred got up from the table. "We won't be long, Patricia. Shall I send someone over to join you?"

Patricia glanced past him and saw Richard Marquez walking to towards the table. "No thank you," she replied, "I'm sure I'll be all right. You two run along."

When the three of them got to the library John Taylor was already there.

"Sam," the Senator began, "I'm sorry to take you away from the party but I have to be in Washington tomorrow for an important vote, so I'll have to leave. Before going I wanted to fill you in on the status of several things."

"Don't worry about it, Senator. This is more important than the party. What's up?"

John Taylor looked at Alfred. "Maybe I should give a little background for Alfred's benefit. We have asked the Senator to help us with three things, Alfred. One is the annual migrant labor issue. Every year there is legislation introduced to require better treatment of the workers. Each year the pressure becomes greater, making it more difficult for us to defeat it. And each year the changes in the law would make it more and more difficult for us to comply and still operate at a profit."

"Profit hell," Sam interjected. "If these bills got passed it would make it impossible to use the valley to grow vegetables."

"Why is that?" Alfred asked.

McNamara spoke up. "It would require the county to provide bilingual education for the children. It would add great cost to the school district. The bill would make the workers eligible for welfare. That would be a cost passed on to the taxpayers. With benefits like these they would be inclined to stay all year. That would mean added costs of sanitation and health care. They would get higher wages under the bill. The feds would gain some jurisdiction over the camps and probably expect each one to be turned into some kind of resort."

"Where do we stand on this year's migrant labor bill?" Sam asked when he finished.

"I feel sure I can bury it in committee, Sam, but each year it grows more difficult. Every year there are louder screams on the part of the liberals to reform the laws in favor of the migrants."

"Hell, if those bastards had their way we would just give the whole damn country away," snorted Sam.

Alfred smiled at his father's outburst. It amazed him that he could be so forward thinking on many topics and so narrow on others. Everyone was aware of Sam's vehement opposition to any legislation that forced him to treat the migrants in any way different from the way he and his father had done for decades.

"What's the solution?" Alfred asked.

"Change," replied the Senator. "Change brought about by you that you can live with. Then I can keep them at bay forever. What you need is someone to institute a plan of action that I can point to and convince the people on my side that enough is being done without more legislation. This way you control the change and do it the way you want to. Throwing them some bones like this will be a hell of a lot easier than having an army of bureaucrats telling you what to do."

John Taylor spoke up. "That will take a lot of time and money."

"I know John," said the Senator. "But it beats the alternative. I can kill this years' bill but without some change by the next session we may not be so lucky."

"What about the water?" Sam asked, changing the subject.

Taylor interrupted again. "Alfred," he said, "as you know, the Sangre de Cristo sits on an immense underground lake that dates back to the times this valley was an inland sea. No one knows how much water. It may be the largest aquifer in the country. For years now the cities in this part of the country have been trying to buy the water and pipeline it for their own use."

"Alfred knows about that, John," Sam interjected. "We've always agreed that we won't sell the water. No one knows what effect it would have on the valley and we don't need the money."

The Senator spoke up. "The problem is that it may not be your decision much longer if you don't do something. The cities are trying to introduce legislation that would give them the right to condemn the water for their own needs. Then you'd have to give it to them whether you liked it or not."

"Is that a serious possibility?" asked Alfred.

"I'm afraid so if we don't launch our own counteroffensive," the Senator replied. Alfred looked at his father and John Taylor. He was sure any counteroffensive wouldn't come from them. It was becoming more and more clear to him that they were tired of the fight.

"Damn, Senator!" Sam exclaimed. "Don't you have any good news?"

"I'm happy to say I do have some good news. All the permits you need for importing the winter vegetables from Mexico have been issued."

"That is good news," Sam responded and turned to Alfred. "We've been trying to get these permits for several years."

"Why do you want to do that?" Alfred asked.

Sam responded quickly. "If we can supply winter vegetables and our summer vegetables we can control the markets for the entire year. As it is, since we can only provide summer vegetables, we run the risk of losing customers during the winter season. If we have twelve month contracts we ensure a market for the Sangre."

"What happens now that you have the permits?"

"We finalize the contracts with the suppliers in Mexico. Someone will have to go to Mexico to finalize them," Sam answered as he stood up. The others followed suit. Sam shook hands with Senator McNamara. "Senator I appreciate all your help. We'll do what we can to make your job a little easier." He reached into the breast pocket of his coat and withdrew a check. Handing it to the Senator he said. "Here is something I hope will make sure that you will be in Washington next year to keep up the fight."

The Senator looked at it discreetly and smiled. His campaign would be $100,000 richer when it was cashed.

"Thank you, Sam," he said gratefully. "This will be a big help."

"One hand washes the other, Senator," Sam said as he led the group out of the library. When they reached the foyer, a driver was waiting to take the Senator to the airport.

While Alfred and the others were meeting in the library, the table had been cleared and chairs had been placed along the balcony wall of the terrace. The guests were getting ready for the fireworks display that would be the finale of the evening.

Alfred excused himself from the group and walked out onto the patio. He found Patricia seated near the balcony wall with Richard Marquez. He managed to take his seat next to her just moments before the first Roman candle burst into a flood of colors. The first explosion was like a single note of music to open a symphony. Then more and more joined it until the night sky was a carpet of colors, dazzling the eye.

Patricia viewed the growing crescendo of colors and patterns exploding over the semi-desert landscape. She had a feeling of excitement and well being that wasn't just the result of the alcohol and pills. Something new had happened. Each explosion sent a shudder and sense of erotic excitement through her. As the number of explosions increased so did the pressure of Richard's leg against her thigh. The pressure she returned was just enough to encourage him.

CHAPTER 8

At the end of the fireworks display Alfred joined his father to say good night to the guests. He then hurried to the bedroom he shared with Patricia hoping to see her before she went to sleep. When he entered the room he saw immediately that he was too late. It seemed to him that more and more Patricia was getting to sleep very quickly after an evening out and avoiding any chance that he might want to make love.

She was only partly covered and her nude body was beautiful in the glow of the moonlight coming through the window. He sat on the edge of the bed and stared at her with a look of complete love. Then he put a hand on her shoulder and slid it down and cupped her firm breast. She didn't move and he realized that nothing he could do would arouse her.

Alfred got up and put the cap on the pill bottle that was beside the bed. He took the bottle and the half-finished glass of scotch into the bathroom and poured the drink into the sink. He put the pill bottle in the medicine cabinet then turned out the light and left the room.

He stopped at the small bar in the library and poured himself a snifter of Remy Martin, then walked to the far end of the terrace where it was dark and he could be alone. He found a place near some jasmine bushes. They were in bloom and the sweet evening scent perfumed the clear fresh air. The luminarios along the garden and road from the gates to the hacienda were still burning and gave off a warm glow. The valley beyond was dark except for the lights of several small communities. It was like a great river dotted with small islands of luminarios. Above, the night sky was perforated with pins of light in more abundance than he could ever remember.

The past day had been an important one for Alfred. When he arrived at the hacienda he had no intention of leaving a lucrative law practice in New York for what seemed to be a sterile cultural existence in the valley. Now he wasn't so sure.

He'd left the valley when he was twelve to go prep school in the east. It hadn't been difficult for him. After his mother had died his life with his father had been distant. While he loved Isabella and Eduardo as father and mother the apparent rejection by his father had stung. From the moment he'd arrived at Mahechnie Preparatory School until he was graduated from Harvard Law School he'd thoroughly embraced life in the East.

His visits to the valley during that period had been few and brief. While he was there he longed for the lights and bustle of the city, and he thought more of the valley as a place to get away from than one to be drawn to. He took a sip from the snifter and assayed his feelings.

He could feel a change in himself since his arrival. His love of the excitement of New York was still with him of course, but the challenges of the problems the valley faced were suddenly of deep interest as well. Besides, he realized how frail his father was becoming and that his last chance at a relationship with him was here and now.

The valley air had cooled considerably since the early evening, and he went to the kitchen in search of coffee. It was the first chance Alfred had had to visit this room since his return. Doing it when he would be alone with his memories had special appeal to him.

It was a large kitchen, big enough to serve any restaurant. The hacienda needed it. Besides being used to serve forty or more guests for a sit-down dinner or hundreds for hors d'oeuvres and cocktails, it was also needed to serve the hacienda staff of twenty.

Everything about it was redolent of his childhood; the
wonderful mixture of colors and spices and the textures of the
food that was the mainstay of this part of the world; brilliant
reds of ripened chilies hanging in *ristras* along the wall, braids of
garlic, and the smells of sauces that mixed ingredients like cloves,
cinnamon, dark chocolate and green chilies.

All his life Alfred had found refuge from life's disappointments
in the kitchen, just as he'd celebrated his joys there as well. During
all of his childhood whenever he came into the kitchen Isabella
greeted him. Even when he came home late or got up in the
middle of the night and went to the kitchen, Isabella would appear.
She never began a conversation and sometimes they would be in
the kitchen for hours and not exchange a word. He would sit on
a stool at the large butcher-block workstation and she would
busy herself in some way. Just her soothing presence would
comfort him.

Isabella, the wife of Eduardo, his father's valet, had managed
the hacienda all these years. She was the mother of Father
Augustine Romero. She was also the closest thing to a mother
that Alfred had. When his own mother died, Isabella and Eduardo
immediately took over the day-to-day chore of raising him.

He heated water and found some instant coffee. He took the
cup and sat at the large butcher-block table and let his memories
flood over him.

When Alfred was growing up, Sam had suppressed the anguish
he felt over the death of his wife by burying himself in the work
of the Sangre and there was little time for Alfred. His thoughts
were interrupted as a door opened and Isabella came into the
kitchen. Alfred put his coffee cup down and walked over to her.
He put his arms around her and kissed her on each cheek. Her
hair had some streaks of gray but her skin was as smooth as it had
been when he first began this ritual many years ago.

"*Mama, esta bien?*"

"*Si, Alfred, con la ayuda de Dios. Gracias.*"

Isabella moved away from his embrace and busied herself at
the stove. She quickly heated some beans and warmed two small

tortillas. She added chopped serrano peppers and cheese and rolled them into tubes. She put them in front of Alfred, who had resumed his seat at the counter. "Have you missed our food now that you go to those fancy restaurants in Paris and Rome and New York?" she asked.

"Mama, all of that is just food," Alfred said, taking an eager bite of the soft tacos. "This is a part of my life. It's not the same!"

"Nevertheless, it appears you do not deny yourself 'just food' as you call it." Isabella lovingly patted the roll of fat around his waist. He wasn't the slender Alfred that had gone off to school.

He winked at her. "I only eat it because I'm unhappy that I can't have your food." She laughed. "I had a wonderful visit with Augustine tonight," he said. "He's very dedicated to his work."

"Perhaps too much," Isabella answered. "I'm a little worried about his safety."

"His safety!" Alfred exclaimed. "Why should you feel that way?"

"You don't know, Alfred, because you have been away so long. There are many bad things happening in the valley. The workers are treated very badly and they are trying to bring about change. Augustine has taken up their cause. I'm afraid he'll be hurt."

"By whom?" Alfred asked.

Isabella made the sign of the cross. "By *La Mano Negra*."

"The black hand? What is it?"

"A secret society and here it's very evil. But I can't tell you more. You must talk to Augustine about it." He could see clearly the concern and fear on her face. "Chico," she continued. "There are many bad things going on and your father isn't strong enough to control them. Eduardo tells me your father wants you to come home. Please do this for us."

Alfred took her in his arms again and kissed each eyelid. At that moment Alfred knew exactly what he would do. Everything in his life pointed to the Sangre de Cristo. As soon as he made the decision all the reasons he'd put forward for staying in New York vanished. It was here with his father and Isabella and Eduardo that his destiny lay.

The only major concern that remained was Patricia. The time at the hacienda had made him realize that the marriage wasn't on the uphill swing. If anything it was deteriorating and needed an infusion. Perhaps a move would give it new life. He felt sure that continuing their life style in New York would lead to divorce. He couldn't say that a move to the valley would save their marriage, but he loved her desperately and thought it was his best chance.

He held Isabella close to him for a moment more then drew back. "Mama," he said looking into black moist eyes. "I'll come back. This is where I belong."

A tear fell on Isabella's cheek. "*Gracias a Dios, chico,*" she replied with deep emotion. "*Gracias a Dios.*"

CHAPTER 9

Alfred's concerns about Patricia's reaction to his decision to move back to the valley proved unfounded. He broke the news to her over coffee the following morning. Not only did she put up no resistance but actually seemed to welcome the decision. She pointed out many of the things he'd already thought about. The challenge of something new. Her feeling that as prominent land owners their position in New York, when they visited, could only be enhanced. Alfred didn't agree with all her reasons but was happy with the result.

His father responded with warmth and enthusiasm. He wanted Alfred to begin work without delay. There were several problems that needed immediate attention. The labor union elections were to take place in October, at the end of the season, and Sam wanted to go all out to defeat the union. There was also the issue of the contracts with the Mexican growers. If they were to take advantage of the next winter's season it was imperative that Alfred finalize their contracts by the end of September. Meeting these schedules meant that Alfred had only three months to get up to speed on the business of the valley.

Once Alfred and Patricia agreed to return to the valley events moved quickly. Alfred and Patricia returned to New York the following day. She arranged for the sale of the flat while he wrapped up his law practice. It turned out that Patricia seemed as eager as Alfred to resolve things in New York and get back to the valley. Her enthusiasm pleased Alfred. He had the feeling that she also felt returning to the valley was an opportunity for a new chapter in their lives. She took care of the sale of the flat and the shipment west of their art and antiques before Alfred was able to tie up the loose ends of the law practice. She returned to the Sangre several weeks before he was free to leave.

Alfred's withdrawal from the law firm went much smoother than he'd expected. Reassured that Alfred would be available for consultation his partners took the news of his departure calmly. The idea of increased shares in the partnership pie helped them be gracious.

It was the end of July before Alfred was able to devote his full time to the affairs of the Sangre. He engrossed himself in the task of learning as much as he could about the business management of the valley. He drove each morning to El Centro and in an office provided by John Taylor studied the books and papers of the family holdings.

He'd always assumed the grant produced a great deal of income but he wasn't prepared for just how much it was. The annual income to Alfred and his father was enormous. Every transaction in the valley generated income. Six thousand square miles of rich agricultural land, and all of it owned by him and his father. The fields were leased to tenants and the Currans received rents and a share in the production. When the vegetables were processed it was done in plants owned by the Currans. When the processing plants sold them to the distributors the profits came to the Currans. And when the tenants bought their food and medicine and cars and tractors they did so from businesses that rented their space from the Currans.

Alfred recognized that it would take him several months to get a handle on all the business relationships between him and his father on one side and all the other entities doing business in the valley.

Alfred's days were devoted to reviewing documents and preparing flow charts and organization charts to familiarize himself with the family business. His contacts with Patricia were limited to the evening meal they shared with Sam.

Their relationship had settled into a polite tranquility. Because Alfred was in bed early and up at dawn, Patricia suggested separate bedrooms until his hours became more in line with hers. He agreed it would be a good idea. He felt the relationship had improved since they left New York. They didn't argue and their conversations were conducted with extreme civility. She showed great affection for his father. But her treatment of anyone she considered her inferior was always indifferent and sometimes ugly. It was clear she had no compassion for working people and it never occurred to her that servants were human.

Soon after Patricia arrived in the valley, Richard Marquez showed her around the land grant. After Alfred's return from New York she continued her explorations on her own. Using one of the jeeps that belonged to the hacienda, she spent most of her days wandering over the valley. Alfred was surprised at her transformation. Instead of the well-manicured made-up New York socialite she took on a much more natural look. Her hair, which in the past had always been curled and sprayed to keep it in place, was now straight down her back. It was bleached by the sun and had a natural sheen that made it even more beautiful.

Patricia had always been careful not to do anything that might blemish her skin. She carefully protected it from the sun, using covering or protective lotions. But she was willing to pay the price to enjoy the rugged life of the valley. Quite often Alfred noticed marks on her body that revealed her enthusiasm for hiking and climbing through the sage and the boulders in the foothills of the mountains.

Once Alfred noticed several bruises on her thighs. She told him that she'd fallen and slipped down a small hill where she'd been looking for arrowheads. Another time he noticed a discoloration on her wrist. She explained that the holding log struck her wrist when she was opening a gate. All of this interest in knowing everything she could about the valley pleased him, and he liked her much more in this kind of tomboy role.

He was also pleasantly surprised by her interest in learning what she could about the history and operations of the valley.

He assumed she'd spent time with his father during his absence learning the facts she often alluded to during their dinner table conversations. She certainly shared Sam Curran's attitudes about the migrant workers in the valley. She also showed a great deal of interest in how the original grant came into being. And she often questioned Alfred about the history of the grant and how it had ended up in the possession of the Currans.

After his work with the accountants Alfred compiled an organizational chart that reflected the interlocking relationships between the various entities in the valley. In early September he met with his father and John Taylor in Sam's library to discuss Alfred's work and the status of the Mexican contracts.

"Alfred," Sam began, "while you've been getting up to speed John and I've been putting the final touches on the contracts for winter vegetables from Mexico. I've taken the liberty of informing them that you will be there in a week to formalize everything and sign the final contracts. Is that all right with you?"

"That's fine," Alfred answered.

"Good," Sam said. "You and John will have plenty of time between now and when you leave for a full briefing. Now tell me how you're doing in figuring out the workings of the Sangre."

Alfred stood up and walked to an easel set up where they could all view it. "Here is a chart of all our contracts in the valley," he said, beginning the discussion. "At the top of the chart is a box labeled Curran. Below it I've divided the operations into ten categories. Agriculture, land leases, labor, canning operations, shipping, marketing and so forth."

"I like this very much," Sam interjected. "It gives us a very good overview of the entire operation. Nice work."

Alfred continued. "Doing this has helped get a much clearer idea of how the system is organized, but it has also raised some questions."

"In what way?" John Taylor asked.

"Let me answer that by way of one example," Alfred responded. "As you can see here on the left of the chart I've charted the shipping operations. At the bottom we have small companies that pick up in the fields and deliver to small collection centers, which do the preliminary sorting. From these small centers the vegetables are then delivered to the main warehouse in El Centro. After processing and packing, the vegetables are transported in refrigerated trucks to market. Each of these steps is governed by a contract."

"How does that raise a question?" Sam interjected.

"Because all these contracts are not with us. In the case of all the operations in the valley these contracts are with a separate management company which in turn contracts with us."

John Taylor spoke up. "There is a reason for that, Alfred. Many years ago we decided that it would be much easier for us to spend our time having to review only the ten or so major contracts with management companies and let them worry about the details of all the lesser contracts. We felt it a more efficient use of your father's time."

"I understand that," said Alfred. "What bothers me is that I've had some difficulty in finding out the details of the contracts between the management companies and the other entities. Don't get me wrong. As far as I can tell the management companies are completely open and above board with us. And they seem to be very efficient, so our profits are good."

"Then is there any problem?" Sam asked.

"I don't know," Alfred replied. "I just don't feel that I can understand everything that's going on in the valley unless I can see exactly how these minor contracts work."

Sam spoke. "I don't see why that would be a problem. John, do you know the people in charge of these management companies?"

"Yes, of course," Taylor responded, "but we don't have to go to each of them. They're all owned by a holding company and we can talk directly to them."

"Who owns the holding company?" Alfred asked.

"Anthony and Richard Marquez," John Taylor replied.

CHAPTER 10

John Taylor arranged a meeting between Alfred and Anthony Marquez on the following day.

Alfred began the meeting. "Anthony," he said. "In reviewing all the business arrangements of the Sangre I realize that under the present arrangement we contract with several management companies and they in turn contract with everyone else. John Taylor tells me all these companies are owned by one holding company named Conquistador."

"That's right," Anthony replied. "Many years ago your father decided that his job would be easier if he only had to worry about the big picture and leave the details to me. I formed Conquistador, which in turn created the other companies. This has been the system for fifteen years." He hesitated and Alfred sensed a concern, then he went on. "The current contracts have twelve years more to run. Is there anything wrong?"

Alfred was quick to respond. "No, no, not at all. Just the opposite. The contracts provide for annual fees plus a percentage and everything seems in perfect order. It's just that I don't feel I'll have a complete understanding of the workings of the grant unless I completely understand the contractual relationships between all the parties."

"You realize of course," said Anthony, "that there may be over one hundred contracts. It will take some time to get them all together. When do you want to see them?"

"I'm leaving for Mexico in three days and may be gone a week. Will that be enough time?"

"I'm sure it will be," said Anthony. "Is there anything else?"

"Yes, one other thing. I would like to visit a field or two that are being harvested. I'd like to see it being done."

Anthony thought very quickly. He was in a hurry to get back to Richard. The idea of letting Alfred see all the contracts terrified him. He couldn't be sure that the skimming he and Richard had built in would stand scrutiny. Besides, the latest contracts had been handled entirely by Richard, and Anthony felt pretty much outside the loop. The second problem wasn't letting Alfred get too close to a field of workers. There was a lot of unrest over the treatment they got from Anthony and Richard. He didn't want Alfred to hear what they were saying. Also Anthony didn't feel safe going among them without his own bodyguards.

"There is a section near Linda Vista," he finally responded. "We can drive there if you like." Anthony decided that field would be safe. It was a small crew and the boss had them well under control.

The two set out from El Centro for the thirty-minute drive. Alfred insisted they take the gravel farm roads along the east of the valley rather than the one paved road that bisected the valley north and south. Alfred wanted to get a feeling for the fields and their crops.

Alfred noticed that Anthony was preoccupied. His driving was inattentive and he behaved as if his mind was far from the issues at hand. About halfway to Linda Vista Alfred saw a group of men standing in one corner of the field. Anthony seemed not to have noticed.

"Anthony," he said. "What's going on over there?"

"It's a meeting of workers. The union is trying to get certified as representative of the workers, and I suppose one of the organizers is there. They have been given the right by the National Labor Relations Board to hold meetings in the fields from time to time. I wasn't aware of this one."

"I would like to go over there. I want to hear what this organizer has to say. I hear that he's been spreading lies about us."

"I don't think it's a good idea." Anthony replied slowing the vehicle only slightly.

"Why?"

"There's a lot of labor unrest right now. You might not be welcome."

"Anthony!" Alfred bristled. "I own this land. I can go where I want. If there's a problem so great it prevents me from going where I want, then I want to meet it head on. Let's go over there."

Anthony reluctantly slowed the truck and turned around. They drove back to the field where the men were congregated and Alfred got out. Now panic showed on Anthony's face as he reluctantly followed.

The two men walked toward the group. As they grew nearer they could tell that one man was speaking to the rest. He had his back to Alfred but Alfred could tell he was a young Hispanic dressed in work clothes. His jet-black hair hung to his shoulders. He was speaking in Spanish and Alfred began to make out the words as he grew closer. His voice had the intensity and passion of a Pentecostal preacher.

"Without the protection of the union," he said, "you will always live as you live now. Nothing will change. You will be paid less than the minimum wage. You will pay more for your houses and your food than you will make. You and your women and your children will work twelve hours a day, seven days a week and at the end of the season you will not have enough money to take you to the next place. You will never have water or sanitation or medical care. And your children will have no education and no chance to get out of the fields. If you join the union we'll fight together to end these slave labor conditions. We'll bring down the Currans, who are no better than the most corrupt dictators."

As Alfred and Anthony got closer, the men listening to the speaker began to fidget anxiously until he noticed. He stopped speaking and looked their way. Recognizing Anthony, he spoke to him.

"Marquez," he said. "These men are on their own time and under the rules of the Labor Board. I have a right to speak to them."

"I know, I know!" growled Marquez angrily. "But you won't always have a Labor Board to protect you."

"You mean like last July when your thugs beat me at Linda Vista? You can beat me, Marquez, and you can kill me, but there will always be someone to take my place."

Alfred was shocked at the seething anger and sense of impending violence that was present. "This is our meeting!" Chacon shouted. His voice rose and became more threatening. "You two get away and stop trying to intimidate these workers."

Alfred spoke for the first time. "Wait a minute. No one is trying to intimidate the workers. I don't even know what you are talking about."

"And who are you, gringo?" Chacon asked.

"I'm Alfred Curran." Alfred said. Chacon looked at him for a moment in disbelief. Then turned back to the workers and resumed speaking in Spanish.

"Comrades," he shouted. "This is the man that keeps you in slavery. This is the man that lives like a king while you and your family die like pigs. This is the man who won't pay honest wages. This is the man that won't give you medical care, or running water. This is the man that sucks your blood. He dares to come here and show his face. He's the head of the snake that coils its body around you and squeezes the life from you. If you cut off the head the snake will be gone."

"That's a lie." Alfred shouted in Spanish. "Nothing he says is true. We pay a good wage. We pay for medical care and sanitation. You are treated well." There were looks of shock on the faces of the men. Chacon moved away from the men toward Alfred. There were murmerings. When Chacon got close, Alfred was frightened by the sheer hatred on his face.

"I can't believe that you think so little of these people to come here and lie to them," he said. "After these men pay the bribery they have to pay they make one half the minimum wage set by law. There is no running water where they live. There are no septic tanks, only holes in the ground. When a child is sick, they can only pray. The children can't go to school. They work in the fields because the money you pay the family isn't enough to live on." Alfred stood in stunned silence. Anthony Marquez grabbed his arm.

"We better get out of here!" he said urgently. Alfred shrugged his hand off angrily and yelled at Chacon, "You're nothing but a communist agitator, what you're preaching is lies and class hatred. I intend to see to it that you are put in jail where you belong." Anthony was desperately pulling Alfred toward the truck.

Chacon was following them. "You and your corrupt family are history!" he yelled. "Dead meat!"

The two men had reached the truck and Anthony was behind the wheel. Alfred looked back at Chacon. "Is that a threat to kill me?" he asked.

"It means you and your dictator father are finished. It will happen one way or another!" Chacon yelled.

"I would be careful," Alfred hurled back as he got in the truck. "People who live by the sword often die by the sword." As he finished, a visibly shaken Anthony set gravel flying as he sped away.

CHAPTER 11

The next day Alfred met with his father, John Taylor, and Anthony Marquez. The four men had gathered early to review their position and their strategy in advance of Alfred's trip to Mexico. Alfred recounted the events that had taken place in the field the previous day.

When he finished, Sam Curran turned to Anthony Marquez. "Is any of what this Chacon says true Anthony?"

"No," said Anthony. "It's just the propaganda this Chacon is spreading around to drum up support for the union." Alfred thought he sensed some discomfort on the part of Anthony.

Alfred turned to John Taylor. "John what is the minimum wage we pay these workers?"

"Two dollars above the minimum wage set by law," he answered.

"How does that compare with other farms?" Sam injected.

"Most pay the minimum," Taylor answered.

"What about the condition of the camps and benefits?" Alfred persisted.

"Our records show substantial payments each year for health costs. We also show substantial expenditures each year for camp upkeep. Based on the payment, I would assume the camps are well maintained." Alfred looked at his father.

"It's been many years since I visited a camp," Sam said. "Maybe fifteen years. But they seemed good to me then."

"Chacon said something about paying kickbacks. Is that possible?" Alfred directed the question to Anthony.

"No," he answered. "It's impossible. Believe me these are unfounded lies."

"I don't like to have my life threatened," said Alfred looking at his watch. "Before I leave I'll try and have a meeting with Mr. Chacon."

"Do you think that's a good idea?" asked Sam. "Will it be safe?"

"I doubt if he'd do anything crazy this close to the election," Alfred responded, "but in light of what happened yesterday I've decided to carry protection." Everyone knew he meant a gun. "Whether I see him or not I promise you one thing," he said. "When I return from Mexico I intend to find out for myself what's going on. Then I expect to take some strong measures to put a stop to this situation."

The four men spent several hours reviewing the documents that would control the Mexican venture. They made minor changes, but both Taylor and Alfred believed they were of no major consequence. They all agreed that everything was ready for Alfred's trip. As the meeting was breaking up Alfred addressed John Taylor and Anthony Marquez. He looked at both men with a determination they had not seen before. "When I return," he said in a tone of voice that left no doubt that he meant what he said, "I want full documentation of what we pay for the workers. Then I'll visit the camps personally. I mean to see to it that this Chacon is taken care of. Is that understood?" Both men merely nodded.

The next day Alfred tried to find Chacon but time and circumstances prevented a meeting. He returned to the Hacienda later in the afternoon and said goodbye to his father and Patricia. Then he went to the charter plane office and left for Mexico.

From Denver Alfred flew to Houston and then nonstop to Vera Cruz, where he was met by Jaime Isita, the lawyer they had retained to represent them in Mexico. From Vera Cruz they drove inland towards the town of Orizaba. Isita informed Alfred that there had been a small change in the plans. The meeting had been moved from the larger town to a small station named Valle Hermosa, which was the headquarters for the cooperative that was to supply the vegetables. Once they left the coast the route took them though land much like the Sangre. It was flat rich agricultural land. Bordered on one side by the Pacific Ocean and on the other by the southern Sierra Madre Mountains.

Alfred was taken to the Hotel Benito Juarez located just off the town square. That evening and the following day he and Isita met with the representative of the growers. Everything went as smoothly as one could expect in Mexico. It was decided that the remaining issues could be resolved in two days. Isita agreed to go to Vera Cruz for a day and oversee the final contract changes while Alfred remained in Valle Hermosa

The next morning he inquired at the desk of the hotel about excursions outside the city. He was told there were several. One of which was a drive into the mountains of the Sierra Madre. He was told the route traveled through a canyon much the same as the famous Barranca de Cobre in the state of Chihuahua. When it reached the top there was a magnificent panoramic view, and on a clear day one could see as far as the ocean.

Alfred decided this would be an ideal way to spend the day. Isita had left their rented car and, armed with a map, Alfred headed west toward the Sierra Madre Mountains. Thirty miles from the city the mountains began to rise quickly to seven thousand feet. The road he took entered the mountains through a canyon named Barranca de Banderas. It was a steep and narrow one that began an immediate and arduous climb along switch backs through heavy overgrowth. As the road got higher he caught glimpses of the canyon. It had sheer cliffs on either side and few guard rails along the edge of the road.

Near the top he passed a small village. Isita had told him that most of the revenues received by the inhabitants of the mountains came from profits derived from sale of marijuana. He said it was the largest marijuana-growing region in Mexico. The area was under the control of a drug lord who was in many ways more demanding of law and order than the government. Alfred had been mildly surprised at the lack of distress by those he talked to over the presence of an illegal activity so close to the town.

Alfred continued past the village onto the top of a mesa and then drove to the west until he came to a lookout point that had been his destination. It was a magnificent view. The agricultural plane stretched beneath him much as it did from the hacienda at the Sangre de Cristo.

He ate the lunch the hotel had packed for him and then walked along the edge of the mountain for several miles. He returned to the car and sat there looking at the scene that stretched before him. He realized he was happy with his decision to return to the Sangre and sitting there viewing similar agricultural land only heightened his happiness. He knew he would commit his life to managing the land grant and renewed his feelings of love for Patricia. When he returned he would devote much of his time proving his love. A slight chill made him realize the sun was dropping past the horizon. He wanted to get down the steep narrow road before dark and started immediately.

When he passed the village at the top of the steep narrow road down into the canyon it was nearly dark. Alfred had not traveled very far after the village when he found it blocked by a small transport truck with its hood up. Two men dressed in police uniforms were standing by the truck. Alfred parked his car and walked to the truck.

"*Como estan?*" he said as he approached the two uniformed men. "*Algun problema?*"

"Yes," answered one of the men in Spanish. "The truck has broken down. The driver has gone for help."

"Do you mind if I look?" asked Alfred.

"Of course not señor," the same officer replied, walking with Alfred to the truck. Alfred leaned over the fender to look at the engine. The policeman that had not spoken stood behind him. He pulled his gun and hit Alfred on the side of the head with all the strength he could muster. For Alfred everything went black and he collapsed. The two men dragged his unconscious body back to his rented car and put him behind the wheel. One of them returned to the truck and backed it down the hill. It had been parked on the sharpest switch back. He then returned to Alfred's car and the two of them began to push the car down the road. One of the men was at the driver's side. As the car gained speed and approached the switch back he gave the wheel one turn to the right towards the canyon then jumped clear.

The car reached the edge of the mountain with enough speed to travel nearly the length of the car past the canyon wall before the nose dropped forward. The two policemen ran to the side of canyon and watched from the road as the car hit the side of the canyon on a small ledge then bounced outward. At the next ledge it bounced again and burst into flames. Now it was a fireball careening from ledge to ledge until it came to rest on the rugged canyon floor several thousand feet below.

The two policemen stood and watched the car burn. "What do you think?" the one Alfred had spoken to asked.

"I think he was dead when we put him in the car. If he wasn't he is now."

"Should we climb down and see?"

"Are you crazy. No one can climb down there. Believe me they'll take our word for it."

"You know considering we had such short notice for this job I think we should have a bonus," said the one that had knocked Alfred out.

"Fat chance of that happening," the other replied.

"Don't be so sure. I took his wallet."

"How much is there?"

"A thousand dollars."

"*Hijole!*" A good bonus."

CHAPTER 12

Prisoner number 215 is in the commandant's office at the federal prison of Los Altos in Chiapas, Mexico. He sits facing a desk. The simple desk has one file on it and a nameplate: Col. Rufino Mendez. Behind the prisoner stands Lt. Borrego, the cousin of the commandant.

Col. Mendez has not arrived. Number 215 knew this tardiness was calculated for its psychological impact. Time for 215 to ponder the torture he'll receive if he doesn't give Mendez the information he wants.

On the wall behind the desk is a map of the Los Altos prison. 215 knows it by heart. The small building he's in is the main administration building. On each side and across from it are tin roofed shacks for the prisoners. One small shack is set apart and is the infirmary where he and Dr. Francisco Suarez live and where Dr. Suarez treats the prisoners, the prison staff, and their families.

Two metal fences topped with razor wire surround the entire compound. Between the two fences the Chiapas jungle has been cleared. The outer perimeter is also cleared for a hundred feet before the land was engulfed by jungle. Several towers are positioned to give the guards a clear field of fire into all cleared space. No one had ever escaped from Los Altos and survived.

The door behind him opened and he hears the footsteps of Col. Mendez coming to the desk. Mendez is a short, fat man. He tries without success to put his size twelve body into size 8 clothes with comic effects. This is deceiving. He's devious, ruthless, and brutal. He's maintained control of Los Altos for 15 years and has amassed a small fortune through extortion and bribes. And human nature being what it is what he has isn't enough.

He takes his hat off revealing straight black hair of medium length. The hat is too small like the rest of his clothes and has left a circular mark in the hair and a red mark on his forehead. As he sits down he looks directly at prisoner number 215, then at a file in front of him on the desk. He studies it for a moment as if for the first time.

"Alejandro Cordero, prisoner number 215," he reads from the file. "Arrested in the state of Chiapas at the clinic of one Francisco Suarez. The clinic was built and operated with the funds of Octavio Mendoza leader of the Yucatan drug cartel. The prisoner claims to have no memory of who he is or how he came to be at the clinic. His identity papers said he was Alejandro Cordero, born in the state of Sonora."

Mendez looked at Cordero now and continued speaking. "The records that were found showed that you had been at the clinic over two years and Dr. Suarez had performed plastic surgery on your face no less than four times. Since you could offer no other explanation the court decided this was surgery to change your identity and that you were a major part of the Mendoza cartel. It sentenced you and Suarez to life in prison. I consider it my duty to discover who you really are and how much money you should pay for the privilege of being here."

"We've been over this many times before," Alejandro finally spoke.

"That's true," Mendez responded. "We left you in the punishment shed for two weeks. And that didn't work." Alejandro inwardly winced at the memory. The five feet by four feet tin shed, with temperatures that sometimes reached 120 degrees, would have made Alejandro reveal his past if only he knew what the past was. After the shed there was the use of the whip on his back that flayed the skin. After each of these punishments Dr. Suarez had threatened to withhold medical treatment of anyone if the torture didn't stop. The threat had worked long enough for him to treat Alejandro and nurse him back to health. Now Mendez was beginning again.

"Then there was the whip, but still you refused to cooperate." Mendez said.

"Have you considered that it may be because I really can't remember my past?"

"Yes I've considered that," Mendez replied. "But I don't believe it. What I believe is that you're young, in very good physical condition and able to withstand much pain. Today we'll see how you tolerate electricity."

What Mendez found out was that Alejandro could tolerate a great deal of electricity until he passed out and couldn't be revived. Then he was dragged unconscious to the infirmary where Dr. Suarez was faced once again with the job of bringing Alejandro back from the brink of death. He wondered how many times he would be successful.

CHAPTER 13

Alejandro remained unconscious for two days. All the time Dr. Suarez was at the side of his cot doing his best to give aid and comfort. When Alejandro awoke it was another day before he could tell the doctor in detail what had happened. After he finished Dr. Suarez looked thoughtful.

"Alejandro," he said, "the way you explained everything just now seemed different somehow than the way you have recited things in the past."

"What do you mean?"

"I don't know exactly. You seem to have a grasp of more detail. And your way of thinking and speaking seems clearer. Perhaps Mendez' use of the electricity has helped us in some obscure way. Let's try again to recover your past. I know it seems like a waste of time. We've been through it so many times but we must not give up. If we don't find out who you are soon I'm afraid Mendez will go too far and kill you."

"All right, I'll try," Alejandro replied. "I'll do anything to avoid another session with Mendez."

"Good," said Don Francisco. "Here's what we'll do. I'll tell you again how you came to my clinic. Try and concentrate your powers on recovering any small thread that we can." Dr. Suarez began his story.

"You were brought to the clinic by some farmers from the village of Esperanza. They found you along the trail that they used to go from the village to their fields in the canyon. Your condition was near death. You had cuts on most of your body and your left arm and leg were fractured. The greatest damage was to you head and face. Almost every bone in face was broken and there was a severe fracture to the skull. With some effort I managed to stabilize you. When it was clear you'd live we began the job of restoring your face. You had no identification on you so there was no way to tell what you looked like before your injuries. In some ways that was good because I looked forward to rebuilding your face as I wished without regard for having you look as you did before. It was five operations and two years before the restoration was complete. Complete except for your memory."

"Did any of the villagers know what happened to me?"

"They told me that one of the boys in the village had seen two policemen push a car over the side of the canyon. He didn't see whether there was anyone in the car. That was where they ended the questions. Once they discovered that the police were involved they wanted nothing more to do with it."

"Why didn't they report finding me? For that matter why didn't you report finding me?"

"Many reasons. The villagers discovered some years ago that they could earn more money growing five marijuana plants than an acre of corn. They pay *mordida* to the police and usually the police look the other way. On the other hand they don't trust the police and will do nothing to call attention to themselves. As for me the clinic was, as they say, financed by drug money. I've known Mendoza a long time and many years ago I went to him with the proposal that if he'd finance the clinic I'd operate it. He agreed. In this part of Mexico many children of poor people are afflicted with cleft palate. It's a gross disfigurement of the face and any child with it will be an outcast all his life. I have the surgery techniques that reconstruct the faces but it's very expensive and none of the families can afford it. It could only be done with Mendoza's money. Besides, you were a project yourself. My first goal was to restore your handsome face."

Suarez paused for a moment to review his handiwork. What he saw was a face that held a certain fascination. The eyes were not exactly in line with each other and the nose had angles not usually found in nature. One eyebrow was shaped differently from the other and the mouth slanted slightly downward from left to right. Suarez had no idea what Alejandro looked like before the injuries but he was sure he looked completely different now.

"Did Mendoza know who I was?" Alejandro asked.

"No," replied Don Francisco. "We were all sure that you weren't involved with the drug trade. Mendoza said he would look into the events in Vera Cruz but the raid on the clinic took place before I heard anything."

"Why do they think I'm Alejandro Cordero?"

"One of Mendoza's people had left phony papers at the clinic in the name of Cordero. They expected someone to come to the clinic and pick them up. When the federal police raided the clinic they found the papers and assumed they were yours. We had no way to prove otherwise."

"I remember being fingerprinted. They must have checked them."

"I suppose so. But if you didn't have a record it's unlikely they would have found a match in Mexico." Suarez paused then asked. "Has any of this helped?"

"I'm not sure," answered Alejandro. "I feel there's a memory bank in the deep recesses of my subconscious that is getting closer to the surface. Maybe it's just wishful thinking."

In the weeks following the torture at the hands of Col. Mendez Alejandro's sense of recovering his memory grew more intense. He experienced brief flashes of a connection between his past and the coffee plants that he worked among each day. These flashes of remembrance always occurred so quickly that he was unable to discern anything concrete other than the fact they meant something about his memory. Each time it occurred he desperately tried to build on it and see all of it. It was like a dream that he knew he'd had but couldn't remember. One day while he was working in a remote part of the plantation he had a mental image of fields. He couldn't distinguish much about them. It was as if he was viewing them very close up and had to draw back to put them in perspective.

That night he and Don Francisco were seated on mats that they used for yoga and meditation. "The visions of fields I told you about are happening more frequently," Alejandro said to the Dr. when the meditation was finished. "I still can't decipher them but they seem to be of fields that exist somewhere other than here. The landscape and the vegetation are different."

"That's encouraging," Don Francisco responded with enthusiasm. "You must try to remember everything about these scenes. Especially anything that is out of the ordinary; something that might give a clue to the location. This might be the end of the thread we've been seeking. If we can just get a small hold it may allow us to unravel the entire tangle."

Each day at work Alejandro would concentrate his thoughts on fields and crops. With each image he had he would try to remember some detail. Each time he felt that he saw more of the field as if his view had gone from a few plants to a much larger field. It was like going from viewing the field from the perspective of an ant to that of a cow. He tried as hard as he could to gain a better perspective. He wanted to feel as if he was on a hill viewing the field. In this way he hoped to get an even greater idea of what he was seeing.

Each night he discussed this thought with Don Francisco. "Tell me what's happening?" said Don Francisco.

"When these visions first came to me," Alejandro explained, "I felt I was very close to the ground and could only see small things. Now it feels as if I'm standing up and looking down at my feet. I see more but still not enough to give me a sense of where I am."

"It's very interesting that your perspective seems to be getting farther above the fields. Why don't you try each day to imagine you're taller, or that you're climbing a building, or that you're an airplane? Try to get further and further above the ground. I hope that once you're viewing the place of your visions from a great enough height you'll recognize it. And if you recognize it then all the pieces of the puzzle should come together."

In the following days Alejandro did as Dr. Suarez had

suggested. He had limited success and then one day he had a major breakthrough, or so it seemed at the time. He'd tried to imagine getting higher above the ground and finally managed to see the field from high enough to realize that the field was a circle within a square. The circle was green and lush and the corners of the square were brown. As his perspective grew he saw that all the fields were in this pattern. He concluded that the crops had been deliberately planted in circles.

One evening during their meditation he imagined he was a bird flying high above the ground. He felt he was a large bird and was surrounded by other large birds with long necks, wide wing spans, and long legs that trailed behind them as they flew. When the meditation ended he was anxious to tell Don Francisco about the round fields.

Don Francisco couldn't explain the significance of the field being round but was encouraged by the progress Alejandro was making and begged him not to stop trying.

Each day brought more and more imagery to Alejandro. He could see fields stretching out to the horizon. Flat fields that reminded him of a tapestry. He was now at a point where the fields were entirely visible to him.

One evening while he and Don Francisco were meditating together he was imagining himself as one of the large birds looking down on these large round fields. He began to sense other birds with him in the air. "Don Francisco," he said. "Something very different just happened." He stopped. Don Francisco was looking at him in a shocked way. "Don Francisco what's wrong?" he asked.

"Alejandro," said the doctor, "say that again." Alejandro repeated it. "Alejandro you're speaking English to me. You've never done that before. I wasn't aware you knew how to speak English. What made you speak English?"

"I don't know" Alejandro reverted to Spanish.

"No! No!" Don Francisco said. "I think it will help if you continue in English."

As they discussed this new event it became clear to them that whenever Alejandro now had the vision of the fields and the birds his thoughts were in English. Everything else he did or thought about was in Spanish. Don Francisco came to the conclusion that Alejandro had spent his past in an English-speaking environment. But Don Francisco wondered why when he'd regained consciousness from his original car wreck he began speaking Spanish fluently? All of this was confusing and raised more questions than it answered.

"Alejandro," Don Francisco finally said. "All of this puzzles me very much. I've always assumed you were Latino and your life had been spent in Mexico. If you didn't come from Mexico then why were you in Mexico? And why did someone try to kill you? I'm sure they think they succeeded. Indeed it was a miracle that you survived. For the time being I think it will be best if no one knows you speak English. Please promise me you will only speak Spanish unless we are alone."

"Of course I'll promise you. But why do you think so?"

"I feel something very sinister surrounds your accident. I want to think about it carefully. Whoever was responsible for your accident has acted on the assumption you are dead. If they find out you're alive their only choice will be to kill you. If you're still here when they find out it will only make it easier."

CHAPTER 14

Alejandro didn't make the rapid progress that Dr. Suarez had hoped for. As a result Alejandro began to feel he would never recover his memory. Other than always thinking of the round fields and birds in English he didn't seem to be able to recover any other threads or clues about his past. So far all he knew was that his background was Anglo instead of Hispanic or at least that he'd grown up speaking English as well as Spanish. He was also aware he had some connection with a place having lots of fields that had a peculiar growing pattern of circles within squares. Any more than that remained out his reach. In the past the belief that he would regain his memory had sustained through the grim days at Los Altos. Now he began to think that the memory might never come back and his only hope was escape. He knew the chances were slim but to die trying was preferable to spending his life there.

When he was working in the fields he thought more and more about ways to escape. He continuously reviewed the situation. Two fences surrounded Los Altos. The first one was twelve feet high made of heavy chain metal and topped with two rolls of razor wire. Once he was past the fences he would face fifty yards of clearing and then there was another fence and more razor wire. Every inch of the fence was in the view of some guard outpost and lighted all night long. He knew that even if he were able to scale both fences successfully he would be faced with another hundred yards of cleared land before reaching the jungle.

Once in the jungle he would be without shoes, shirt, or water and have no idea of where to go. It was doubtful that he would be able to survive.

If he were going to escape it would have to be in a way different than merely breaking out of the prison. He must have a plan that would insure his survival until he could escape from the country.

One evening as Alejandro was returning from the fields Lt. Borrego called his name.

"Cordero," he said. "Colonel Mendez wants to see you in his office." For the past weeks Alejandro had been able to put out of his mind the torture by Colonel Mendez. Suddenly it all came back and the thought of another session sent chills of fear through him.

As they entered the office he was relieved to see that Mendez wasn't in the room. It was odd, he thought, how the mind worked. He found himself hoping that he would merely receive a beating rather than the electricity. He knew from past experience that he could force his mind into a state that would allow him to survive clubs and fists. He wasn't so sure about the electricity.

Mendez entered the room before Alejandro was seated and began speaking at once. "Sit down Cordero," he said pointing to the chair in front of his desk. "Don't worry, Lt. Borrego and I only want to talk to you. We've decided that beating you is of no use. We've decided to try reason instead. Don't you think this is a good idea?"

"Yes, of course," was all Alejandro could say as he sat down.

"You must understand something Cordero," the colonel continued. "Here at Los Altos we receive very little money from the government. It's very difficult to live on the pay we receive. To make life better for everyone we expect contributions from the prisoners. The greater the contribution the better we all live. Do you understand?"

"Yes," Alexander replied. "That's why Dr. Suarez arranges for payments for him and me." Mendez put his hand in the air to stop Alexander.

"It's not fair that Dr. Suarez pays for both of you. Why should he have to pay for you and himself?" Alejandro didn't respond.

Mendez went on. "For many years everyone in this prison got a lot of money from the drug trade. Now they are expected to return some of it to us. You are the only one in Los Altos who doesn't pay. You say it's because you don't remember anything about your past. We don't believe you. Anyway you're taking space here that could be taken by someone who does remember their past and can pay their fair share. What this means is that in sixty days if you don't remember enough to pay your way you will be sent to Isla Magdalena." He paused.

Alejandro knew about Isla Magdalena. It was the island prison where the very worst of Mexican criminals were sent. Being sent there was dreaded by even the most hardened inmates of Los Altos. For Alejandro the thought that he would be separated from Don Francisco was even worse than the horrors of the prison.

"I'm sure you can see how reasonable our position is," Mendez looked past Alejandro at Borrego and gave slight nod. "Will you cooperate?"

"Please understand Colonel Mendez," Alejandro answered. "If I could I would."

"I would carefully reconsider your position over the next sixty days," Mendez said as he opened one of the desk drawers. Alejandro saw the battery cables only for a moment before Borrego covered his head with a mask. Alejandro forced himself to think of round fields and large birds before the first pain shot through his body. Finally the pain was too much for the mind to deal with and it shut down. Alejandro lost consciousness and Borrego, with the help of a guard, half carried, half dragged him back to the cell.

Alejandro regained consciousness while Dr. Suarez was trying to make him comfortable. In his delirious state he began speaking in English. Suarez managed to quiet him and then gave him something to make him sleep.

The following morning Alejandro awoke with the doctor at his bedside and before he could say anything Suarez spoke.

"Alejandro! Speak only in Spanish. No matter what you tell me say it only in Spanish. Do you understand?" Alejandro nodded his assent.

"Alejandro," the doctor went on, "we must invent a past for you and pay Mendez more money. I have more than enough for both of us. I can pay it in a way that it appears to come from you. We must stop these beatings. Worse, there is a rumor that if you don't start paying you will be sent to Isla Magdalena."

"I know," said Alejandro. "But don't worry. I have a better solution."

"What do you mean?" asked Suarez.

"I mean I know who I am!" exclaimed Alejandro. "Do you understand, Don Francisco I know who I am? I know how I got here. I'll now be able to leave and go home. I . . ."

Don Francisco interrupted. "This is wonderful news, Alejandro!" he exclaimed happily. "When did happen? How did it happen?"

"This time before they used the electricity I tried desperately to concentrate on the images of the round fields and the birds. For some reason I couldn't do it. Each time I tried another image kept presenting itself. It was a market stall or something like that. Food and pans were hanging from the walls. Then something very strange happened. As I looked around an old woman appeared. She was Latin in appearance but she spoke to me in English. She called me Alfred and suddenly as if a floodgate was opened it all came back to me. I know who I am."

"I'm very happy for you Alejandro. I want to know everything, but we can't say anything about this at the moment. We have to be sure that no one can hear us, and we must think about it very carefully. There are many things we still don't know. Before we let anyone know I want to understand some things that puzzle me about your situation. You must promise me that you will remain quiet for the time being."

"But why Don Francisco? I'm sure I'll be released when they discover who I am. Everyone will realize it has been a terrible mistake." The pain and despair of the last years had been taken away like a drawn curtain and Alejandro wanted to shout his existence to the world and return to the Sangre and his wife, his father and his friends.

"Don't be so sure Alejandro. We must meditate over why you were put here, and find out what forces are at work."

"Meditate!" exclaimed Alejandro the rising despair evident in his voice. "I'm tired of meditation. I'm innocent and I want to return to my home. I'm going to report this as soon as possible."

"Please, Alejandro. There is more to this than meets the eye." Don Francisco answered. "I don't say you shouldn't tell Mendez. I only mean that we must take a few days to decide the best way to proceed. Please give this old man his wish. Just a few days. Will you do this for me?" Alejandro was too tired and hurt too much to put up any resistance.

CHAPTER 15

Alejandro slept all that night and most of the next day. From time to time during the next several days a guard would come to the cell and demand that Alejandro report for work. Dr. Suarez would take the guard into the room where Alejandro was asleep and let him see the still unconscious Alejandro. The guard would only mutter something about throwing Alejandro into the jungle so that he wouldn't use precious medicines, but made no more fuss about it. This behavior was more out of deference to the doctor than any care about Alejandro. All the guards relied on the doctor to treat them and their families and they didn't want to offend him.

When Alejandro awoke he was groggy from the drugs the doctor had given him. He remembered the details of his past that had come to him during the torture but wasn't as adamant about telling the authorities.

When Doctor Suarez saw that he was awake he made sure there were no guards that overhear them. "Alejandro you must tell me everything about your past. I'm sure this will give us the information we need to help set you free."

Alejandro sat up in the bed with some difficulty and after a long drink of water began his story. "I remember everything. My name is Alfred Curran. My father and I own a large agricultural land grant in the United States. The fields were circles within squares because of the irrigation systems that rotate in circles and don't cover the corners. The family I come from is very wealthy and powerful. I'm sure that when they find out I'm alive they'll inform the authorities. Then it will be known that a horrible mistake has been made. I'll be returned to the U.S. and then I can use my influence to get you released even if I have to pay all that I have to do so. Why won't you let me tell them?"

"I don't mean you shouldn't tell them. I only mean we should plan our strategy very carefully. Your story only confuses me more. If your car going into the canyon was an accident why were the police there? Why wasn't more done to recover the remains? Why did someone want you dead? It's important that we review all the events leading up to your being in Mexico before we say anything. If you won't keep quiet for a short time for yourself please do it for me."

"But I know why I came to Mexico. It was to sign contracts for the importation of winter vegetables. Jaime Isita the lawyer in Vera Cruz will testify to that."

Don Francisco thought for a moment and then spoke. "This causes me even more concern. Why didn't the matter receive more attention in Mexico? If the villagers are correct you were murdered by two men dressed as policemen. In Mexico this can only happen for one reason: money.

"I had money. I often carry a lot of cash. I'm sure I would have had close to a thousand dollars with me. Surely that's enough for murder."

Dr. Suarez thought for a moment then said. "Yes, a thousand dollars could be motive for murder but how did they know about it? And why wasn't more done to recover your body. It must have been assumed you wouldn't survive the crash. An American family with so much money would have spared no expense to recover the body. It's a matter of national pride." What had been the bright color of determination in Alejandro's face gave way to pale doubt.

Dr. Suarez tried to reassure him. "Alejandro I still have many contacts in this part of Mexico. The man who delivers the food to Los Altos lives in Vera Cruz and he owes me a favor. Let me contact one of Mendoza's lieutenants and try to find out what I can before you do anything. Now, please tell me all you can about yourself before you came to Mexico."

It took Alejandro a long time to tell his story. When he finished Don Francisco was convinced that Alejandro should remain quiet about his past for the time being. It was obvious to him that the only way Alejandro's murder could have been covered up was with the collusion of someone in authority. He explained all of this very carefully and Alejandro was finally convinced that they should find out as much a possible before disclosing who he was.

It wasn't easy. With each moment a new recollection of his past came to him and it was difficult to reconcile the fond memories of that idyllic past with someone wanting him killed. The only ones he felt might be behind the murder attempt were Richard and Anthony Marquez. He was certain when he left the valley that things weren't right and that what he'd been able to discover pointed to them. But why? Killing Alfred wouldn't get them the grant. Alejandro's father was still alive and could very easily sell or give the grant away. His wife Patricia would get it if the father didn't change his will. He was sure his father had nothing to do with this and he was sure Patricia was innocent as well.

He had no doubt that if he could get back to the United States he could clear things up immediately. The cold dish of revenge lay on his palate for hours on end as he contemplated his triumphant return and the exposure of Richard for the murderer he was. But how was he going to do that? Don Francisco was sure that if he told the authorities who he was it would probably lead to his death. On the other hand, not to disclose who he was meant a living hell at Los Altos or somewhere worse. If he told them who he was he might at least have some chance for survival. Escape seemed to be out of the question. It had never been done and he'd thought about it for two years and couldn't see how it would ever be done.

The hopelessness of his situation enraged him and it was the thought of revenge that sustained him. Alejandro's vacillation between disclosing his identity to Mendez and waiting for another possibility was resolved for him by Don Francisco. He and the doctor were in their cell after the day's routine.

"I told you I know the driver of the food truck. Do you remember?" Don Francisco asked.

"Yes," Alejandro answered.

"After you regained your memory I asked him to make some inquiries for me," he paused when he saw the look of concern on Alejandro's face. "Don't worry. He's someone who's sympathetic to us who I can trust. Besides he knows nothing about you and I told him nothing that would connect you with my questions."

Alejandro looked relieved. "Has he found out anything?" he asked.

"Enough to convince me that when Alfred Curran came to Mexico the arrangements were being made to have him murdered." Dr. Suarez still spoke as if Alfred Curran and Alejandro Cordero were different people. In many ways, such as in their looks and in their philosophy, they were different people. He went on. "Whoever attacked him and pushed his car into the canyon has collected the money for killing him. The rumors are that a captain and two policemen were able to build lavish homes just after the reports of Curran's death. No one tried to retrieve the car or body. They said one of the policemen had made the difficult climb down to it and that it had incinerated. He said whoever was in the car was destroyed. The car was traced to the rental company and it showed that Jaime Isita had rented it. The official conclusion was that Curran was dead and there was nothing to recover."

"But my father would have spared no expense to retrieve my remains no matter what the cost," Alejandro injected.

"I'm sure that is true if he'd known the real facts. We don't know what story was given to him." Suarez responded. "What we do know with some certainty is that you were set up to be killed by someone in the Sangre and they paid a great deal of money to the killers. What is most important is this. If it's discovered that Alfred Curran did not die then it would be absolutely necessary that the job be completed."

"But if I told the authorities don't you think they would protect me?" Alejandro asked.

"I don't think so and I wouldn't trust my fate to that chance. You have seen how corrupt Mendez and Borrego are. If we could notify some authorities in Mexico City it's certain they would inform Mendez and I'm sure they would arrange your death during an imagined escape. We must think of something else."

"Death would be better than staying here forever. I would almost rather take the chance. There may be a chance that I could get to someone in authority that isn't corrupt. Surely everyone is Mexico isn't as corrupt as those that tried to kill me."

"I agree Alejandro. Everyone in Mexico isn't corrupt. But everyone here at Los Altos is. Even if they believed you they would try and find out who wanted you dead and how much they were willing to pay to have the job finished. Please, we must take our time and find a way for you to escape. Once you are out of Los Altos I can arrange to get you out of the country. I've already started the wheels in motion."

"Then let's find a way to do it," said Alejandro.

CHAPTER 16

During the next several days Doctor Suarez busied himself making sure of the arrangements to get Alejandro out of the country in the event they could arrange a means for his escape from Los Altos. One evening in the cell Suarez asked Alejandro a strange question.

"Have you ever read anything by Mikhail Lermontov?" he asked.

"No," answered Alejandro. "He was a Russian poet wasn't he?"

"Yes. Around 1840 if memory serves me correctly. It has been many years since I've read him," said Suarez. "I remember an episode from his book *A Hero of Our Times* that may help us find a way out of here. Let me tell you about it."

Alejandro listened intently as the doctor recounted the tale. He saw immediately how it might be adapted to his situation considering what had gone on with Mendez and Borrego up till now.

"I'm afraid that the plan will work only if you are willing to suffer another beating," he said to Alejandro when they had agreed on a plan. "Otherwise I'm afraid they'll not be convinced of your truthfulness."

Alejandro thought for a moment. He'd suffered so much at the hands of those sadistic guards that the thought of more torture made him shudder. "It won't be easy," he answered. "But if it means my freedom and a chance to return to the valley I'll do it.

The question is how do we get them to undertake another interrogation. It hasn't been very long since the last one?"

"I believe I know a way," Suarez answered. "I'll pretend we've had a falling out and I'll refuse to pay for you any more. I think this will prompt another visit to the commandant."

The following day Dr. Suarez told Mendez that he would no longer pay for Alejandro. Two days later Borrego put the handcuffs on Alejandro and took him to Mendez' office. Alejandro was put in his usual chair. He tried to make himself believe that the torture he was about to receive was a small price to pay if it led to his freedom. It was important to concentrate on the plan he and Dr. Suarez had devised. For it to work it was necessary that Alejandro make his confession at just the right moment. It couldn't be too soon or Mendez might be suspicious, and if he waited too long he might be unconscious and unable to tell them anything at all.

"Cordero," Mendez began, "you'll leave for Isla Magdalena next week. The only thing that can save you is to pay for the privilege of staying here. I promise you won't like Magdalena. Now that Suarez won't pay for you any longer it's even more important that you arrange for payment. This is your last chance. Will you pay?"

Alejandro was relieved not to see the battery cables and hoped they would use fists this time. He prepared himself for the blow he knew was coming and said "no". Borrego struck him between the shoulder and the neck with a truncheon. His arm went numb and his spine felt as if scalding water had been poured through its center. He began to fall to his knees and on the way down Mendez hit him with a closed fist just in front of the right ear. His senses became disoriented. In the past he would have welcomed this feeling as the beginning of unconsciousness. Now he had to fight to prevent it. If his plan was to have any chance of success he had to take several more blows but remain alert.

Borrego kicked him in the side with his heavy boot and Alejandro tasted blood as Mendez kicked him in the face and cut the inside of the cheek. After two more blows Alejandro feared he might pass out and with effort cried out.

"Stop! Please stop. I'll tell you what you want to know." Mendez looked at Borrego with surprise and satisfaction. He stepped away from Alejandro and motioned Borrego to put him on the chair.

He gave him a moment to catch his wind then asked him. "How much can you give us each month?"

Alejandro thought for a moment. "I can't give you anything each month." As he said this Mendez drew his fist back to strike. "No!" said Alejandro. "Let me finish." Mendez lowered the hand. "I can't give you anything each month because all that I have is in one place and I'm the only one that knows where it is. That's why I've taken your beatings all this time. If I tell you where it's hidden you'll take it all and I'll have nothing."

"How much?" Borrego asked.

"Three million dollars in gold." Borrego and Mendez exchanged glances. "I saved it as part of my share of the cartel. I don't trust banks. I thought the safest way was to buy gold coins and bury them. It's safe but I'm the only on that knows where it's buried."

"Then you must tell us," said Mendez.

"Please," said Alejandro. "Be reasonable. If I could give you some each month that amount would keep me here forever. But I can't and once you have it all you'll still send me to Isla Magdalena, or you'll kill me. No, I won't tell you."

"Then we'll beat it out of you." said Borrego.

"You've already tried that," said Alejandro. "You know I won't tell you." Even the thickheaded Borrego had to accept that as fact.

"If you won't tell us where it is why have you told us anything?" Mendez asked.

Alejandro hesitated. "Because I'm prepared to give you all of it if you'll give me my freedom," he said.

"That's impossible," said Mendez. "Do you think we're fools? Don't you know that everyone in this prison could give us that much money? We cannot accept it and not be found out. It's one thing to take monthly amounts in exchange for better treatment.

But we can't just let people go. We would be caught and then we would be the inmates."

"I know," interjected Alejandro. "I've thought of that. But don't you see my case is different."

"How is it different?" asked Borrego.

"First, there's no one who knows who I really am. So no one would question my death. Second, no one but me knows of the money. It could be done just between the three of us. You could get the money and let me go. Then you could say I had escaped into the jungle. No one ever survives there and I would be given up for dead. That would be the end of it. I'd be long gone from Mexico and you would have three million in gold."

Mendez took time to think about what Alejandro had said. Finally he said. "Tell us where the gold is hidden. Once we get it and are convinced that what you say is true we'll arrange for you to escape."

"The gold is buried deep in the ground near the village of Oriente," Alejandro responded.

"I know the village," said Borrego. "It's about halfway from here to Vera Cruz."

"That's right," said Alejandro. "I own a small finca there. That's where I buried it."

"Good," said Mendez. "Draw a map for us showing the exact location. We can leave in two days. When we get back you'll be a free man Cordero." The look in his eyes told Alejandro that the Colonel was already spending the gold. It also told him that as soon as they had the gold he would be dead trying to escape.

"I have a better idea," said Alejandro. "Take me with you. Just the three of us. I'll show you exactly where it is. After you have it you'll leave me in the village of Oriente. It's been a long time since the gold was buried and I must be there to show you the exact place."

"When you return to Los Altos you can report my escape. That will be the end of it."

"You forget one thing Cordero. While we are gone the acting commandant will know you're missing."

"I've thought of that as well," Alejandro replied. "Send me back to my cell tonight as if I'm unconscious. That's always been the case in the past. Dr. Suarez will say I'm unable to move for the two days we're gone. That's also happened in the past. No one will question it."

Mendez thought for a moment. "It might work," he said finally. "I must think more about it. For now we'll send you back to your cell as you suggested. If I decide to do this thing we'll leave on very short notice so be ready. Also I think we must be very convincing." Before Alejandro could move the truncheon Mendez was holding in his hand crashed against the side of his head. Alejandro wouldn't have to fake being unconscious when he was returned to the cell.

Borrego closed the door behind the guards who had been called to carry Alejandro back to his cell. He looked at Mendez. "*Hijole!*" Three million in gold! No one knows about it and no one can trace it. This is a miracle. Can we do it?"

"Why not, cousin? Why not? We can leave tomorrow."

"But how can we be sure that Cordero won't report us when he's free."

"Don't worry," Mendez replied. "I've been thinking about this. Three million in gold must take up a lot of room in the ground. When we fill the hole back in we should put something in there to replace the gold."

"You mean rocks or something like that?"

"What would be better than Cordero's body?" Mendez said as he smiled and put his arm around Borrego's shoulders.

CHAPTER 17

Not long after Alejandro was returned to the cell he regained consciousness. Doctor Suarez anxiously waited to hear what had happened. After Alejandro had recounted the conversation the doctor was ecstatic.

"They'll do it Alejandro. I knew they would. Of all the vices greed and lust are the strongest. Since greed finances lust it usually takes first place. They'll come. We must be prepared. Let's go over the plan one more time." Alejandro shook the remaining cobwebs from his brain and sat up in his bed.

"I'm ready," he said and began to recite what Don Francisco had prepared him for. "The road we take is five kilometers after Oriente. The road is marked by a small *tienda* on the right. We turn right there and follow that road for five kilometers where the road climbs to the top of a small mesa. On the mesa is a large field used to graze cattle. On the left side of the field is a large ceiba tree. This is the landmark where we'll dig."

"Perfect," said Don Francisco when Alejandro finished. "Now if all goes as planned you'll go to Vera Cruz from Oriente. I have a friend there who will provide you with a passport, money, and clothes to get you to the U.S." He paused for a moment then continued. "His name is Miguel Angel. He lives at Calle Primavera number 12. He provides passports to all the couriers for the cartels."

"Can we trust him?" Alejandro asked.

"I've no reason to believe otherwise but just in case I've offered him a great deal of money and where principal fails money does not." There was a noise outside the cell and Don Francisco stopped. After a few minutes he resumed.

"I've arranged for you to fly directly from Vera Cruz to Houston and then to Baltimore."

"Why to Baltimore?" asked Alejandro.

"That's where I went to medical school at Johns Hopkins University. It's a very good school even though it's located in Baltimore. I have good friends there and when I began to run the clinic for Puerta I decided to get a safety deposit box where he could deposit my money. Everyone else does it in Miami, which seemed very foolish to me. When you arrive in Baltimore you're to contact Manuel Gallardo. He lives on Dumas Street and his number is in the phone book. When you see him tell him you come from me. You'll tell him that I have a tattoo on my left thigh that says Angelica. That's our code. He'll give you an envelope with a key to a safety deposit box at the Maryland State Bank. I don't know how much money is there. For all these years Puerta put money in the box for me but never told me how much. He was a very generous person so I believe it will be substantial."

"How much do you think?" Alejandro asked.

"I'm sure it will be over a million," Suarez answered.

"Good," said Alejandro. "It'll be enough for me to return and obtain your release. After that we'll return to the valley together."

"No Alejandro, that isn't what I want. I'm too old." He saw the disappointment on Alejandro's face. "Listen Alejandro I don't mind finishing my life here. I've reached a peace that I can't find elsewhere at this time in my life. I'm allowed to practice my medicine. I live a very simple life and can meditate as I wish. I don't mind. After all," he continued, "the only difference between a prison cell and a monk's cell is a state of mind."

"But Don Francisco, you're the father of my new life. I can't leave you here."

"You're right Alejandro. I am the father of your new life.

Because of that I'll always be with you and we'll always be linked by a spirit. But you must go. There is a deep trouble in your soul and it will continue until you've solved the problems that brought you here."

"I also believe you have a mission," he continued. "Not of revenge but of healing. Whatever caused you to be sent here is a cancer and it's causing great misery to many people. You're not the person that came to Mexico. You don't look like him and you don't think like him. The person that came here didn't care what was happening to other people in his valley so long as he received the income. That person was able to look at ideas and things but wasn't able to see them. He was like someone who knew the world by looking at a map. He knows the contours of the land and the limits of the country but he doesn't know the flesh and blood. You know that now and you must promise me you'll return to the valley not just for revenge but to make it a better place to live."

"Don Francisco, please let me come back for you."

"No, Alejandro. Please don't ask me again."

They sat for a moment each with their own thoughts. Alejandro wasn't sure in his heart that he wanted anything more for the rest of his life than to be with this man who had given him a new birth physically and mentally. At the same time he knew he must return to the valley at all costs and seek his revenge.

Don Francisco looked away so that Alejandro wouldn't see his face. This was the first time he'd lied to Alejandro. Dr. Suarez was a physician and he knew his cancer had reached a stage where the time left in his life would be measured at best in months and perhaps only weeks. He was certain that if Alejandro knew this he wouldn't go and he must keep it from him at all costs no matter how painful the lie.

"Alejandro," Doctor Suarez broke the silence. "I want you to use my money to regain what's yours in the valley. When you've done that I want you to repay the money in the following way. I want you to build a clinic in the valley for the poor people. Will you do this for me?"

"Yes, Don Francisco, I'll do it. It'll be the finest clinic in the world." Suarez couldn't see the tears but he could hear them in the Alejandro's voice.

"Thank you," he said. "One more thing. I believe that you must spend time finding out the circumstances of your disappearance before you tell anyone who you really are. It can be done easily enough. Go to the library and look through the newspapers from your state for the time around your accident. The death of one so prominent as you must have generated a lot of news. This information will help you decide how you should proceed."

"I agree. I won't identify myself as Alfred Curran until I understand all there is to know about my coming to Mexico. And I'll not rest until I've righted whatever wrongs have resulted."

"Good."

"There is one other thing," Alejandro continued. "I know you won't go with me or let me return for you. I've accepted that and I understand. It's something else I wish to tell you. When we first came here and you asked me to share your yoga and meditation. I was skeptical and must say did it mostly to make you happy. But you said something to me that made a profound impression. You told me that the birth of a person didn't take place when they passed from their mother's womb. You told me that a person wasn't born until they had developed all their capacities to their fullest. And you said the tragedy of our lives was that most people died before they were born. In many ways my road to birth began then.

"What you have taught me about the meaning of my life has made my existence meaningful. I don't know whether I'll ever be born before I die as you have said. But I promise it will not be because I haven't tried. I'll never forget you and what you have done for me. I would have endured ten times the misery of these years for what I've gotten from you. I love you more than you can imagine and I'll never forget you."

"Thank you Alejandro. Now try and rest. I believe they'll come for you before dawn."

Alejandro lay on his cot curiously calm considering the events that lay before him. He imagined that well conditioned astronauts must feel this way before a shuttle launch. Anxious to get going, a deep sense of anticipation and excitement but no fear or sense of the possibility of failure.

Alejandro couldn't believe that his nightmare was almost over. He'd been in this camp over two years. It was over three years since he left the valley. So much had changed. More than just his physical appearance but also his entire mind set.

The out of condition, self indulgent, thoughtless rich man that had come to Mexico had been replaced with a well conditioned introspective soul that understood, through the teachings of Don Francisco, the relationship between the physical and the metaphysical and the understanding that one didn't exist independent from the other.

He'd come to believe that all the agony and despair that had come to him as a result of coming to Mexico had been more than offset by the good that had come. He believed that his real life had started the day he'd been pushed over the cliff and later and taken to the clinic. While he longed for the revenge he was to inflict on Richard Marquez and anyone else responsible for his being where he was he also understood that because of the experience he'd become a person that he might never have become otherwise.

Dr. Suarez was happy that the darkness of the cell hid the tears that slipped down his cheeks. He was spared even more grief by the sound of approaching footsteps. "Hurry, Alejandro. It's time to go." The two old friends embraced; father and son, Mentor and Telemachus, spirits profoundly bound one with the other forever.

The cell door opened and Mendez came in. "Here," he said handing Alejandro some clothes. "Put these on."

When Alejandro was dressed Mendez led him out of the cell and through the gates of Los Altos to a waiting pickup. He shackled Alejandro around the waist and attached handcuffs to his wrists and then to the waist shackle. Alejandro was told to get into the back of the truck where his legs were shackled and he was covered with tarp.

"We will stop at Oriente," said Mendez. "Then you can give us further directions."

CHAPTER 18

The drive from Los Altos to Oriente was pure hell for Alejandro. There was nothing between him and the metal bed of the pickup truck. With his hands and feet shackled he could do nothing to stop himself from being thrown wildly about as the truck careened over the dirt roads. To add to his discomfort there were several shovels and picks in the truck with him. They would slide around as Mendez took curves at breakneck speed. If he wasn't being thrown against the sides of the truck the tools were being thrown against him.

Besides being bruised and battered the dust generated by the truck almost choked him. It was cold and he had only thin cotton trousers and a cotton shirt for clothes. He managed to wedge himself crosswise and brace himself with his feet and head and shoulders but after several hours he wondered if he would ever be able to walk again, or to gain circulation in his hands and feet.

After dawn some warmth from the sun began to penetrate the tarp that was covering him and he began to feel better. Since he'd been in Los Altos he'd been without a clock of any kind. His days were from sunrise to sunset and his nights the darkness. At the latitude of the camp the two were almost equal. Based on what Don Francisco had told him he guessed that Oriente would be reached about an hour after sunrise.

His thoughts were interrupted as the truck began to slow and then came to a stop. He heard both doors slam. The tarp was taken off his head and he was pulled roughly to a sitting position. It was a bright, slightly overcast day and after the dust settled his lungs welcomed the cool fresh air. He wondered if the air would smell the same when he was free.

"We just passed Oriente," Mendez said. "Do you recognize anything?"

Alejandro looked around and saw nothing that gave him a clue as to where the turn off might be. He began to panic. Not knowing anything about the country he'd hoped he'd be allowed to sit up and see where they were going. Now he was unsure. Had they passed the store? Was it ahead of them? How long could he continue this charade before they realized the truth?

He tried to stand. He desperately needed to get some circulation back into his legs. He also thought he might be able to see farther along the road and spot the store that marked the turn off. He began to struggle to his feet Mendez struck him with his fist and knocked him back down.

"If you're not being honest with us Cordero we'll kill you and leave you to rot like a dog in the jungle." Alejandro braced himself for another blow but before Mendez could strike again Borrego interrupted him.

"I don't know about you Colonel but I'm hungry. I'm out of cigarettes too. Why don't we go back to the small store we just passed and find something? Then we can see if Cordero has a better idea of where to find the gold?"

Alejandro held his breath. That had to be the store Don Francisco had mentioned. Whatever guardians had taken charge of his life they were coming to his rescue now.

"Did you say a store, Lt.?" Alejandro asked.

"Yes," Borrego answered.

"Was it just before a cross road?"

"I think so. I'm not sure."

"I'm sure that's the turn," said Alejandro. "It's been a long time," he added trying to cover his confusion.

"All right," Mendez interjected. "We'll return to the store and get something to eat then you can tell us the next step." Alejandro was left uncovered as they turned the truck around and returned to the store. When they arrived the two men left him in the truck and went inside for cigarettes, coffee and something to eat. When they were finished they returned but brought nothing for him. He had time to gather his bearings during their absence and was ready for them.

"It's all clear to me now," he said. "This is the road. Do you see the mesa there?" He gestured with his head towards a tabletop area several kilometers from the crossroad. Both men looked in that direction but said nothing.

Alejandro continued. "The road takes us across that mesa. About halfway there is a large pasture on the left side. If we drive across the pasture to the woods that border it we'll find the place."

"Good," Mendez said. "I'm in the mood to dig. Especially for gold."

As the truck started up the hill leading to the mesa the road became almost impassable with deep ruts and Alejandro feared for his safety as he was thrown about. When they reached the top the road became smoother even though it was little more than a path. Now Alejandro was on his own. This was as much as Don Francisco had described for him. Luckily there was no sign of life on the mesa and on the other side of the pasture the jungle grew dense very quickly. For Alejandro's plan to succeed he needed some time without interruption.

The truck stopped halfway along the side of the meadow. Mendez asked for directions.

"Do you see that large ceiba tree on the other side? The tallest one?" Alejandro asked.

"Yes," Mendez answered.

"Drive to it and then we'll make the necessary calculations."

Mendez turned the truck off the path and drove to the edge of the jungle and stopped. He and Borrego got out of the truck and each took a shovel and pick. "All right Cordero," said Mendez, "tell us where to dig."

"Please, Colonel," Alejandro responded. "It's not that easy. It's been over six years since I buried the gold. The map I made disappeared long ago. I must try and remember exactly where it is. And you must remember it's buried very deep. Besides the jungle has changed. The trees have grown or fallen. There are new vines. It won't be as easy as you think." He paused for a moment. "Please take off my chains and allow me to walk about. I think it will come back to me very soon."

Mendez only laughed. "Cordero," he said. "I've dealt with prisoners much more clever than you. Do you think I'll release you from your chains so that you can try and escape into the jungle?"

"But you'll have to take them off to let me dig," Alejandro replied.

"Don't worry about that," said Mendez as he pulled Alejandro by the ankle chains to the back of the truck. "Borrego and I'll do the digging. You'll sit in chains and watch. After we find the gold we'll release you as we promised." He took a key from his pocket and unlocked the chains that encircled each ankle. Now Alejandro could walk but his hands were still attached to the chain around his waist.

Mendez stepped back and drew his pistol. "Now you can walk and locate the place to begin digging. If you make one false move I'll shoot you in the leg. Now hurry we don't have much time." He pulled Alejandro off the back of the truck onto the ground.

Alejandro needed a moment to steady himself. He'd lost all sensation in his legs and wasn't sure he could walk. Mendez was in no mood to waste time and he pushed Alejandro in the direction of the large ceiba. The fever brought on by the idea of three million dollars in gold had gripped the two guards.

Alejandro stood in front of the tree and moved first to his right and then to his left. In the jungle he spotted another large tree whose trunk split into a 'v' near the top. "I remember that the edge of this large tree near us had to have one of its sides in line with that tree with the large 'v'," he said as he lined it up first to the left and then to the right. "I also remember that a forty-five degree angle is then made and fifteen paces counted into the jungle and that marks the place." He hesitated.

The accuracy of all this impressed Mendez who stood waiting, his eyes glistening at the thought of the gold. "Yes," he said, "go on. What else? Which side of the tree? The right or the left?"

"That's the part I don't remember," Alejandro replied. "All we can do is dig in both places. I know it's one or the other." With that Alejandro walked to the left side of the tree and then fifteen paces away from it. He stood looking back at Borrego and Mendez. "It's here," he said. "Or it's in the same place but on the other side of the tree. I'm not sure. If you'll undo these handcuffs I'll help you dig."

Mendez only took the leg irons from the truck and made Alejandro stand by the tree where he chained him once again. This time he added another chain and wrapped it around the tree so that Alejandro couldn't go anywhere even with his short steps. Mendez then joined Borrego and they both began to dig frantically.

It was more than two hours before the two men had dug a whole several meters in circumference and four meters deep. The sun was growing hotter and both men, badly out of shape, were growing tired. Alejandro watched from his vantage point near the tree. Soon both emerged from the hole. Both were tired and unhappy. Their faces were streaked with dirt and sweat. Their tan uniforms had turned dark from perspiration.

"Cordero," Mendez spoke. "There is no gold here. We've dug to the depth you told us and there's nothing."

"Colonel, I told you I wasn't sure which side it was on. It must be the other side. Why not let me help you dig. It'll be easier and faster." Alejandro could see that Borrego, who had been doing most of the digging, would gladly have let him but Mendez refused.

"We'll dig one more time," Mendez said. "But if we don't find the gold in the next hole then your body will be in it." He nodded to Borrego to follow him and counting the paces, as Alejandro had done before, he located the spot and once again began digging.

Alejandro, in the shade of the ceiba tree, was cool and rested.

He could see that both men were suffering from the sores the shovels were wearing on their unprotected hands. Neither man had done any physical labor the past several years and they weren't used to the toil. Each shovel full took longer to lift and the pace grew slower and slower. The second hole was now to the depth of their chests and they had to lift the shovel over their shoulders to throw the dirt out.

"Colonel," Alejandro said during one of their many stops. "I'm in good condition. Why not let me into the hole to dig. It's too deep for me to run away. Besides you have guns. I only want to find the gold so you'll be rich and I'll be free." No response came for a moment and then Mendez turned to him.

"All right," he said finally. "I'll take the chains off so you can dig. But remember we'll be watching. If you do anything suspicious I'll kill you. Then I'll have the gold and you won't even have your miserable life. *Comprende?*" With difficulty he and Borrego pulled themselves out of the hole. Both men seemed ready to drop from their exertions. Mendez released Alejandro while Borrego held the gun on him. Alejandro did nothing but take the shovel and get into the hole where he began to dig. Satisfied that he was working both men sat down at the base of the tree and were content to see the dirt fly out of the hole. Alejandro worked with a frenzy and they were satisfied he was as anxious to complete the job as they were.

The minute Alejandro was in the hole he started to execute his plan. He didn't have much time and had to work quickly. Instead of taking dirt from the bottom of the hole he began to dig underneath the edge of the hole nearest the tree where the two men sat. He worried that any minute one or the other might come to check his progress.

Carefully he removed dirt from beneath the bank almost three feet deep and as far back as the shovel would reach. He took as much dirt as he dared from underneath the overhang. When he finished digging towards the two men he began to chip away at the roof of the new hole. He wanted to undercut the bank enough so it would collapse under the weight of either of the two men. He was fearful of taking too much and having it collapse by itself. As soon as it was thin enough he dug some more at the bottom of the hole until he came across one of the few rocks.

He reviewed quickly in his mind what he was going to do. He wanted to get both men to rush to the side of the pit where the bank was undercut. He hoped it would collapse under their weight and throw them into the hole. Then if he struck fast enough with the shovel he should be able to knock both of them out before they could recover.

He gave careful thought to whether to kill them or not. He'd decided to avoid it if at all possible. But if it meant a choice between their lives and his freedom the decision would be easy.

The shovel found the rock. He took a deep breath and put his desperate plan into action. He struck the rock several times with the edge of the shovel. He hoped it would sound like the shovel hitting a metal box.

"Mendez! Borrego!" he yelled. "I've found it! Here it is!" He stepped away from the undercut bank and waited. The two men were semi-dozing when they heard Alejandro. He shouted again.

"Quick!" he said. "I've found the gold. Come quick!" Both men struggled to their feet. Tired and groggy they were gripped with the prospect of three million in gold and raced each other to the side of the hole. Borrego was the first to reach the bank. His weight caused it to collapse and his momentum carried him into the hole. Mendez who had been just behind him had been able to stop just in time and began fumbling for his pistol. Borrego fell face first into the dirt and Alejandro swung the shovel with as much strength as he could muster then turned to Mendez who was just removing the gun from its holster. Alejandro quickly scooped some dirt onto the shovel and threw it towards the face of Mendez. It was off target but distracted Mendez long enough let Alejandro swing the shovel sideways against the his knee. Mendez cried out in pain and tried desperately to point the gun at Alejandro as he was falling to his knees. He fired too soon and the shot struck the bank near Alejandro's head. Alejandro grasped

Mendez by the feet and pulled him quickly into the hole. Mendez still held the gun but Alejandro was able to pull it from his hand before he could fire again. Then, it was with great pleasure that Alejandro hit Mendez several times on the jaw with his fist. Alejandro jumped out of the hole and located the chains that had been used to restrain him, and then he chained the two men securely to each other. He took Borrego's shoes for himself and both pistols. Borrego who was most nearly his size had taken his shirt off to dig and it still lay by the tree. Alejandro discarded his own tee shirt and put on the cleaner shirt. The shoes fit nearly enough. He found the papers of both men in the truck. He hoped that if he was stopped he might be able to bluff his way by using Borrego's papers.

He left the two men chained together in the hole. He didn't think anyone would find them very soon. He would tell Don Francisco's friend where they were and leave it to him to make an anonymous call after he was out of the country.

When Alejandro was ready to leave he checked on them one more time. They were both unconscious. He resisted the desire to shoot both of them in the knees as a pay back for the beatings and torture he'd suffered.

Alejandro got in the truck and began the drive to Vera Cruz. He wasn't free yet but the tears on his cheeks told him he was closer than he'd been in over three years.

CHAPTER 19

Alejandro Cordero waited in line to show his passport to the immigration officer seated behind the counter. He kept repeating the name on the passport to himself. Another name. He wasn't sure how to refer to himself even in his thoughts. Alfred Curran killed near Vera Cruz? Alejandro Cordero prisoner at Los Altos? Or now another name on a phony passport given to him by a forger in Mexico? When could he reclaim the Curran name? Tomorrow? The next day? He couldn't be sure of the answer to these questions but at least in the next few days he would know the circumstances surrounding Curran's disappearance.

He forced himself to focus on what was before him now. Ever since he'd left Mendez and Borrego and driven away in the pickup truck his nerves had been frazzled.

The drive to Vera Cruz was without incident and he found the house on *Calle Primavera* easily. The friend of Don Francisco was discreet and efficient. He promised to dispose of the truck and to be sure that Don Francisco was told of his success. He received the news of Mendez and Borrego without expression. Alejandro had the clear impression that no phone call about their whereabouts would be made. This didn't surprise him. A great many people had friends or relatives at Los Altos and the treatment there was notorious for its brutality. The death of the commandant and his lieutenant would be welcome news.

He spent only two days in Vera Cruz. He was given clothes, enough money to hold him over until he was able to get into

Don Francisco' safe deposit box, and the forged passport he now clutched in his hand. This was worth all the money in Don Francisco' safe deposit box and the value of the Sangre de Cristo combined. This small book was all that stood between a jail term and his freedom to regain what was his and to take revenge on Richard Marquez. He had no idea whether it was a good forgery or not. He could only trust that it was and take his chances.

His anxiety level moved up several notches. Now would be the greatest test of his nerves. At all costs he must maintain the appearance of an innocent man. It was difficult. He'd been in jail for the past three years.

He felt unsure of himself. How much had changed? Would he give himself away? He felt someone would know him or his secret and expose him. Maybe he would make a slip that would give him away. His hands were sweating and he was sure the immigration officer would feel the wetness of the declaration form and become suspicious. All these fears ran like a river through his mind. To make things worse he was traveling from a country that was always under scrutiny by US officials for illegal documents or for people that were involved in the drug trade. He had a phony passport, a phony identity, and he had no experience at this sort of thing. It was stage fright, pure and simple. As he got closer to the desk he began to question his ability not to fall apart in some physical or mental way.

The American businessman behind him in line tapped him on the shoulder and nodded towards the desk. It was to let him know that it was his turn to cross the yellow line and give his passport to the officer.

Alejandro stepped forward and handed the officer the passport and his customs declaration. The officer looked at them then handed the customs declaration back. He placed the passport next to a large three-ring notebook and thumbed through the pages. Alejandro couldn't see what was on the pages. He mind began to race again. What would come up? Was the name on the passport one that was known to the U.S. authorities? He had no idea who he was supposed to be. If there was statistical information in the book about his family and he was asked about it he would be dead. If only he could read the pages of the book. His nerves were reaching the breaking point.

"How long will you stay in the US?" the immigration officer asked.

Alejandro hesitated. "I'm not sure," he finally managed in English.

"What is your purpose here?" This threw Alejandro off.

"Well," he began. "I'm going to see some people about . . ." The officer interrupted him. "I mean is it business or pleasure?" Relief spread over Alejandro. "Business," he answered.

"Well don't let it be all business and no pleasure," said the agent as he passed the passport back to Alejandro.

Alejandro fought for control. Don't scream for joy he told himself. Don't show emotion, just be calm. Next there was the obstacle of customs. He had nothing to declare. His only baggage was his carry on. He gave the declaration card to the man at the door. The agent looked at it only briefly and waved him on.

Alejandro slept the entire way from Houston to Baltimore. From the airport he took a taxi to the Society Hill Hotel on St. Paul Street.

It was early evening when he got to his room and after putting his bag away he looked in the phone book and located the name of Richard Gallardo. Alejandro called the number and the voice that answered said he was Gallardo. He showed no surprise and seemed as if he'd expected the call. He arranged to see Alejandro first thing in the morning.

Gallardo's shop was on Dumas Street. From the map it looked like a distance of several miles. The weather the next day was cool and the light was filtered through a thin layer of clouds that only occasionally allowed patches of robin's egg blue to peek through. Alejandro needed the exercise and decided to walk. He could also use the time to plan the next few days.

Based on what Don Francisco had told him he assumed there would be a lot of money in the safety deposit box. He worried about going into the bank and taking the contents of the box even though he realized that others had been making deposits for many years without a hitch. He told himself that he'd passed all the hurdles necessary for the time being, and that he could behave naturally. He didn't have to look over his shoulder all the time.

Now Alejandro could see the Chesapeake Bay and the warehouses along the waterfront. The exercise felt good and his muscles were responding after several days of sedentary existence. The flat expanse of the bay brought to mind the great underground lake of the Sangre and made him think again of his future.

The temptation was to return to the Sangre de Cristo and disclose his identity. He could easily prove everything that had happened to him the past three years. On the other hand something told him this would be dangerous. In any event he'd promised Don Francisco he would read the papers from the time surrounding his disappearance before taking any other action. His walk took him along the side of the main downtown area of Baltimore, past Camden Yards, and after another mile or so to the small neighborhood store of Richard Gallardo.

He found Gallardo sitting behind the cash register. He was an older man who had moved to Baltimore from Mexico over forty years ago. He'd befriended Dr. Suarez when the doctor was a student at Johns Hopkins and they had maintained contact ever since. After Alejandro introduced himself and gave Gallardo the message about the doctor's tattoo the two of them went across the street to a small coffee shop. It was self-service and they both got coffee in paper cups and went to an out of the way table. After they were seated Gallardo told Alejandro that several years ago when the doctor had been given the clinic by Puerta he'd come to Baltimore for a visit and while he was there had made arrangements for the deposit box and for access to it by presentation of the key.

Gallardo was sure that Alejandro would have no trouble getting into the box. He pointed out that over the years there were many different people who had placed items there without any questions being asked by the bank.

It was evident to Alejandro that Gallardo was as fond of the doctor as he was and they spent some time exchanging expressions of their affection. Alejandro was enjoying himself but wanted to get the money as soon as he could and then go to the library. After Gallardo gave him the key and directions for the bank Alejandro thanked him and retraced his steps to the center of the city where the bank was located.

When he arrived at the bank he was directed to an officer named Bonnie Kinney. From her appearance he guessed she'd been with the bank for several years. She was pleasant and made him feel at ease. After he presented her with the key she led him to the safety deposit vault and showed him the box. He saw that his hand was trembling lightly as he took the box from the vault into a private room. It was a large box and in it were several smaller boxes. None of the smaller boxes were locked. He selected one and opened it. When he saw what was in it his heart plunged. It was filled with pieces of white paper folded into rectangles much like small envelopes. One of the edges was folded so it fit into the other edge, which served to keep it from springing open. He recognized what cocaine users called bindles. They were small packages of cocaine for individual sale.

It appeared that Mendoza had rewarded Dr. Suarez with cocaine. Alejandro couldn't believe it. Now in order to have enough money he would have to become a drug dealer. He picked up one of the bindles and felt rocks instead of powder. From the feel of it the cocaine was in the form of crystals. He didn't know if this made it more or less valuable. He opened the bindle and got an even greater shock. What Alejandro assumed to be cocaine crystals turned out to be several beautiful large emeralds.

Alejandro stood for a minute and made a random check of each box. Each one was filled with the same kind of envelopes containing large emeralds. He put one of the bindles in his pocket, locked the box and left the bank. He visited several jewelry stores and after getting a good idea of the value of the stones he accepted the best offer. It provided him with more than enough money to see him through the coming weeks.

After buying some new clothes Alejandro returned to the hotel, changed, and then walked a few blocks to the Eisenhower Library. The woman at the information counter was very helpful and asked one of the students that worked there to show him where to find the copies of the Denver Post he wanted. After a quick demonstration of the filing system and the use of the microfilm machine the student left him alone.

Alejandro chose a month of papers beginning with the date he arrived in Mexico. He felt his hands shake as he began to search his past in order to determine his future.

CHAPTER 20

It didn't take him long to find what he was looking for but nothing had prepared him for what he read. He could only stare at newspaper in front of him in stunned disbelief. It was front-page news. The headline was dramatic. 'Land Grant Heir Named as Suspect in Murder of Labor Organizer'. The story beneath the headline said that the district attorney had announced that Alfred Curran, heir to the Sangre de Cristo land grant, was a suspect in the murder of Michael Chacon. Investigation showed that the victim of the murder, Michael Chacon, was suspected by the police of dealing cocaine. He'd been shot once, execution style with a 38 cal. Smith and Wesson revolver.

The district attorney, Richard Marquez, announced that the police had strong leads and believed there were two murderers. Besides Curran they identified Alberto Falcon a Chicano activist who had been posing as a labor organizer but whom the police had determined was a drug dealer. They believed that Falcon had fled to Mexico and was now the subject of a manhunt.

It was three days before Marquez announced the conclusion of the investigation. The murderer suspected of the actual killing was Alfred Curran heir to the Sangre de Cristo land grant. At the press conference, which was called by Marquez and the chief of police, they announced that the investigation showed that Curran's pistol had been the murder weapon and that there was evidence to link Curran with a Mexican drug cartel.

Alfred stared furiously at the paper. No wonder Don Francisco had warned him that something was wrong and that he shouldn't disclose who he was. He would have walked into a murder frame up. He forced himself to read on and with each new disclosure his anger rose.

Further investigation revealed that Curran had been involved in large scale drug trafficking for several years beginning with his years at law school. The DA further said they could only speculate that it was the aura of international intrigue and drug dependency that had ensnared the young scion in this odious business. They announced they had issued a warrant for Curran's arrest and that the Mexican authorities had been alerted to the fact that Curran had left the U.S. for Mexico.

Related stories mentioned that the suspects' father was in seclusion at his hacienda and unavailable for comment and that his wife Patricia had declined to be interviewed and was said to be in shock and had directed all questions to Richard Marquez who besides being the district attorney was also a life long family friend.

Several days after the announcement that Alfred Curran was a drug dealer and that he had participated in cold-blooded murder the Mexican authorities reported that he had been killed when the car he was driving had plunged into a deep river canyon in the state of Vera Cruz.

Marquez held another press conference and provided the passport of Curran and other identifying papers and announced that the family had been notified by the Mexican authorities that the burnt remains of Curran couldn't be recovered. The family decided to leave the decision regarding recovery to the Mexicans. The hunt for Alberto Falcon was continuing but it too was now in the hands of the Mexican authorities who promised full cooperation.

For Alejandro it was like viewing the scene of a battle with the dead and wounded lying about in various horrible ways. The scene repulsed him but he found it difficult to turn away from it. How and why did it happen? Was it because he told everyone he was going to investigate the workings of the valley? But what could he possibly have uncovered that required him to be killed to prevent it? If Richard and his father were corrupt he couldn't imagine that murdering him was the answer? It just didn't make sense. But it was clear to him that the murder and his being framed for it had to be the work of Richard Marquez.

The number of stories in the paper dealing with the circumstances of his death and his life before fleeing to Mexico grew less and less and finally disappeared altogether for six months. Then there was the announcement that Arthur Curran had suffered an aneurism immediately after the news of his son's death and after several months in a coma had died. This was too much for Alfred and he left the library to hide his grief.

Later, he returned and finished the review of the papers for the months following. By now there was a certain sense of inevitability. At least he found a reason why Richard had gone to the trouble of killing him. Patricia and Richard were married three months after his father's death. Now Alejandro had the answers to his earlier questions. Richard's fear of Alfred uncovering corruption hadn't driven him to having him killed. What he wanted was to own the Sangre de Cristo. He wanted to get back what he thought had been stolen from his family. He'd seen a chance to get rid of Alfred and had taken it. Except for some Mexican peasants and the miracle of Dr. Suarez it would have worked perfectly.

Alfred's despair over the death of his father and his situation turned to rage. He'd been stripped of everything; his inheritance, his father, his looks, his identity, three years of his life, and his wife. He felt helpless. If he returned to the valley and proved that he was Alfred Curran he would face a murder charge, and if Richard had been as careful in framing him for the murder as he had been in everything else, he would be convicted for a murder he hadn't committed.

He sat thinking at the table with the pictures and stories in front of him. In one paper there was a large picture of Alfred Curran. It was the picture of someone fifty pounds heavier than Alejandro. There were other significant differences. The surgery by Dr. Suarez resulted in the left eye socket appearing to be placed differently in the face. The eyes were farther apart. The left ear was smaller and shaped differently. Both faces were pleasant to look at but anyone who had known the old Alfred would never see him in the new one. Alejandro was convinced that if he returned to the valley no one would recognize him as Alfred Curran. Maybe the answer of what to do next was in that fact.

CHAPTER 21

On the one hand the task seemed simple. Adopt an identity, return to the Sangre, investigate the murder of Chacon, find evidence that would help prove that Curran was innocent, and then disclose his identity. On the surface it seemed easy but as they say the devil is in the details. What identity? As a stranger in the valley how could he hope to investigate a murder that was almost four years old? What authority would he have to get anyone to even discuss the case with him. At each turn of his mind the task seemed impossible.

He needed an identity that would also give him some power and that was the rub. Assuming the false identity of someone that would not be active might be easy, but having one that would give him power to make a criminal investigation seemed impossible.

The obstacles grew each time he thought about it. He remembered Don Francisco telling him once that he often tried to solve problems by imagining a solution and then working backwards to see if it was possible to create the circumstances to reach that solution. He asked himself what kind of person could appear in the valley and have the authority to ask questions about a murder over three years old? Under the circumstances probably no one. Forging identity papers saying he was a government agent was a sure way to get caught. He wondered what he would be in this situation if he had his choice? The answer, someone who had a legitimate purpose in the valley doing something that would be a good cover for investigating the murder. It occurred to him that if he was a lawyer he might be able to force the issue into court. Then under some pretext, and using subpoenas and other legal tools, he might be able to get into the files. This idea seemed worth pursuing. Alfred Curran was a lawyer and if there was someway for Alejandro to return to the valley as a lawyer it might be the ideal solution. He quickly realized that it was completely mad to think there was a way to obtain the identity of a lawyer and be admitted to the Colorado bar.

He spent each day thinking of ways to gain an identity and his impatience was growing. Each time that it seemed hopeless he remembered the teachings of Don Francisco and knew he must obey the admonition to be patient. When he thought of a plan and then rejected it he kept coming back to the idea of returning to the valley as a lawyer. No matter how impossible the idea seemed he knew that if it entered his consciousness with such regularity there must be a way to bring it about. His subconscious was telling him that this was the way to proceed, and he knew that his conscious must now devise a way to do it.

One day he retraced in his mind what Alfred Curran had done to get a license to practice law in the state of Colorado. As a member of the New York bar it had been remarkably easy. He'd sent an application for admission to the Supreme Court of Colorado along with proof that he was a member in good standing of the New York state bar. Because several states, including New York, had reciprocity with Colorado and a member of one bar could be admitted to membership in the other without taking the bar exam again.

Alejandro realized that none of what he'd done as Alfred Curran applied to him. He wasn't a member of any bar and to become a member he would have to attend law school and pass the bar exam. He couldn't get into law school even if he was prepared to wait the three years it would take to go through law school again and the additional year to gain admission to the bar. That was out of the question.

All right, he told himself, start again. Alfred had passed the
bar in New York. From that moment he was a practicing lawyer.
From then on all that was required of him was to obey the rules,
fulfill his continuing education requirements, and pay his dues
each year. Once a person was admitted to practice law in the state
he was assigned a registration number by the Supreme Court of
that state. Each year in January the lawyer had to reregister and
pay a fee. The system served several purposes. The money raised
was used to fund projects relating to the administration of justice.
It also gave the court information on an annual basis about the
lawyer; whether he was still practicing, retired, or had died.

In reviewing this procedure it began to occur to Alfred that if
he could find a way to forge documents that showed him to be a
lawyer in one of the states that had reciprocity with Colorado he
might then be able to use those forged documents to gain
admission to the bar of Colorado. Then he could return to the
valley and begin his quest to redeem himself.

The obstacles to doing this seemed insurmountable. He had
no doubt that if he appeared in the state and presented documents
and an application for admission there would be letters between
the courts to confirm that he was a lawyer in good standing in
the other state and they would find out that no such person
really existed. Once that happened he would be discovered.

He went over the scenario again and again. Somehow the
key to the puzzle lay in the registration system. What did the
court use the system for? One was to raise money, another was to
track the lawyers and assure they were not under some impediment
to practice. For instance what if an older lawyer suffered a stroke
and was hospitalized? Chances are no one would inform the court.
But the court had a built in system of finding out. This was
because when it came time for the annual registration and they
received no application or registration form from the person they
would strike him from the rolls until he complied with the
registration.

What if someone died during the year and no one told the
court? The process would be that when it was time for the annual

registration and none was received they would take the lawyer off the rolls of licensed practitioners. If he were deceased that would be the end of it. If he had merely failed to register he wouldn't be able to practice until he did register.

The more Alfred thought about it the more certain he became that the only mechanisms the court had for knowing that a lawyer was dead was someone informing them of the fact or waiting until the lawyer failed to register and be stricken from the rolls.

Suddenly he thought he had the solution. If he could assume some lawyer's identity immediately after their death and then inform the clerk of the Supreme Court that he was moving from the state they would place him on inactive status and not expect a registration statement. In that case if no one informed the court of the death they would always assume the lawyer had moved to another state and was no longer practicing in the old state.

Now Alfred had the key. First he would determine which states had reciprocity with Colorado. Having done that he would read the newspapers from states until he saw an obituary of someone that he thought would suit his needs.

CHAPTER 22

Alfred discovered that the District of Columbia had reciprocity with Colorado. He decided to stay in Baltimore for time the being and see what happened. Each morning he read the obituary columns of the Washington Post as well as papers of surrounding communities. While the mortality rate among lawyers seemed to be as high as with any other profession none suited his particular needs.

He needed to find someone who was nearly his age, had been practicing law at least five years, and was a sole practitioner. He assumed that if the deceased person was in a firm there would be a greater likelihood that someone in the firm would inform the court of the lawyer's death. He also wanted someone that was unmarried and without close survivors.

He knew it was a long shot but he was determined to wait. If his analysis was correct, and with the right amount of luck, he would soon be in a position to return to the valley as a practicing lawyer.

Most of the obituaries he read involved people over fifty, a group he couldn't fit into. On the one or two occasions that someone in their thirties died it turned out they were married or had close survivors. It was six weeks before he hit pay dirt. It was in the Baltimore Sun. "A traffic accident claimed the life of Baltimore attorney Alexander Courage on Tuesday. Courage was thirty-eight years old and was killed instantly when a car running a red light near the inner harbor struck the car he was driving.

Courage was a member of the Maryland bar and the bar of the District of Columbia and had offices at 1620 Andrews St. in the District of Columbia."

This might be it. There was no indication of a family and a hunch told him this one was worth checking out. He caught the next metro liner from Penn Station to Washington then took a taxi to the address listed in the paper. It was a row house in a low-income neighborhood. The house had been converted into several offices, and the name of Alexander Courage was on the door along with that of a collection agency, a realtor, and an accountant.

Alfred went in. What had been a foyer was now a reception area with a desk and filing cabinet. No one was in the room. He waited for several minutes and then a young woman came in from an adjoining room.

"I'm sorry I didn't hear you come in. May I help you?" She asked as Alfred turned towards her.

"I hope so. I'm here about Mr. Courage."

"Oh yes. Isn't it terrible? One day you're here and then suddenly you're gone. I don't know what we're going to do? He didn't have any family and I don't know what we're supposed to do when something like this happens."

"Were you his secretary?"

"Not really. I work for everyone here. I'm the receptionist and do some typing, and answer the phones when they aren't here. Mr. Courage did most of his own typing. I only did it if there was an emergency. I really didn't know anything about his work except . . ." her voice trailed off.

"Except what?" Alejandro asked in his most engaging way.

"Well maybe I shouldn't be telling you this. He didn't have many clients. Whatever he did wasn't the usual lawyering. Anyway it's going to be a problem because all his stuff will have to be moved or sold and I don't know who will do it."

"I think I have the solution for you on that," said Alfred. "It's the reason I'm here. I work for the attorney dispute resolution department of the court here in DC. When a member of the bar dies unexpectedly we step in to protect the interests of any clients he was representing, and make sure his affairs, such as court dates, are taken care of in an orderly way. Will that help?"

"You're a godsend," she replied. "I was so afraid I'd be getting all these phone calls demanding files or money or information and I wouldn't have a clue about what to do."

"Well we'll take care of everything. I must insist you make sure no one goes into the office until there has been a complete inventory, and I've finished my work. Do you understand?"

"Oh yes, that's no problem."

"Good. I have two other offices to stop at for the same reason then I'll return and begin the inventory. By the way if Mr. Courage receives any calls please don't volunteer any information. Just take a number and tell them someone will return the call. We wouldn't want to give someone some wrong information would we?"

"No! I won't say a word." She was obviously relieved not to have any further obligation.

"By the way I neglected to learn from Mr. Courage's file where he was born. Do you know?"

"Baltimore," she replied.

Alejandro quickly decided this was as close as he might get to the right situation for a long time and he had to work fast. He left the office and in the next block he found a pay phone. His first call was to the department of vital statistics in Baltimore. He gave them the name of Alexander Courage and his birth date and told them he was traveling to Canada and needed a certified copy of his birth certificate. The woman on the phone said there was no problem and that he could pick it up the following day. Alejandro didn't know if Baltimore had a system for matching death certificates to birth certificates. He thought it would be unlikely and even if they did it would be months before it was done and by then it wouldn't matter.

His next call was to the clerk of the court for the District of Columbia.

"This is Alexander Courage," he said. "My registration number is 93524. Could I have some information please? I'd like to move to another state to live and would like to go on inactive status here. How do I go about that? Just a letter? Fine. Oh, by the way even though I'm on inactive status will you be able to forward my records to the Supreme Court of the state where I'm moving? No Problem? Good. And one other thing. I'm sorry to be a nuisance, but I've misplaced my license. Could I get a duplicate. Thank you very much. I'll pick it up this afternoon."

Alejandro returned to the law office. The receptionist let him into the office and he began to sort through the files. By all appearances Courage wasn't a very successful lawyer. So far as Alfred was able to determine he had a few clients that he'd prepared wills for but his calendar showed no appointments scheduled and no court appointments at all.

Alfred pulled out those files that had identifiable clients and wrote a form letter on plain paper informing them of Courage's death and returning their file along with a money order for $200 in case he was holding any money that belonged to them. It seemed unlikely but Alejandro didn't want someone writing a grievance letter to the court because Courage had some of their money. Based on what he could tell about the clients he was sure $200 would assuage any concerns.

The receptionist told him that Courage owed some rent to the accountant who was also the landlord. He spoke to the accountant who agreed that the Courage's furniture would satisfy the debt. Alejandro then sent a letter to the clerk of the court informing the court that Alexander Courage was moving to Colorado and wanted to be placed on the inactive list effective immediately. When he was finished he packed everything from the office that was of a personal nature.

"I believe everything has been taken care of," he said to the accountant and the receptionist.

"Thank you so much for your help," said the young girl obviously relieved.

"Yeah," added the accountant. "Thanks for everything. I sure wish my profession had this much concern for their fellow accountants when one of them died."

The next day Alfred picked up the certified copy of the birth certificate, went to the Baltimore Airport and took the first nonstop to Denver.

He was now Alexander Courage, lawyer.

CHAPTER 23

In Denver Alexander Courage rented a furnished apartment in the Capitol Hill area and then began the work of becoming a lawyer in Colorado with his new identity. It proved much easier than he thought it would. He filled out an application, and paid the fees. The only difficulty presented itself when he had to provide letters of reference from three members of the District of Columbia bar. He would have to forge them and hope the letters would be accepted at face value. He had no idea how thorough an investigation there would be into his application. Maybe the fact he was a lawyer in good standing with the D.C. court would be enough. All he could do was cross his fingers and hope.

He returned to Washington to search for three likely candidates whose name he could use in the forged letters of recommendation. He drove around the neighborhood where Courage had his office and randomly selected three lawyers from signs on windows and doors. He felt confident that they would have similar low scale practices as Courage and that they were not active in bar association functions. Both of which suggested to him that they wouldn't be too concerned with the niceties of the law practice and even if contacted might pass the matter off with an affirmation that Courage was in good standing.

He called the bar association and determined that the three lawyers he'd selected as references had no problems with the court and then ordered separate stationary for each of them. On each letterhead he altered the telephone numbers slightly as if it might be a typo. Maybe if the person handling his application called one of them this slight error would put them off enough to pass over the follow up.

He mailed the letters to Colorado, saved a few sheets and envelopes of the stationary just in case, and returned to Denver.

He was told by the clerk's office that the process might take three to four weeks. It seemed like an excruciatingly long time to hold his breath but he had a lot to do before returning to the Sangre. There was the question of what he could do in the Sangre when he did get his license. There was always the possibility of going there and opening his own office but he knew it would be a long and difficult task to establish himself. He thought a job in some agency would be a quicker path. If there was some legal aid society that operated in the valley that he could be a staff attorney for it would give him credibility and, with any luck, a better opportunity to discover what really happened the night Chacon was murdered.

He discovered there were several state agencies that had offices in the valley. The one that struck him as being the most likely was the Rural Legal Services Program. It was funded by the state and its lawyers represented poor people in rural areas that couldn't afford private attorneys. He called the office and discovered that the pay was next to nothing, the hours were long, the struggle was great and they could always use someone with his experience and dedication. As soon as he was admitted to practice they wanted to hear from him.

There was another problem that was much more serious. He'd never worked for a living. The income from the Sangre had been more than enough for his life style. His role in the New York law firm was to bring in business. Once the client was signed up his job was to keep them happy, he didn't practice law. Now he was faced with the prospect of actually representing people and didn't know enough to fool anyone. He had to use the time waiting for news to give himself a crash course in poverty law and court procedures. Every day he went to the Supreme Court library and read everything he could get find that dealt with those subjects.

He worked night and day reading the rules of court procedure, and the statutes that he might be involved with. He read the case law and law reviews on the subjects of poverty law and civil rights. He devoured every book he could find about trial lawyers and the arts they employed. He bought a copy of the classic *Anatomy of Cross-Examination* and kept it on his night stand. Slowly what had started as an exercise of desperation became a fascination with the subject. He began to gain a different insight into how the valley had operated all the years and how insulated he'd been with respect to basic human dignities and equality before the law.

Finally, in May, a letter came with the news he'd anxiously been waiting for. The Supreme Court of the State of Colorado wished to inform him that they had reviewed the application of Alexander Courage for admission to practice before the bar of the state of Colorado and everything appearing to be in order had approved his admission. If he would call the clerk they would arrange for his being sworn in and, with payment of the appropriate fees, he would receive his license.

He took care of all the details by the end of the week, gave up the apartment, got in the used Chevy blazer he'd purchased, and headed southwest on highway 285 to the valley, to his valley, to revenge years of captivity, multiple operations, the theft of his land, the taking of his wife, and to solve a murder.

CHAPTER 24

The road from Denver to the Sangre de Cristo wound its way into the Rockies and across their spine at 10,000 feet through the Icelandic expanse of South Park, and then over the rugged mountains that separated the park from the Arkansas River drainage. Antelope, deer, elk and mountain sheep punctuated the scenery as he moved ever closer to his lost home.

Thoughts sped through his head with the blur of a grand prix race. He realized that he'd been so immersed in escaping and finding a new identity that he hadn't spent much time preparing himself for the moment he would see the valley again. Nor had he faced the prospect of assuming a strange identity among people he'd known and loved all his life.

The past few years had at least prepared him for living a lie. For three years he'd lived as someone else and now the art of dissembling came naturally. He felt as if Alexander Courage, Alejandro Cordero, and Alfred Curran were just three persona of the same person. Sometimes even he wasn't sure which was the real him. It would be easier to play the part knowing that in physical appearance he looked completely different than the Alfred Curran that had disappeared three and a half years ago. But there was something else. He *was* a different person. His time with Dr. Suarez had made him a different person.

The route turned south at Buena Vista and then hugged the Arkansas river until it veered southeast to Salida and he continued south over the pass that separated him from his home. The Sangre de Cristo began at the north end of the San Luis Valley and extended a hundred miles south. At the north entrance to the Valley he stopped at the small village of El Monte. He bought gas, some sandwiches and iced tea. He then drove east across the valley and took a dirt road into the mountains. The road climbed the side of the foothills until it reached a switch back where he could park and gave him a panoramic view of the landscape

He backed the blazer onto the pullout and lowered the tailgate where he sat and ate and thought about his future. The words of Don Francisco had once quoted came back to him. "We can only live our life forward," he said, "and we can only reflect on it backwards." With this recollection Alexander's thoughts were overwhelmed by deep feelings of love for his teacher and the fear that he would never see him again. He shook himself back to the present and his need to live forward and the urgency of preparing himself mentally for all the emotional shocks that lay before him.

He gazed lovingly down on the valley that stretched before him like a beautiful carpet. As far as the eye could see there were fields in their familiar circular pattern. Here and there he could see small rainbows created by the mist of water as it was sprayed on the fields. The transportation trucks pulled small clouds of dust. Along the northwest edge of the grant the lakes and ponds that were sanctuaries for hundreds of species of birds glittered like jewels in the afternoon light. In the foothills to his left, well in the distance, he could make out the outlines of the family hacienda. In the valley below him was the town of El Centro where his new job waited.

He suppressed his desire to hurry; to get started with the business of revenge and the rescue of his wife. He knew deep within himself that he must think about the events ahead. He must be mentally prepared for whatever he found. He must have a reservoir of confidence and strength to overcome any challenge.

He reviewed the newspaper reports about his disappearance. A migrant worker named Michael Chacon who had been posing as a labor organizer had been murdered. The report issued by the

district attorney was that he was a cocaine dealer and worked for
Alfred Curran, the heir to the Sangre de Cristo land grant. There
was another person involved in the drug dealing named Alberto
Falcon. Curran and Falcon had a falling out with Chacon and
had murdered him at the house where he and Falcon lived. The
gun that was used was traced to Alfred Curran and his fingerprints
were the only ones on it. The investigation showed that Curran
had fled the scene and traveled to Mexico by air. Falcon's
whereabouts were unknown but he was presumed to be hiding
in Mexico. Later the Mexican authorities reported that Curran
had been killed when the rented car he was driving had plunged
several thousand feet into a gorge in southeastern Mexico.

Curran's father suffered an aneurism and was in a coma until
his death a few months later. After Alfred Curran was officially
declared dead his widow married Richard Marquez, the district
attorney.

Alexander pondered the facts for some time. He could see
no immediate way that he could prove his own innocence. He
decided that a specific plan would depend on events as they
unfolded. Now all he could do was start his job as a legal aid
lawyer and hope he could drive events in the right direction.

The sun dropped behind the Fremont Mountains that
formed the western border of the valley. Now was the time that
Don Francisco called the *crepusculo.* The time at dawn and dusk
when there was light but the sun wasn't visible. It was during
these times of day that Alexander and the Dr. had spent most of
their reflective moments together. They did so in the morning to
prepare for the day, and in the evening to reflect on their successes
or failures. It brought a special feeling of poignancy to Alexander
and a warm breeze crossed his cheek like the gentle caress of Don
Francisco's hand when he'd nursed Alexander.

Alexander stirred himself, closed the tailgate, and started down
the mountain to El Centro and to begin his quest.

CHAPTER 25

"Colorado Rural Legal Services," the voice that came to Alexander through the phone was that of a young woman with a slight Hispanic accent.

"This is Alexander Courage," he replied. "Is Miss Chavez in?"

"Oh, Mr. Courage, we wondered when you would arrive. Celia is having a breakfast meeting at Melina's restaurant. It should be nearly finished. Anyway it's with members of the board and I'm sure she wants you to meet them. Why don't you go over there? Do you know where it is?"

"Yes," he answered. "I saw it last night when I arrived. I'll go right over."

The restaurant was in the same block as the hotel where Alexander had taken a room. The restaurant was simple and was decorated with southwestern decor. The letters on the window said that it served Mexican and American food. Alexander pulled open the screen door and stepped inside. On each side there were tables and chairs and directly ahead a counter with stools. Three men were seated at the counter having coffee and a few of the tables were occupied. He glanced around the room and saw only one woman. She was seated at one of the large tables near the wall. Obviously the table had been used by several people but now there was only one other person at the table. When Alexander recognized him he had to call on all his discipline not to turn on his heel and leave. It was Augustine Romero, his childhood friend and now priest to the Sangre de Cristo. All of Alexander's planning could very easily go out the window in the first minutes if Augustine recognized him.

Alexander nervously walked to the table. Augustine and the woman were in serious conversation and it was a minute before they realized Alexander was standing near the table. The woman looked up.

"You must be Mr. Courage our new lawyer," she said with what Alexander thought was a touch of resigned sarcasm in her voice. Father Romero got to his feet.

Alexander could only marvel at how little Augustine had changed over the past four years. 'If I haven't changed anymore more than he has,' thought Alexander, 'I'm about to be found out.'

The woman, now standing, introduced herself. "I'm Celia Chavez," she said extending her hand. Alexander shook it and was mildly surprised at the strength. She looked at him with a certain indifference as if she didn't feel he would be in the valley long enough for her to invest much time in getting to know him. Alexander was puzzled. He had the impression from the state office that there was a serious need for lawyers in the office, but this initial welcome seemed distant and unenthused. Celia quickly removed her hand and turned towards Father Romero who in turn had been watching the scene unfold with studied interest.

"Augustine," she said, "I'd like you to meet the latest temporary employee of the legal services office. This is Alexander Courage from Washington."

"Now Celia save your sarcasm for someone that doesn't know you so well." Augustine replied smiling at Alexander. "I'm sure Mr. Courage isn't just a temporary employee. I'm sure he'll be here for sometime. I'm Augustine Romero," he said offering his hand to Alexander who was relieved not to see any hint of recognition in the priest's face. He'd passed the first and most important test. If Augustine didn't recognize him he was sure no one else would. Maybe he could relax a little now.

"I'm very pleased to meet you *padre*. And I'm from Baltimore not Washington."

"A distinction without a difference I'm sure," said Celia as the three of them sat down.

"I'm sorry you didn't arrive a little sooner," Augustine said. "We just finished our monthly board meeting but the other two members had to leave for work." He changed from English to Spanish and asked, "Your resume says you are fluent in Spanish. Did you learn it in Baltimore?"

Alexander smiled. "No," he effortlessly changed from English to Spanish. "I studied it in college, then I spent several years in Latin America."

"What were you doing in Latin America?" Augustine asked.

Alexander thought for a moment. "I was doing research for a doctoral dissertation on the plight of political prisoners."

"How interesting. Is it complete?"

"Not yet."

"Please let me see it when it's finished," Augustine responded and then glanced at his watch. "Goodness," he said. "I'll be late for confessions. Alexander, I must go now but I want to know more about you and help you understand the valley. Why don't we all have dinner tonight? Let's say seven o'clock here?" He didn't wait for an answer. He stood up, kissed Celia on the cheek, and left.

Alexander watched him leave then turned his attention back to Celia who had a wry smile on her face and was imperceptibly shaking her head. "You like him very much," commented Alexander. It was a statement not a question.

"Yes," Celia replied. "He's a devoted and courageous humanitarian. A vanishing breed."

Alexander changed the subject. "When you introduced me to him you said I was the new temporary lawyer. What did you mean? Am I on probation and you have already decided to fail me?"

"No!" answered Celia emphatically. "I'm sorry if it sounded that way. Let me explain my cynicism. Over the past five years there have been four lawyers that have come to work in the office and all of them are gone. Frankly, I think it would be easier to do all the work myself than train someone only to have them leave just when they become useful and have gained the trust of the people we serve."

"Why do they stay for such a short time?"

"There are many reasons. They come here because they have a romantic sense of riding their white charger into the valley and triumphantly winning the distressed damsel, called justice, from the lair of the dragon. Then they find out that things don't work that way. They discover there is no glory, just nitty-gritty hard work. Our victories are measured with teaspoons not buckets. Soon they are disillusioned and the lure of money and the city are rationalized into helping society where they can truly make a difference. They cash in on the experience and then leave."

"Surely that doesn't account for all of them?"

"I suppose I'm not being completely fair. I think what I said is true but it may not be all the truth. There are other factors. Fear is one."

"Fear of what?"

"To understand that you must understand the dynamics of the Sangre," she replied. "And to understand that you must spend a lot of time in the valley." She looked at him expectantly.

"I intend to be here for a very long time," said Alexander.

"They all say that," she responded. "Time will tell," she continued "but we'll only know that by living it won't we?" She didn't expect an answer. "Well, let's get started," she said.

CHAPTER 26

Celia and Alexander spent the rest of the day familiarizing Alexander with the legal services offices and indoctrinating him in the operation of the program. Celia did her best to describe the work. The kinds of cases the office handled were ones that the legal profession would consider small potatoes. It was rare that a dispute involved more than five hundred dollars, an amount that most lawyers wouldn't consider worth their while. For a migrant worker though it was proportionally more in terms of survival than ten thousand was for the man that made a hundred thousand. Cases usually involved landlord-tenant disputes or rental agreements. Sometimes disputes over payment of wages came up. There was the large category of how each of the small towns in the valley treated the workers. Celia explained that major crime involving the poor, such as drug dealing, theft, murder, spousal abuse and so forth was handled by the public defender. But there wasn't much of that. The migrants, she said, were extremely law abiding. It was the cases of minor violations of town ordinances that she and Alexander handled and these were plentiful, as he would find out over time.

Before either one of them were aware it was time to meet Augustine for dinner. It was a short walk back to Casa Melina, the restaurant where they had met earlier.

Augustine wasn't there yet. They chose a small table near the window and ordered two Tecate beers. Alexander picked up the thread of the earlier conversation. "Why are town ordinance violations so plentiful and so much of our work load?" he asked.

"It's one of the major patterns of corruption in the valley," Celia began. "It works this way. The labor camps are all located near small towns like La Garita and Del Norte. These are municipal corporations that contain little more than a grocery store, a gas station, a bar and restaurant, maybe a mercantile, a city hall and a fire station, plus fifteen or twenty homes. The towns themselves are owned by the Sangre de Cristo which means Anthony and Richard Marquez." Alexander felt a gnawing in his belly. To hear of the Sangre referred to as belonging to the man who had tried to kill him and stolen his wife was nearly more than he could take. He took a sip of beer and tried to calm himself. Celia went on.

"Most of the ways the Marquez's exploit the valley is legitimate although on the windy side of the law. In this case they use ordinances against public drunkenness to exploit the workers even more than what they have already done through wages and kickbacks. Actually every aspect of the operation of the valley is worthy of some mafia controlled borough in New York."

"Is this part of the fear you had mentioned earlier?" Alexander asked.

"Most of the time the fear is based on more explicit facts," Celia said. Just then they were interrupted by Augustine Romero who excused himself for being late as he sat down and told the waitress he would have a Tecate.

"Padre," Celia said to him. "I was just about to tell Alexander how Richard Marquez and his gang take care of anyone who tries too hard to help the migrants in the valley. Specifically I was about to tell him about the murder of Michael Chacon and how they framed Alberto Falcon"

"Please, Celia you know that I feel as you do about that incident, although for different reasons, but I wish you would be less strident in your description. It can only lead to trouble for you."

Alexander saw this as a good opportunity to find out more about the murder of Chacon. He turned to Augustine. "You just said you had different reasons for believing what Celia said about the death of Chacon. May I ask what they are?"

The waitress delivered the beer and Augustine took a drink before answering. "Please don't misunderstand me, Alexander. I agree with Celia that Michael Chacon's death wasn't because of drugs. I believe that for two reasons. First, because I knew Michael and worked with him and Alberto Falcon, and they were dedicated to the problems facing the migrant laborers. I promise you they were not involved in drugs. Second, and even more importantly, in order to believe the two of them were involved in drugs I would have to believe that my dear friend Alfred Curran was involved in drug trafficking. I know that was an impossibility."

"How can you be sure?" asked Alexander relieved to know someone believed in him.

"Because Alexander and I were like brothers. I grew up with him. My mother was his mother. Alfred's mother died when he was two years old and my mother raised him. We were inseparable until he went away to prep school and I went to the seminary. Believe me it's inconceivable that he would be involved in such things. It wasn't in his character."

"Padre," Celia interjected. "I agree with you that Alfred Curran couldn't have been involved in drugs because if he was then Michael and Alberto were and I don't believe that. But when you say it was out of character for Curran aren't you overlooking the fact that he didn't seem to have much character at all?"

"That's not true, Celia. Oh, I admit that before Alfred had returned to the valley his interests and values were shallow. He married a woman that was an eastern debutante and it seemed all they were interested in was a fancy eastern social life. He didn't want to stay in the valley. He just wanted to take the money from his inheritance and live between New York and Europe. He wasn't very serious or ambitious and didn't care much about anything other than his own pleasure. But at the time of the murder I saw that this was changing. I found out later he'd decided to stay in the valley and was very energetic in learning all there was to know. It was just a matter of time before he would have discovered the corruption. I knew him. Within him there was something good. He only needed to find it. He needed someone to bring it out of him, but it was there, I promise you."

"Why were they sure that Alfred Curran murdered Chacon? What was the evidence?" Alexander asked.

"The best way to answer that," Augustine said by way of response, "is to tell you the whole story and let you draw your own conclusions. First, let's order. May I order for you?" Alexander said yes and Augustine engaged the waitress in a lengthy conversation in Spanish. Celia smiled and in an aside to Alexander explained that southwestern cuisine was Augustine's passion. While they were waiting for the food Augustine told the story.

"Not long before the murder of Chacon Alfred and his wife, Patricia, returned from New York for his father's eighty-fourth birthday celebration. It was a grand time. I had just been assigned as parish priest here in El Centro." He paused for a moment as reliving that night then he continued. "Besides being a birthday celebration it was also a chance for Arthur Curran to invite some politicians and to do some arm twisting against the migrant labor bill that came before congress every year.

"My mother was still managing the hacienda, which she'd done all my life, and my father was still the valet to Arthur Curran. The party was a huge success. We met Patricia for the first time and Alfred and I were reunited after many years. Nothing unusual happened that night except Alfred made it clear that he was only going to stay in the valley for a short time and then he and Patricia were going to make their permanent home in the east and travel between there and Europe. This wasn't much news since we assumed that to be the case all along.

Richard Marquez was also there. Richard was a few years younger than Alfred and me but we had known him as we were growing up. His family was one of the original land grant recipients. His father worked for Arthur Curran and in many ways managed the valley. I hadn't seen Richard for several years and I noticed a change that I found troubling. Perhaps change isn't the right word but he was different. He came from a very violent and abusive family and always had a mean streak but that night I sensed that he'd become much more hardened and bitter."

"Why would he be bitter?" Alexander asked.

"Richard was always of the opinion that the Sangre de Cristo land grant had been stolen from his ancestors."

"Is that true?"

"There was some justification for him thinking that. But so could descendants of ten or twelve other Hispanic families. Richard's family was one of the original families that had applied to the Spanish crown for the grant. Over the years his family and the others had abandoned it and after the war with Mexico the Curran's and others came here and perfected the grants in their names. So while there was some history to support his feelings it wasn't much. And besides the Currans had treated his family very well. They always had first choice at all the ways to make money in the valley and Richard's father took advantage of that."

"In what way?" Alexander asked.

"In every way possible. By the time Richard returned from law school his father managed the day-to-day operation of the valley and had corrupted it in a way that produced enormous income for him and Richard. He controlled all the jobs. He took kickbacks from everyone that he hired. He got kickbacks from the canneries, the stores, the police, and the court personnel, even the judges. He controlled everything. And he maintained his control in very violent ways. He'd always been a sadistic man and often we saw the evidence of that violence on Richard.

"When we were young and Richard became angry he would inevitably tell us that the valley belonged to him and someday he would get it back. Of course we always attributed it to a temper tantrum and never took him seriously.

"Also at this time Michael Chacon and Alberto Falcon had come to the valley for the second year in a row. In the first year they had made great progress in organizing the workers and Richard and his father knew that if they were any more successful it could destroy their whole empire.

"One night after an organizational meeting a group of vigilantes took Alberto Falcon to a remote place and beat him horribly. The word among the migrants was that Richard or his father were personally responsible. Since it happened the night of the party and Richard and his father were both there we knew they were not involved. Many of us were prepared to believe that Richard's father was capable of such an act but felt Richard was different.

"In any event the beating did not have its desired effect. It only caused Michael and Alberto to increase their efforts. Many of the migrants began to think that perhaps they could bring about the change that was so desperately needed. More and more workers joined them. This caused Richard and his father even greater concern and I believe they made the decision to get rid of Chacon and Falcon. If it meant murder I think Anthony Marquez was capable of that."

"But how is Alfred involved in this?" Alexander asked.

"I don't believe he was." Augustine replied. "During the months leading to the murder and Alfred's disappearance I saw him often. He was busy learning how the valley functioned. He spent most of his time with the Curran's lawyer, John Taylor."

"So Curran had decided to live in the valley?"

"At the time I didn't know that. My father told me later that Alfred had agreed with his father that his future was here and that he and Patricia would live here. In fact my father said that his trip to Mexico had been planned for some time and that it was to sign some contracts."

"Did your father tell the DA that?" Alexander asked.

"Yes," replied Augustine, "but nothing came of it."

"Where is your father now?" Alexander asked hesitantly.

Augustine made the sign of the cross. "Dead these past two years," he replied. "He seemed to lose the will to live after the death of Alfred's father and of Alfred. Alfred was like a son to him. May their souls rest in peace." This somber moment was relieved by the delivery of the food. Augustine quickly put the memories behind him and began to wax eloquent about the dishes before them.

"These," he said pointing to a colorful plate, "are stuffed poblano peppers in a red chili sauce, and these," he said pointing to another dish, "are strips of beef simmered in a chipotle pepper sauce. With the rice and black beans you will find it's all very delicious."

The three of them ate in silence, each savoring the wonderful combination of flavors that suffused their palates. Alexander wanted desperately to hear more but controlled his eagerness. Finally he asked Augustine about the details of the murder.

"The police said they received an anonymous tip that there had been a shooting at the house near La Garita," Augustine began. "It was the temporary home of both Chacon and Falcon. The police said that when they arrived they found Chacon shot to death. Alfred Curran's gun with his prints on it was near the body. The ballistics stated categorically that it was the gun that had been used to shoot Chacon. The police also found significant amounts of cocaine that they concluded was from a larger shipment. Falcon was never seen again but his car was found abandoned just across the New Mexico state line. The police found cocaine in it and established that it was part of the same shipment found with Chacon.

"Naturally no one believed that Alfred was involved. Everyone believed there was some explanation. His gun could have been stolen and the prints carefully preserved in an attempt to implicate him or embarrass the Currans.

"We all waited for the explanation. Then to our amazement it was announced that Alfred had flown to Mexico the night of the murder and that his whereabouts were unknown. Then we were informed that he was killed when the car he was driving plunged into a ravine and was burned."

"What proof was there that the remains in the car were those of Curran?" Celia interjected.

"Richard announced that the dental records proved conclusively that it was Alfred."

Alexander reflected on this. Obviously if Richard could bribe Mexican police officials to murder Alfred it would be simple to get them to prove it through phony dental comparisons. Both Patricia and his father trusted Richard and it would have taken serious suspicions by his father and wife to override Richard.

"Everyone was in shock," Augustine continued. "Alfred's father suffered a stroke and died several months afterward. Alfred's wife mourned his death for several months and eventually resumed her life and later married Richard. And Richard had what he'd always said he would have. He had the Sangre de Cristo."

"Do you believe he somehow lured Alfred into a trap assuming he could either marry the widow or gain control in some other way?" Alexander asked.

"Yes. In my heart I believe it but I can't prove it and with Alfred dead and Falcon gone I'm sure we will never know the truth."

The three of them sat silently for a moment. Alexander had one more painful question. "Is your mother alive?" he asked.

"Yes," said Augustine, "thanks be to God," as he made the sign of the cross again. "She's alive and strong. She cooks for me at my home. You will meet her soon and have the best food in the valley."

The story Augustine had told was helpful to Alexander but he couldn't concentrate on it. He was suddenly filled with emotions he found difficult not to betray. He managed to control himself until dinner was over, then he excused himself and walked back to the hotel.

Augustine watched him leave. "You know I think this one is different than the rest. I think he has the mental and physical toughness to fight Marquez. Also he's quite handsome. Maybe he was sent here for two purposes."

"Such as?" Celia asked.

Augustine had a glint in his eye when he answered. "To help the people in the valley and to win your heart."

CHAPTER 27

Celia and Alexander spent the next day at the Los Arboles migrant labor camp. Their job was to determine what legal problems the workers had and provide them with the legal services they needed. The camp itself shocked Alexander. It was nothing more than a slum that wasn't part of a city. In contrast to the hovels called houses the setting was beautiful. It was next to the banks of a dry riverbed. The water below the surface was plentiful and nourished the large cottonwood trees that gave needed shade. The buildings that were rented to the workers and their families were nothing more than tar papers shacks. Ramshackle one-room affairs built with less care than the average farm outbuilding. In most of them six or more members of a family lived on top of each other. There was no running water. A well with a hand pump was all that served the entire camp. There were no toilet facilities except outhouses. In many cases these had long outlived their usefulness. He hadn't seen poverty in Mexico that was worse than this camp.

In the center of the camp there was a picnic table and it served as Celia's office. She and Alexander sat there and several of the workers came to her with their problems. Often it had to do with complaints of being mistreated by a work foreman or the fact that a child wasn't allowed to attend school. For the most part the problems stemmed from the fact they were migrant workers with no political power. They were at the mercy of who they worked for. He could see the frustration on Celia's face as she listened the problems knowing that there was little she could do to help. They stayed at the camp into the early hours of evening then started back to El Centro.

Not long after the drive began Alexander vented his anger. "I can't believe that these people are exploited like this," he said. "Cattle are treated better. Why is this allowed to go on?"

Celia was quite for a minute. When she spoke her voice was measured in a way that gave the impression she was deliberately hiding rage. "These are the dispossessed," she began. "Someone in the food chain gets screwed in our society and these are the logical ones. They don't vote; partly because the system prevents it, and partly because of their nomadic existence. They are illiterate and in many cases can't even speak English. Every year is a struggle to survive and there's no time to break the cycle."

"But how can the owners allow it?" Alexander exclaimed. "This valley produces enough money. These people could be treated better than they are and everyone could still make a lot of money"

"The answers to that are tradition, greed, and power." Celia responded. "Tradition because ever since the Currans began to develop the agriculture in this valley they exploited the migrants; greed because Richard and Patricia Marquez can never seem to have enough money; and power because they control so many lives. For them it's like an aphrodisiac."

"That part about the Currans isn't true!" Alexander exclaimed. He quickly he realized his error but before he could say anything Celia spoke.

"How do you know whether the Currans exploited anyone or not? You just got here yesterday." Celia said. Now she was worked up and didn't wait for Alexander to answer. "Do you think these pathetic camps were just built since the Currans died? It's clear they have been here for more years than most people in the valley can remember. They haven't been maintained since they were built. Of course it was going on when the Currans were here. They started the tradition. Old man Curran was notoriously opposed to improving their condition. He spent more money bribing legislators to prevent change than it would have taken to change the situation. Before he died, Alfred Curran, the old man's son, was a fat, lazy, eastern effete snob who cared more about going to the opera and symphony, and playing bridge and golf, than about the valley. He sure as hell didn't worry about the plight of the migrants."

Alexander could barely control himself but he knew he must. This picture of his father and himself was painful and yet somehow he wasn't sure it was false. With a superhuman effort at self-control he moved to another subject.

"The Currans are both dead so why haven't things changed? Richard Marquez is Hispanic. Why doesn't he change things?"

"Are you kidding?" Celia almost laughed. "As bad as the Currans were Richard Marquez is worse. No matter how much the valley produces he and his wife want more. The Marquez family and their crooked helpers can't get enough money. They'll go to any ends to get more even if it means destroying the valley. They are corrupt and have corrupted the police, the courts, the factories, and the health care system. They have their cronies in every job of importance or power and they see to it that there will be no change. Anyone who tries to bring change is eliminated in one way or another."

"But you have been here five years and haven't been harmed. From what I've seen you care for the people and help them. Obviously they haven't tried to get rid of you."

"That's because I'm their token. I'm allowed to have minor victories so they can point to me just as you have and say 'see we allow people opposed to our viewpoint to work here without problems'. But it's bullshit. I put band-aids on chest wounds. I treat symptoms. The disease remains. Believe me if anyone seems to be bringing about real change they are gotten rid of."

"You also mentioned power."

"Yes, power may be the worst of all the reasons why change doesn't come about. Richard Marquez is a vicious sadist. He has built a police force that is the same as he is. He's happy in the presence of pain and suffering. He has managed to gain control of enough land and people to form a small country and he's nothing more than an evil dictator. He'll stop at nothing to prevent his power being eroded."

"But doesn't anyone try and do something about it?"

"They used to. But nothing has gone on for several years."

"Why not?"

"Because of what happened to the last ones that made any progress at all."

"You mean Chacon and Falcon?" asked Alexander

"Yes." Celia said as came to a stop in front of a small cafe on the outskirts of El Centro.

"I'm hungry," Celia said. "How about some food?"

"Sure." Alexander replied getting out of the truck. They entered the small cafe and Alexander was overwhelmed with the smells that had so pervaded his childhood. Chilies roasting, refried beans cooking, tortillas being grilled, and sopapillas being fried. It gave him the same comforting feeling he had when he was in the kitchen of the hacienda with Isabella. He and Celia took a table near the counter and after getting two Corona beers with wedges of lime he resumed the conversation.

"Why do you think Chacon was murdered because of his attempts to organize the poor?"

"I've been told the story too many times to doubt it," she answered. "He and Alberto Falcon had been organizing workers in the valley for two summers. They were making real progress. Once Chacon was taken out of a meeting, tied to a tree, and beaten by Marquez and his men. In the past that had been enough to get rid of troublemakers. In this case it didn't work." She squeezed the lime into her mouth and then took a drink from the bottle of Corona. Alexander waited for her to continue.

"When Falcon and Chacon didn't quit the workers gained even more confidence in them. I believe the Marquez bunch decided that they had to take more extreme measures. Anyway Chacon was murdered. You know the rest of the story," she finished just as the waitress brought the dinner.

"What ever happened to Falcon? Was he ever found?"

"Alberto wisely split for Mexico."

"Why didn't he stay and fight the charges?"

"Because Marquez, who was DA at the time, ran one of the most efficient railroads in the country. He controlled the judge and the jury. It would only have been a matter of asking for a verdict of guilty and Falcon would have been history.

"So Falcon has never been caught?"

"No."

"Do you know where he is?"

"Mexico."

"Mexico is very big."

"So is your curiosity." Celia responded. Alexander realized he'd pushed too far and quickly retreated. Happily he could concentrate on the food in front of him. Enchiladas for him and chilies relleno for Celia. A basket of warm flour tortillas was set between them. They ate in silence for a while then Alexander ventured.

"You don't believe that Chacon, Falcon and Alfred Curran were involved in drug trafficking in the valley?"

"I don't know anything about Curran but I'm sure that the other two weren't. They were doing to good a job of organizing. They had to be eliminated so Chacon was murdered and Falcon forced to be a fugitive and leave the valley. What the situation with Curran was you'll have to find out from someone else."

CHAPTER 28

During the night and the following morning Alexander thought over what Augustine and Celia had told him about the murder of Michael Chacon. Obviously Richard had decided that he had to get rid of Chacon and Falcon. It was also an opportunity to get rid of Alfred Curran. Once that was done he could take the chance that Patricia would marry him. That wasn't much of a gamble. He and Patricia had struck up a relationship before Alfred's disappearance and it was only logical that with his rugged good looks he would be able to win Patricia's vulnerable heart.

The central issue for Alexander was how to prove that Falcon and Alfred didn't murder Chacon. At the moment he didn't have a clue. He was positive that Richard and the police had made sure that evidence against him and Falcon would be overwhelming. He was equally positive that he couldn't reveal himself before he had the facts to prove his innocence. The more he thought about it the more difficult the problem seemed to become.

Maybe, he thought, he would just continue as Alexander Courage for the rest of his life. Maybe the question wasn't of proving his innocence but rather just to use his abilities to bring down the Marquez Empire. He rejected that thought almost as soon as he had it. The fact was that he was still in love with Patricia. He couldn't imagine living in the valley without getting her back.

At the office the next day Celia's attitude was all business. "Good morning, Alexander," she said. "Today I'd like you to go to the La Garita camp. Just do what we did yesterday. Speak with whoever needs legal help and begin files on them. When you come back this afternoon we'll go over them and I'll supervise any action we take. One other thing, do you remember the old gentleman that was here yesterday?"

"Yes. I overheard him talking about an assault."

"His name is Estaban Guerrero," Celia said. "His nephew, Geraldo, was beaten rather badly on his way home from the bar in the small village at La Garita. He believes the police are responsible and he came to us for help. He wants to do something about it but I don't know what it would be. We could sue the police and the town but there were no witnesses and it will be the word of Geraldo against the police. Any judge or jury in the valley would believe the police over Geraldo." She paused to put a file away then continued. "Getting back to Mr. Guerrero. He has been coming to the valley to work in the fields for thirty years. The migrant community respects him, and we must have his confidence if we expect the migrants to come to us for help. He's an overseer now and he'll be at the camp. You should meet him and try and gain his confidence. He's sort of an elder among the workers and if he thinks you're all right it'll help you gain the trust of the others."

"What should I tell him about his nephew's case?" he asked.

"For now just tell him that I'm still looking into the circumstances of the assault and I'll let him know what I find out. Now you better go, it's a long drive." Alexander started out the door.

"Wait a minute," Celia called. He turned to look at her. "Don't you want to know where it is?" Another mistake he thought. He'd only been here two days and shouldn't know so much. He needed to be more careful. He recovered quickly.

"When I drove into town I saw the sign to La Garita on the highway. I assume it's near there."

"It is," she said and turned back to her desk.

The La Garita camp was a forty-five minute drive from El Centro. Alexander welcomed the time to himself. The drive was to the west side of the valley. It was there that the shallow lakes were located. During the spring and fall great numbers of birds stopped during their migrations. He'd always loved the birds. Keeping the ecology in tact had been one of the things that he and his father had agreed on most strenuously. They had always vetoed the sale of the water in the valley. They were afraid that it might upset the surface water and thereby affect the birds' habitat. His feelings about the birds had grown in intensity because of the role they had played in his regaining his memory at Los Altos prison.

When he arrived at the La Garita camp there were very few people to be seen. An occasional child came out of one of the houses for water but otherwise all was quiet. He found the building he was to use as his interview room. He took a yellow pad from his briefcase and waited for his first client. After an hour had passed and no one had come to see him he decided to take a walk around the camp. He asked one of the children where Mr. Guerrero lived.

When he got to the house he found the door was open. "Señor Guerrero?" he said in Spanish through the screen door. "My name is Alexander Courage, I saw you yesterday at the Rural Legal Services Office." He waited but there was no reply. He went on. "Celia Chavez asked me to see you and speak with you." Apparently the use of her name was enough to get him an audience because a voice responded by telling him to come in. He entered the room and found the old man seated next to a heavily bandaged young man lying on a sofa. Alexander assumed it was Geraldo, the nephew that had been assaulted.

"*Sientese, por favor,*" said Guerrero. Alexander found a straight back kitchen chair and sat down and waited while the old man finished feeding the nephew some soup.

"Mr. Guerrero," Alexander began. "I'm a new lawyer with the rural legal services and I'd like to help you and the other workers."

"That's what we always hear. Every new lawyer that comes tells us the same thing. And we trust them, and talk to them, and before long they're gone, or they go to work for Marquez and we're betrayed."

"But I'm different," said Alexander.

"Words are the tools of the lawyer." Guerrero replied.

"You're right," said Alexander. "I must show you, not tell you. But to show you I must have a chance."

"He's right uncle." The nephew spoke for the first time. "We should give him a chance." The three sat in silence for a while. Finally Alexander spoke again.

"Celia asked me to tell you she's learned nothing about the beating but was still trying and will let you know."

"There is nothing to find out," said Geraldo from underneath his bandages. "They don't like me helping the workers. Every time I drive some one to the camp after a night at the bar it takes money from their pocket. They believe that beating me will stop me."

"Who beat you?" Alexander asked.

"The two policemen from La Garita."

"Were they in uniform?"

"I don't think so. It was dark and they jumped me from behind."

"Did you see their faces?"

"No, but I recognized the voices."

"Do you mind if I look into it?" asked Alexander.

"Why not?" Geraldo replied. They were interrupted by a knock on the door.

"What is it señora," Mr. Guerrero asked, addressing the older of the two women standing on the porch. She answered rapidly in Spanish and told him that the other woman was a friend who was a permanent resident in the valley. She'd rented a mobile trailer house in La Garita and had been evicted for being late with the rent. She'd been required to make a damage deposit when she rented the trailer and now the landlord refused to return it.

Alexander spoke in Spanish. "Mr. Guerrero, this isn't right. Will you tell the señora that I'm a lawyer and I'll help her if she'll tell let me? I promise you won't be sorry." The old man thought for a moment and looked at his nephew. Geraldo nodded and the old man agreed.

When Alexander interviewed the woman he discovered that what had happened to her was a pattern in the valley. Landlords rented poorly maintained trailers to tenants and made them pay a substantial damage deposit when they moved in. Then he would evict them for the slightest reason and refuse to give the deposit back even though the tenant had been careful not to cause damage. In most cases the tenant simply accepted the loss and moved in with friends or relatives until they could find another place to live and the cycle would begin again. The victims rarely sought legal help because they believed the courts would be on the side of the landlord.

Alexander thought this might be the chance he was looking for. After listening to her story he took the few documents she had and told her he would do what he could. It wasn't much of a case but it was something. It was a beginning, and it would give him a chance to get into court and see how the system operated.

Alexander left the camp and drove the mile or so into the town of La Garita. It was a small town. There was a run down trailer park where he assumed his new client had lived. The main street had a general store, a bar, cafe, and several other buildings. One of the buildings had a sign that said La Garita Municipal Building. Alexander parked his blazer in front and went in.

At one end of the hall was a door marked municipal court and next to it one marked "clerk". He went in and was faced with an older Anglo woman seated at a desk.

"Can I help you?" she asked.

"Yes ma'am," Alexander responded. "I'm new here and would like some information. I'm a lawyer with the Rural Legal Services," he noticed a stiffening in the posture of the woman. "I need information about filing a suit in the court for recovery of a damage deposit for one of my clients."

"Did you say you were a licensed attorney?"

"Yes."

"Well you haven't been practicing very long," she said. "If

you'd been around very long you'd know this is a municipal court and cases like this are filed in the county court over in El Centro."

"Oh, I'm sorry." Alexander felt embarrassed that he didn't know such a basic point of law. "By the way," he asked, "how many policemen work for the town of La Garita?"

"Two," she answered curtly. "One is down the hall now if you want to see him." Alexander had been dismissed.

Alexander walked down the hall to the policeman and introduced himself. The policeman had a body that was like a Michelin tire ad, defined in its parts by creases at the neck and the waist. What he lacked was the warmth. Alexander asked the cop if he knew any thing about the assault of Geraldo Guerrero.

"That's being handled by the DA," he answered managing to convey menace and disdain in just a few words. "If you want to know any thing he should go to him. But you can tell Guerrero that if he stayed out of other people's business he could probably avoid another whipping." Alexander began to ask how the policeman knew that but decided to let it go. He said a cursory thank you and left.

CHAPTER 29

It was evening when Alexander got back to the hotel at El Centro. There was a note from Augustine waiting for him.

"Dear Alexander, I hate to dine alone and would like to have you join me tonight for supper at my house. It's next to the church. I finish with confessions and counseling about 7:30. Would that be too late? I hope not. We will eat simply so don't worry about letting me know if you can come, just come. If you aren't there I'll understand.

Yours in Christ, Augustine."

Alexander smiled to himself. He couldn't think if anything he'd rather do than enjoy a quiet evening with Augustine. Besides it would be a chance to see Isabella. He went to his rooms, showered and changed clothes. He'd been given what must have been the grand suite in the glory days of the hotel. It had a large bedroom that was closed off from a large sitting room and a small buffet kitchen. It was all that he needed and he found it quite comfortable.

After getting dressed he fixed a very dry martini with an olive and sat near the window looking out onto the main street of El Centro. He was looking forward to his dinner with Augustine. The question of seeing Isabella was more difficult. On the one hand he couldn't wait to see the woman who had been a mother to him since the age of two. On the other hand he wasn't sure he could control the emotions he knew would come. If it was difficult not to tell Augustine who he was, it was doubly difficult not to tell Isabella. Would she recognize him? To himself he felt like the old Alfred. He knew his appearance had changed dramatically but deep down he couldn't believe that he wouldn't be recognized by someone who knew him as well as Augustine and Isabella did. Obviously Augustine hadn't and he could only pray that Isabella wouldn't either.

He savored the dry cold taste of the martini and his thoughts turned back to his predicament. Alexander knew that the way to prove his own innocence was to prove the innocence of Alberto Falcon. If he concentrated on trying to prove the innocence of Alfred Curran it would raise too many questions. Besides, people in the valley that could help clear the name of Chacon and Falcon, such as Celia or Mr. Guerrero, wouldn't care about an effort to clear Alfred's name. Any show on his part that his real motive was to vindicate Curran would only raise suspicion and alienate the people whose help he desperately needed.

When it was time he walked the short distance to Augustine's house. When he arrived Augustine was just coming out of the back door of the church.

"Alexander!" Augustine said as he approached. "I'm happy you could come. You said last night that you wanted to know more about our southwest cuisine and my mother is the best cook in the valley." He hooked his arm through Alexander's and they went into the house together.

"Please sit down. I'll get us a glass of wine. Will that be all right? I like a glass of wine in the evening." He didn't wait for an answer and poured a glass of red wine for both of them. "Now I'll bring mama in to meet you."

While Alexander waited he tried to control his nervousness. It wasn't easy. For the first time in four years he was going to see the woman that was a mother to him. If she recognized him his chance of succeeding in his quest would be over. His palms grew sweaty. Finally she appeared in the doorway with Augustine.

"Mama," said Augustine. "I want you to meet the newest

member of the legal services office, Alexander Courage." Alexander watched closely but there was no sign of recognition on Isabella's part.

"I'm pleased to meet you Mr. Courage," was all she said.

"And it's very nice to see you," Alexander replied. "Augustine tells me you are the best cook in the valley. I'm looking forward dinner."

Her response was a self-confident one. "Augustine!" she said. "Only in the valley?" Alexander and Augustine laughed.

"All right, mama, I'm sorry," he said her. He turned to Alexander and with emphasis said. "What I meant to say Alexander it that she's the best cook in the state."

"That is much better *niño*," said Isabella. "Now I must begin the *antojito*s," and with a slight bow to Alexander she left the room. The two men returned to their chairs and their wine.

"Tell me what brings you to this valley," Augustine said when they were settled. Before Alexander could answer he went on. "I must tell you in advance that it doesn't seem quite right. You are well educated and have the looks of someone that could make his way quite successfully in many places that are more glamorous and financially rewarding than working here for starvation wages."

"It's all very long and boring." Alexander responded.

"You forget that I listen to confessions all week. I'm a good listener and not easily bored."

"All right," said Alexander. "I'm here at the Sangre de Cristo by accident. I intended to be in a rural community doing something like legal aid but being here is mostly circumstance."

He took a sip of the wine and continued. "Some years ago I went to Mexico and by chance became interested in the question of political prisoners. During my stay in Latin America I developed a fondness for the Latino culture. When I returned my decision was to live in the southwest. Frankly, Colorado was the state that I could most easily transfer my law license to. Money wasn't the issue. I have what I need from generous parents and what I wanted was to help the poor and disadvantaged. I made a lot of calls and this was the first job I found."

"A very interesting story," said Augustine. "I hope your commitment is deep enough to keep you here."

"What do you mean," asked Alexander.

"The problem we have with outsiders who come to help is that they are motivated by some ideal that they have formulated elsewhere. They have a romantic version of what they can accomplish here. Then when the change doesn't happen immediately they're discouraged. They suddenly realize that decades of the abuses and corruption will not yield to change overnight and they become discouraged. They don't understand that the change necessary in the valley requires incremental change over a long period of time."

Isabella came in with a plate of *antojitos* and put it on the small table between the two men. "These are small snacks," Augustine said as he pointed to each one individually. "These are empañadas, these are little canoes, these are small tacos, and these are quesadillas." Alexander began to sample one of each.

"I hope you'll find me different than the others," Alexander said bringing the subject back to the reasons why he was in the valley. He didn't wait for a reply and went on. "Are there problems in the valley other than the exploitation of the migrant workers?"

"In the past not really," Augustine replied. "Ever since the Currans gained control of the land grant it has been run in a way that rewards everyone involved in it except the migrant workers. Everyone else is well paid, well housed, and the schools are good. This hasn't changed much since Richard Marquez has gained control. The blind spot has always been the seasonal workers and exploitation of them. It has led to a bad situation that has become institutionalized."

"What so you mean?"

"It's all very complex but what it boils do to is this. Many people and institutions in the valley gain much from the exploitation of the migrants. So if anyone can change the treatment of the migrants it will threaten the economic well being of many people."

"In what specific ways?"

"It's hard to be specific. It would be easier to solve if it was specific. It' s more of a ripple effect. Nearly everyone in the valley benefits although some less directly than others. For instance the taxes and kickbacks the migrants pay during their stay here helps keep the property taxes and sales taxes down. The fines they pay in the courts pays for law enforcement. If the migrants didn't pay a disproportionate share of these costs they would be shifted to the permanent residents. That in turn would reduce their spendable income. If the migrants couldn't be exploited for labor the income from the valley would decrease by the amount that would be paid to the worker. So the result is the silent acceptance by a majority of people who at almost every other level of their life are decent good people"

"If they are such good decent people why do they tolerate it?"

"Because it's invisible to them. Because most people wear their heart on their left and their wallet on their right."

Before Alexander could comment Isabella announced that dinner was ready. The two men left their seats and moved into the small dining room. There were two places set with plates and a large soup bowl on top of each one. In each of the bowls were a handful of strips of fried corn tortillas and nothing else. When they were settled Isabella came in with a pan of hot broth that she ladled into the bowl on top of the tortilla strips. Between Alexander and Augustine were several small bowls containing chopped avocados, onions, peppers and cheese. The men then added some of each to the broth.

"Have you had tortilla soup before?" asked Augustine.

"No," Alexander lied. He'd had it hundreds of times in his life. It had always been identical to this. Augustine's mother had always made it.

"I believe the secret to a good tortilla soup," said Augustine, "is having the broth very hot and adding it to the tortillas at just the last moment." And then quickly added. "What do you think of Celia?" Alexander took note of Augustine's habit of combining an off hand remark about food with a penetrating question. It could easily catch one unawares.

"I'm glad you mentioned her," Alexander responded. "I'd like to know more about her."

"I'll ignore the fact that you didn't answer my question," Augustine answered, "and tell you what I know. She grew up in the south valley of Albuquerque to respectable but not educated parents. She's one of the few that escaped the south valley. She got a scholarship to the University of New Mexico and then to the law school. Not only was she a woman taking a man's seat she was a Chicana. Those are deadly odds to overcome. I'm sure all of it accounts for her present toughness. Have you noticed?"

Alexander winced inwardly. He had certainly noticed her toughness. Before he could say anything Augustine sent up another flare. "Have you noticed that she's pretty?" Both of them were surprised at Alexander's response. Augustine was surprised because Alexander did not immediately agree; Alexander because he realized that he hadn't thought about it before now. "Well," insisted Augustine.

Now that he thought about Alexander had to agree that she was pretty, more than pretty, beautiful. Hair the color of a raven's wing, skin as translucent as varnished oak, a figure that was impossible to hide even though she tried. Why hadn't he thought about it he asked himself? Was it because he wanted to keep a professional distance between them? Was it because he could only think of winning Patricia back and simply didn't see other women in that context? Or was he afraid of what might happen if he even thought about the affection he'd been denied for the past four years? He dared not share any of this with Augustine. All he could manage was a simple, "Yes, I've noticed." Then he tried desperately to change the subject. Augustine looked amused and Alexander quickly said. "Earlier I asked about other problems in the valley. Are there?"

"Yes, I'm afraid so," replied Augustine. "When the Currans were in control I believe they permitted abuse of the migrants more out of ignorance than malice. Now I believe there is a growing abuse in the valley that affects everyone, not just the migrants. It's as if Richard, not being content to tyrannize the migrants, is now trying to tyrannize everyone. The police and courts are more corrupt even when it concerns the permanent residents. Also there is the problem of the water. You may have noticed that not all the fields are planted. This is because Richard's company isn't as aggressive as it was under the Currans. The rumor is that he's trying to arrange the sale of the underground water to Denver and Albuquerque. If he does that many people believe it will destroy the valley as we know it."

"That would be a disaster," said Alexander. "The valley is meant for agriculture not to have its water stripped and sold to help some city grow. Besides what about the bird habitats?" He'd finished before he realized what he'd said.

Augustine was looking at him in a strange way. "You know when you said that you sounded just like someone I knew before. It was an uncanny resemblance." His voice drifted off as if he was hearing other voices.

"Is there anything else?" Alexander quickly interjected to take Augustine's mind off his blunder.

"The other is something I can only discuss in the most general way because what knowledge I have of it comes to me through counseling and the confessional." He paused as if choosing his words carefully. "I fear for Richard's sanity. I've been told stories that he suffers from a certain abnormal sexual appetite. I've heard that he pays for young migrant girls and makes them virtual slaves. I hear that like most abnormal appetites his grows in frequency and in violence. Unfortunately this information comes to me in ways that I can't prove. I also hear that many of the beatings of the migrants are done personally by him."

Isabella came and took the bowls away. Augustine asked her what the next dish was to be. "*Pollo pipian*" she said as she left the room.

"Wonderful," cried Augustine. "I'm sure you will like this. It's pieces of chicken browned and then simmered in a thick broth that's flavored with a mix of roasted sesame seeds, cloves and nutmeg. It's something special." Just then the dish arrived and it was all that Augustine had boasted it would be. They ate in silence and Alexander pondered Augustine's concerns about Richard's sadism.

"Do you believe Richard abuses his wife?" He was afraid of the answer and had trouble asking the question.

"I have no proof. But I believe so. Many times she doesn't appear at events where it would be natural for her to attend. The rumor is that she has marks on her face that she's afraid to show. Sometimes she appears with makeup that doesn't quite conceal bruises." Alexander fought down his rage at the thought of Richard abusing Patricia.

"I've answered your questions, Alexander, now answer one of mine. What do you hope to gain from your work in the valley?"

"Redemption and vindication," Alexander answered.

CHAPTER 30

When Alexander met Celia the following morning he was still enthused about the case of Mrs. Sandoval. He thought he might be able to do something to help her and if he did he knew it would lead to greater trust of him by the workers. At the end of the review he told her about his meeting with the Guerreros and with Mrs. Sandoval.

"Is there something we can do for Mrs. Sandoval? He asked.

"Alexander," she said after he'd explained the case to her, "this is a common problem in the valley. There are many landlords who provide meager housing for tenants and always charge a damage deposit. When the tenant moves out they always refuse to return it. The deposit is never less than one hundred dollars and sometimes it's as much as two hundred. This may happen ten or twenty times a year for each landlord depending on how many rental units they own. As you can see it can be substantial."

"Does anyone sue for the return?" Alexander asked.

"Of course! When I first arrived in the valley I did it many times."

"What did the court do?"

"Nothing."

"Nothing? Wasn't it outraged?"

Celia looked amused. "Any outrage the court felt was that we would waste its time with something like this. You have to understand that the courts in the valley are appointed or elected by the permanent residents of the valley. Through networks and

152

marriage they serve each other's interests. They don't serve the interests of the migrant workers because they don't vote and don't have a say in whether they remain as judges or not. Judge Hanson, in the county court, isn't going to rule against someone he knows well in favor of a poor, disenfranchised migrant worker. It doesn't work that way."

"Even if what the landlord is doing is illegal?"

"The courts never find it's illegal. Here is how it works. Let's take this Sandoval case you have. First you have to tell Ms. Sandoval that it will cost her fifty dollars to file the case and have the papers served on the landlord. Usually she'll say she doesn't have the money and would rather take her losses and move on."

"But what about a petition to have the fees waived based on poverty?"

"Good idea. What happens then is that Judge Hanson will require you to bring Ms. Sandoval into court and testify to prove her status as a poor person. First he'll embarrass her and probe into the details of her life. This may include the fact she lives with a man who she's not married to. You know just because these people are poor doesn't mean they have no pride. It's a humiliating experience he puts them through. Most of the time the judge rules that the person has enough assets and income that they do not qualify for indigent status and refuses to waive the costs."

"Can't that be appealed to the district court?"

"Yes of course. But think of this. The county court judge will have stretched the matter out as long as he can. That could be as much as six months. Then you appeal to the district court and that court delays it for another five or six months. Now it has been a year since you filed the case and you haven't even gotten far enough to have the landlord served with the complaint. The district court usually says the lower court did not abuse its discretion and throws you out. Then you can appeal it to the Supreme Court. That may be another year. Now two years have gone by and you have made absolutely no progress. The client has probably moved on or lost interest. But let's assume the

Supreme Court reverses the lower court and permits you to proceed without fees. Two years have gone by and you must now prove to Judge Hanson, who you have gotten reversed, that the word of a poor migrant worker, who he despises, is more credible than that of his buddy the landlord. No way, Alexander."

"But this is more corrupt than if bribes were being paid. Is this the case just in these damage deposit situations?"

"No! It occurs in every case. The fact is that the poor in this valley have no access to the courts. At least not in a way that has any practical value."

"Let's go back to the Sandoval case. Can't the office advance the costs of the suit?"

"We did that in the past but Richard Marquez got the legislature to pass a bill that prevented state funded agencies such as us from financing law suits."

"Can I do it personally?"

"Not so long as you work in this office."

"What about a foundation or some other organization? Couldn't we find someone who would care enough to fund cases such as this?"

"It's very difficult. Most organizations want a bigger bang for their buck than just funding lawsuits that involve a hundred dollar damage deposit. It's very difficult to show a foundation that this is all part of a pattern of discrimination." Celia seemed overwhelmed by the futility of it all. "Besides," she went on. "When people in the past have tried to organize the workers so they could gain strength from numbers they were beaten or, in the case of Chacon and Falcon, murdered."

"It's a horrible cycle of despair," said Alexander. "There must be an answer. What if I found someone to provide funds for these cases? Could we do them?"

"I don't know. I doubt it. But even if we could I'm not sure it would be an answer. It attacks the symptoms but not the disease. No one would want to fund lawsuits forever to get back damage deposits. Unless what we do brings about some permanent change I don't think it makes much sense. It would be better to spend the resources getting the law about damage deposits changed in some way than to fight it piecemeal on a case by case basis." All the time they had been talking Celia was seated at her desk typing a document.

"Celia if you feel this way why do you stay and keep beating your head against the wall?"

"Because," she said, "in spite of all the frustrations it's what I believe in. If I left the office and took a job that paid good wages I'd be haunted by what I knew was going on here and my soul would never be at ease. As futile as it is I've resolved myself to putting on as many band aids as I can until someone comes along who changes the basic system." She took the pages she'd typed and assembled them then stapled them together. "Here," she said handing Alexander the papers. "These are the documents I'll file to try and get Ms. Sandoval's deposit back. Read them over and see if they're right. I'll take care of this if you'll go out to La Garita and see what you can do for Mr. Guerrero's nephew."

Alexander was amazed. All the time she was telling about the futility of filing the lawsuit she was typing it. "What keeps you going?" The astonishment showed in his voice. "Where do you get the energy to come here everyday knowing you'll see the same misery and heartache. Knowing deep down that there is nothing you can do except ease the pain of this one person just a little bit but never change the root causes. What is it that allows you to do this?"

"Pandora's box," Celia replied. Alexander could only register confusion. Celia went on. "Don't you remember the myth of Pandora's box? Zeus gave Pandora a box for the person she married. When she married Epimetheus he opened it and unleashed all the evils into the world."

"Yes," said Alexander. "I remember the myth. And I realize there are evils in the world but how does it apply to you remaining in the valley amid such frustration?"

"To understand that you must remember the only thing that was left in the box."

"What was that?"

"Hope."

Celia closed the office and went to the courthouse to file the Sandoval papers. Alexander set out for La Garita. As he drove he thought about his conversation with Celia. He found her a remarkable woman. She was uncompromising in her commitment and yet realistic about the situation. It was a refreshing combination. Obviously she was totally resolved to fighting for the migrants' rights no matter what the personal cost or whether she had to do it alone.

He also thought about Augustine's question. Yes, she was beautiful. She was also strong, resolute, and committed to her cause without giving away any femininity. In fact her intellectual toughness made her all the more desirable. He let his mind play with the thought of what it might be like if he wasn't married to Patricia and free to pursue another woman. He felt Celia would be the only one on the list. But he had to force himself back to reality. He was married to Patricia and she was as much a victim as he was. The past four years must have been sheer hell for her and now with the added information that Richard was a sadist who beat her made it all the more important to solve the crime a soon as possible. There was no room in the equation for Celia no matter how much he might be attracted to her. He simply had to keep that in perspective.

One thing that Celia had said stuck in his mind. If things were to change it would have to be done in a big way. It wasn't enough to keep putting band-aids on major wounds. If he could find a way to make a major impact then maybe he could kill two birds with one stone. He would accomplish something good in a big way for the workers, and he might be able to put himself in the position of unraveling the murder.

He considered the possibilities as he drove. Maybe there was a way to bring some kind of class action against the landlord's to prevent them getting a damage deposit from the tenants. As he thought more about it he realized he wouldn't be able to win such a case. What then? One source of the frustration was his own inadequacy in the law. Another was a realization that the law was a lot like a spider web. It trapped the poor and allowed the wealthy to break through. Maybe he could find out something in the situation of Guerrero's nephew that would help him untangle the web. There was also the question of seeing Patricia and Richard again. He wanted desperately to be introduced to them, and to see for himself what the situation was. He was sure the key to meeting them was Augustine since he was still invited to functions held the Hacienda. Maybe he could convince Augustine to take him along as a guest. If that didn't work maybe he just had to raise so much hell that Richard would come to him.

CHAPTER 31

W hen Alexander arrived at the La Garita Camp he found Geraldo at home alone. Alexander went in and sat down. "Is your uncle here?" He asked.

"No," Geraldo responded. "There was some trouble at one of the fields and he went out about an hour ago."

"I came to tell him that we're filing papers today to try and get Mrs. Sandoval's deposit money."

"That's nice of you," Geraldo responded in a tone made it clear he didn't expect much to come from it.

"Yesterday when I was here," said Alexander, "you told your uncle to give me a chance. Did you mean that?"

"Yes I meant it. Why not? Celia likes you and I trust her judgment. Besides, even though I don't think anything you can do will change the big picture around here what Celia does helps a lot."

"Why is your uncle so distrustful?"

"Mr. Courage, please try to understand why my uncle and the other leaders feel the way they do. Every year there are new faces here to help us. And in the past we've put our confidence in them. But they either leave the valley or go to work for Marquez. It's better that we try and do this ourselves with the poor tools we have."

"But I'm only asking for a chance. Surely if you trust me on one small thing and I fail you have not hurt anything. On the other hand if I'm as sincere as I say I am and you drive me away because of lack of trust you will have missed a big opportunity. At least tell me more about you're beating."

"What else is there to tell? I've been upsetting one of the valley's favorite ways of making money and they want me to stop. It's as simple as that. First they beat me and if I don't stop then maybe they'll kill me like they killed Michael."

"What do you know about the Chacon murder?" Alexander asked. Geraldo only looked at him and didn't answer. Alexander realized it was too soon to talk about Chacon. He went back to the beating. "What were you doing to upset them?"

"I'm trying to stop them from milking the migrants for money to run their town."

"What have you been doing?

"Every night I go to the cantina with my pickup truck. Whenever I see someone leave to walk back here to the camp I give them a ride. I try to give everyone a ride but that isn't possible. Still I do a lot and the cops don't like it. And they know that if I get more people to help me it will take even more money from them. That's why they beat me. To make me stop, and warn others not to help me."

"Geraldo I know I'm a gringo stranger and I don't know everything that happens in the valley but I can't understand how the fact you give workers a ride home from the cantina threatens the town of La Garita."

Geraldo looked at him for a minute apparently thinking over what he'd said. "You said you drove by the court yesterday. Meet me there tonight at six thirty and I'll let you see for yourself what it means to the town for me to give drunk migrants a ride home."

"Fair enough," said Alexander. "I'll see you there."

Alexander spent the rest of the afternoon in his small interview room at the camp. Three women who had some minor questions visited him but it was clear that he wasn't to be trusted with anything important. At six he locked the door and drove to the court. The town was about a mile from the camp and since few of the workers had their own cars they walked to and from the town.

Alexander went to the door leading to the courtroom and looked at the docket for the evening court session. He counted the number of names on the docket. There were over sixty and all of them were Hispanic. It seemed like a lot of criminal activity for such a small town. Just then he heard some loud voices at the other end of the foyer. He turned and saw that the two policemen were standing next to Geraldo and speaking to him in a threatening manner. Alexander went over and when he got near he heard one of the policeman say to Geraldo.

"Maybe next time you won't wake up." It was the bigger of the two policemen.

"Do you mean next time you beat him?" said Alexander, as he got to them.

"Who the hell are you buddy?" said the cop turning on Alexander.

"My name is Alexander Courage. I'm this man's lawyer. Now tell me did you mean that the next time you beat him?"

The second cop spoke. "No. What he meant was that our friend Geraldo here should be real careful 'cause whoever beat him up may do it again and the next time he might not wake up, ain't that right Jerry? That's all you meant, right?"

Jerry obviously didn't like backing off. He looked at Alexander in a way that said you better never let me find you out after dark on a country road because if I do you are dead meat. The good sense of the other cop prevailed and Jerry let himself be led away.

"What was that all about?" Alexander asked.

"Just the usual warning to stop what I'm doing. Come on let's go in and you'll see how this all works." The two of them went into the courtroom. Alexander was surprised that they were the only ones there.

"Where is everyone?" he asked. "There are over sixty names on the docket sheet."

"No one will be here. That is part of the deal. Just watch."

As Geraldo said this, the clerk entered the courtroom. There was a slight indication of surprise at seeing anyone there. Then the judge came in. He wasn't wearing a robe and was dressed in jeans and a short sleeve shirt.

"Call the docket," he said.

The clerk read the first name on the list, "Manual Aragon " There was no answer and the judge said, "forfeit". Then the clerk read the next name, "Jorge Baca." No answer. "Forfeit," said the judge. And so it went for the entire docket. When the list was finished the judge looked at Alexander and Geraldo and said. "Is there something you have before the court?" "No sir," responded Alexander. "Good," said the judge. "Court's in recess."

The judge and the clerk left the courtroom and Alexander sat in dumbfounded silence. Finally Geraldo said, "Let's go."

Alexander and Geraldo left the building and when they were outside Alexander asked, "What in the world was that all about?"

"Let's go over to the cantina and get something to eat," Geraldo answered. They walked the short distance to the cantina and went inside. There were ten or twelve people inside. Some were seated at the bar and a few in the vinyl covered booths lining the wall. They picked a booth away from the nearest other people and ordered Coronas. The waitress left the menus and went after the beers.

"Geraldo," said Alexander. "What was that all about? There were sixty names on the docket, and they were all charged with the same municipal ordinance violation. None of them showed up for their court appearance and the judge couldn't have cared less. Something doesn't make sense."

The waitress delivered the Coronas and said she'd check back later for their food order. "This is the deal I've been telling you about," Geraldo replied. "Here is how it works. La Garita has a town ordinance against being drunk in public. In every case the fine is a maximum of $300 and a possible 90 days in jail." Geraldo took a drink of his beer and continued. "Every night of the week the town police position themselves between the bar and the camps. Then they arrest the workers as they are walking back to camp. The charge them with being drunk in public and put them in jail." The waitress interrupted them to take their order. Geraldo ordered tacos and Alexander ordered the chicken burrito.

"When they aren't home in the morning," Geraldo continued after the waitress had left, "the wife or friends go to town and post $50 dollars as bail. This bail gets them out of jail and they go to work to earn some money to pay for everything."

"I'm with you so far," said Alexander. "All these names on the docket tonight were people that had been arrested for being drunk in a public place. Is that right?"

"Exactly," said Geraldo. "And then it's understood between the city, the judge, and the defendants that if they come to court and defend themselves they'll be found guilty and get a month in jail. If they don't appear in court the bail they posted for their release will be forfeited and that will be the end of it."

"Beautiful," said Alexander. "Every week the police arrest the workers who have had anything to drink and the city makes fifty bucks. There were about 60 tonight. That's three thousand dollars. Not bad. And right into the city coffers. Over the course of a year it pays for the city government. And the permanent residents don't have to pay for it."

"That's why they're unhappy with me," said Geraldo. "Every migrant worker I give a ride home is one they can't arrest."

"Geraldo this is amazing. All the police have to do is arrest a certain number of workers every week and it pays for their salary and many other town services. Now I see what Augustine meant. So long as this goes on it covers things the residents would otherwise have to pay taxes for. If we could do something to end it that might be the thing I'm looking for." When he said this Geraldo looked at him strangely.

"What are you looking for Mr. Courage?" he asked.

"A way to save the valley," he answered as he signaled for the check. "Come on I'll take you home. I promise you I'll do something about this."

"I hope so," said Geraldo. "I hope so."

CHAPTER 32

When Alexander met Celia in the morning he told her what he'd seen at the court in La Garita. Celia listened to him with interest. She knew all about the problem but the fact he was indignant about it caused her to appreciate him more. When he finished she said.

"Now you've seen one of the greatest exploitation devices the valley has for the migrants."

"Does it just happen in La Garita?"

"No! It happens all over valley. It's a major source of funding for the municipalities. By raising money this way from the migrants they pay for things that otherwise the people that lived here permanently would have to pay for."

Alexander seemed confused. "I don't quite get it," he said. "Do you think it's legal?"

"I've thought about it a lot," Celia answered. "A far as I can figure it's completely legal. The ordinance against being drunk in public has been upheld by the Supreme Court so that part is legal. The limits of a possible $300 fine and or 90 days in jail have been upheld. There is no formal policy by the towns that anyone who doesn't show up for court will only have to forfeit the bail. And even if there were I'm not sure it would be illegal. Each of the workers that are arrested has the right to force the city to prove he was drunk. He has a choice of going to trial or forfeiting the bail. I think that is all the law requires."

"What happens if someone appears and fights the charge?"

"They're found guilty and put in jail for thirty days. Since they don't show up for work they lose their job."

"How many courts are there in the valley that do this." Alexander asked.

"There are ten municipal courts around the valley and they all do it. That includes the one here in El Centro."

"Do all the courts hold sessions only once a week?"

"Yes."

"Isn't there something that can be done about it?" Alexander asked.

"We've tried," answered Celia. "We even took the question of the constitutionality of the city public drunkenness law to the Supreme Court but they upheld it. We tried to organize the workers to appear in court and force the towns to jail them in the hopes that would cost the towns more than they took in but we couldn't get enough support." She thought for a moment then went on. "It's very difficult to make the workers see the long term. They are so caught up on the day-to-day problems of survival. In fact," she added. "It was this very problem that Falcon and Chacon were working on when Chacon was murdered."

"So in this case the powers that be won't even let you put a band aid on the wound."

"Not even a band aid." Celia said. Alexander got up to leave. "Where are you off to?" she asked.

"If you don't have anything you need me to do," he responded. "I thought I might spend a few hours in the law library. There're a couple of ideas I want to pursue."

"No, I don't have anything urgent. But remember a lot of what's in those books hasn't found its way into the valley yet. See you later," she said as Alexander smiled and walked out.

Alexander sat among the books in the law library and thought again about the situation. It was his sense of justice that was outraged. Here was a situation where the individual components were legal but the uses and result of the otherwise legal laws was wrong. There must be something in the equation that held the solution. To find it he had to dissect the problem and find the missing link. A link he could use to the advantage of the workers.

'I'll pretend,' he thought, 'that one of these workers has come to me with one of these cases. He tells me that he was walking to the camp from town where he'd purchased some cough medicine for his daughter. He swears he has not been to the cantina and has had nothing to drink and wants to fight the case. What would I do in normal circumstances? Obviously, I would try to prove he had nothing to drink and therefore couldn't possibly have been drunk. I could call the clerk at the drugstore to testify he'd bought the cough medicine; I could call the bartender to testify he'd not been in the bar that night. But would the judge believe him? Probably not. First, because the judge was paid not to believe the workers when it was their word against the police, and second, because the system has been so corrupted that the courts are not there to learn the truth but only to get a result. It's clear that so long as the judge is the one to decide the facts of the case any defense was hopeless. How can I get around that?' Alexander wondered. 'What would I do if this was a case of burglary and it was the same judge? He knew the answer to that question. He would demand a jury trial. Something clicked in his head, something that he'd read when he was waiting for the decision of the court regarding his application to practice law in Colorado. Suddenly he was on his feet and taking the first volume of the red statute books from the shelf. An hour later he was convinced he had the answer to ending the use of the public drunkenness ordinances to collect money for the towns. He was also sure that the result could give him enough credibility to help convince Falcon to use him as his lawyer.

He left the library and drove immediately to La Garita to see Geraldo Guerrero. Geraldo was parked in his pickup near the cantina waiting for his first passenger back to the camp. Alexander parked behind him and got in Geraldo's truck. He could hardly contain his excitement. "I believe I've found a way to stop the courts from raising money from bond forfeitures," he began.

"You're kidding!" Geraldo exclaimed. "Tell me how."

"It's pretty complicated," Alexander replied. "It depends on a lot of the workers agreeing to let me represent them and do as I tell them. But if you'll help me I think we can give it a try without much risk."

Geraldo debated to himself how far he could go in trusting Alexander. He finally said. "Tell me what you want me to do."

"I want you to get as many people as you can to come to court next week and let me represent them," Alexander said then added. "Geraldo this will not work if only a few agree. We need at least twenty."

"And what happens if doesn't work?"

"It'll work. I'm sure of it."

"We've heard that before. What if it doesn't?"

"They could go to jail. But Geraldo if we have enough people there isn't enough jail space for all of them. And besides it will cost the town a lot of money to feed them. Believe me I'm so sure of this working that I would gladly risk jail to do it. There is one more thing. If they do go to jail I've found a foundation that will pay them twice the wages they would have earned if they'd worked." He hoped Don Francisco would approve of this way of spending his money.

"They'll still lose their jobs," Geraldo said.

"Not if we represent enough of them," Alexander responded. "It's too late in the season to find replacement workers."

"Will they have to come to court?" Geraldo asked.

"Yes," Alexander answered.

"I guess I better get started then," said Geraldo.

La Garita wouldn't have another court session for a week and Geraldo needed that amount of time to enlist the cooperation of the workers that were arrested during the week. Alexander spent most of his time visiting the other camps where Celia introduced him to the workers. All the other camps were like that of La Garita. They all had substandard housing with minimal sanitation and rents disproportionate to the value of the housing.

Alexander never failed to come away from one of them with a deep sense of guilt that he and his father had permitted this situation to exist. He also rededicated himself to winning it back from Richard, and then making sweeping changes in what was nothing more than a feudal system of lords and serfs.

Since the camps were far apart he and Celia had a good deal of time to get to know more about each other. Alexander discovered that besides being beautiful and a good lawyer Celia was interesting in many other ways. She enjoyed literature, music and above all art. Her particular interest was in the early Hispanic art of the region. It was something Alexander, in his life as Alfred, had neglected even though he had spent time and money on art. They had long discussions about *bultos* and *retablos*, those three-dimensional and two-dimensional religious works indigenous to northern New Mexico. Her enthusiasm was infectious and Alexander became interested just from her descriptions. Alexander found himself thinking that he could easily fall in love with her if his situation was different.

As for Celia she was more intrigued by Alexander then romantically inclined. His strong, lean physique and angular, somewhat disjointed good looks were attractive. But Celia believed that love always began above the neck and worked its way down. If she couldn't love a man for his mind she would never be able to love him for his body. It was Alexander's mind that she was uncertain about. He claimed to have been practicing law for several years but had gaps in his knowledge that she found unsettling. And his entire story about why he was in the valley didn't make sense. He had none of the social conscience that drove most people to this work. She felt there was some on the job training going on not only in his law work but his social conscience as well. She would bet anything that before coming to the valley he had not practiced poverty law and hadn't given a damn about the treatment of migrant workers.

For all of that she wasn't alarmed. His heart was in the right place. He was learning very quickly and he had the zeal of the newly converted. She liked him on every level and he made up for many defects in experience by working long hours. He was a big help and she wasn't going to look a gift horse in the mouth.

And she wasn't going to let herself think any romantic thoughts about him either until she knew all the facts.

Celia found out that he and Geraldo were up to something involving the court in La Garita. The court session was the following day and when they got back to the office she asked him what was going on. "I keep hearing rumors that you and Geraldo are planning something important in court on Friday," she said. "Do you think I should know what it is?"

Alexander thought for a moment then said, "Celia I don't want to make you angry but I'd rather not tell you. There're several reasons. If it doesn't work as I've planned I think it will be important that you're not part of it. More importantly, I want to prove to you that I'm not the legal klutz that you think I am." He held up his hand to stop her from speaking. "Don't say anything. I know that I've tried your patience with my endless lack of knowledge about some of the issues that are involved in this kind of law practice. I hope by doing this by myself I'll gain a little of your respect as a lawyer. And I hope I can gain the respect of the workers. So if you don't mind I'd like to keep it from you until tomorrow night. You'll come with me won't you?"

"Wouldn't miss it *amigo. Hasta mañana.*"

CHAPTER 33

Before the day that court in La Garita was scheduled, Alexander had spent time in the law library drafting a legal memorandum supporting his position. He was certain that the municipal judge, who wasn't a lawyer, wouldn't understand it. But the city attorney would understand it and Alexander was sure he would realize Alexander was on firm legal ground.

On Friday when he got to the La Garita camp Geraldo was waiting for him.

"Mr. Courage," he began, "this scheme better work or there are going to be thirty-two very upset workers in the valley."

"Thirty-two! Is that how many said they'd come to court?"

"Thirty-two," Geraldo repeated. "Everyone on tonight's docket."

"You've done a great job! How did you bring it off?"

"Charm, *señor*, charm."

"Thank you, Geraldo," said Alexander looking at him warmly. "I know that if this fails it'll cost you a lot of credibility."

Geraldo looked at Alexander for a moment then said. "For some reason I believe in you Mr. Courage, at least enough to give this a try. But remember if it fails then all the work I've done to organize the people will go down the drain. For both our sakes I hope it works."

"So do I, Geraldo, so do I," Alexander answered. "Well, come on let's go to court and see if this thing flies." They got in Alexander's blazer and drove to the town where they parked near the municipal building. When they got to the front door they saw that there was a commotion going on. The foyer was filled with migrant workers and the two town policemen were engaged in a shouting match with them. Alexander and Geraldo hurriedly entered. Alexander told Geraldo to quiet the workers while he spoke to the police.

"What's going on?" he asked.

"These goddamn *mojados* are about to be arrested for disturbing the peace," one of them said.

"But officer they're here because they have a court appearance. They were summoned here by the two of you."

"They have the doors blocked and people can't move around in here." The cop replied with a menacing look at Alexander.

"That's because the doors to the court room are locked. As soon as the doors are opened they'll go in." Alexander said, holding his ground. "Maybe if you didn't hand out so many tickets to these people for no reason you wouldn't have this problem. Anyway they have a right to be in court and you'll just have to live with it." Just then the clerk opened the doors and the defendants began to file into the courtroom. Alexander followed them in and took a seat at the long table in front of the judge's bench.

Soon a door behind the bench opened and the clerk entered followed by the judge. "All rise," the clerk said. The judge took his seat and said, "Call the docket." If he was surprised that the room was full he didn't show it.

"Jesus Armijo" the clerk called the first name on the evening docket. There was a shuffling in the court but no one answered. The judge had just begun to intone the word 'forfeit' as Alexander rose to his feet.

"Your honor," he said. "My name is Alexander Courage. I'm a lawyer licensed to practice law in the state of Colorado and I'm here to enter my appearance on behalf of Mr. Armijo. Also, I wish to enter a not guilty plea on behalf of Mr. Armijo."

"Very well," said the judge. "I'll hear the case after I call the docket."

"Your honor I have one other request." This was it thought Alexander. Now let's see if the judge can keep a straight face. "I'm demanding that Mr. Armijo's case be tried to a jury of twelve."

The judge exploded. "A jury trial! You can't have a jury trial for a case like this. We've never had a jury trial in this courtroom. We don't even have a jury box. Request denied."

"Your honor I'm new here so I don't know what the past practice has been. But I do know that the constitution of the state of Colorado provides that in any case where the defendant can be sentenced to jail he's entitled to a trial by jury. In this case as you well know Mr. Armijo can be sentenced up to 90 days in jail if found guilty and under the law he has the right to a jury trial. And", his voice began to rise, "he demands it!" This brought murmurs of agreement from those present in the courtroom.

The judge covered his frustration by banging his gavel. "Any more outbursts in the court and I'll have it cleared!" he yelled. He then leaned over to the clerk and whispered something to her and she disappeared. Alexander turned for the first time to look around the courtroom. Celia and Augustine were seated in the front row. Both smiled at him with looks of great satisfaction and Alexander felt better than he had in a long time.

The clerk returned to the courtroom. She and the judge spoke again in a whisper. Alexander presumed she had called the city attorney to get some guidance.

The judge looked at Alexander. "Mr. Courage," he said with undisguised anger. "I'm going to set a hearing on your jury demand for next Friday and will continue the case of Mr. Armijo till then. Next case."

"Luis Baca."

"Your honor," said Alexander. "I also represent Mr. Baca and likewise enter a plea of not guilty and ask that the matter be heard by a jury of twelve." Now the situation began to dawn on the judge and the blood pressure was visibly rising.

"We'll have a hearing at the same time as the previous case. Next case!"

"Armando Barragon."

Again Alexander was on his feet but before he could say anything the judge angrily interrupted. "Do you represent everyone here tonight Mr. Courage?"

"Yes I do."

"And are you going to make the same demand for each one?"

"Yes I am."

"Well, I'm not going to sit here for the next few hours and hear you repeat these frivolous demands." He turned to the clerk. "Just make a note that all the names of the docket have entered a not guilty plea and demanded a jury trial. Set them all for hearing next Friday." He then turned his attention to Alexander. "Mr. Courage, I don't know what game you are trying to play but I can assure it will backfire."

Alexander couldn't control his anger. "Judge, you may think that defending a person charged with a crime by demanding that the constitution be followed is frivolous and a game. I don't. Our forefathers put this provision in the constitution just to prevent the shameful abuses that are taking place in this valley."

"Mister don't you realize that if we have to call a jury for all these cases it will break the treasury of the town?"

"If that's what it takes to bring justice so be it. For decades these hardworking people have come to this valley and this town and left their blood, health, sweat, and their money. Now maybe this town will realize that there is a high cost for exploitation. Maybe it's time for a wake up call." The judge sat for a moment debating how to inflict some punishment on the lawyer before him. Finally, he just stood up and left the bench. As the door closed one of the workers said "all right!' and the rest broke into animated conversation as they left the room.

Alexander busied himself putting his papers into his briefcase and was joined by Celia and Augustine. "Alexander, that was brilliant." Celia was the first to speak. "I've always assumed that petty cases in the municipal courts didn't have the right to a jury trial. Are you sure?"

"I'm as sure as anyone can be about a legal principle. The

language seems to me absolutely clear." The look in Celia's eyes made him warm all over. She was the proud teacher who had seen her prize student excel.

Augustine shook his hand vigorously. "I don't know what all this legal maneuvering is about but from the way Celia reacted I sense we have done something very good. Of course," he added mischievously, "I don't know if she was in love with the message or the messenger."

"Augustine!" exclaimed Celia.

"*Calma*, Celia. It was just a joke, but am I right to believe something very important has happened?"

"I think so," Alexander said as he finished putting his papers away. "It isn't the end of anything but it may be the beginning of the end."

Celia and Augustine offered to buy Alexander dinner at the cantina. When they got there all the workers from the courtroom were celebrating and when they walked in they heard several '*vivas!*' as they went to a table.

"I hope I haven't raised their expectations too much," said Alexander as he held Celia's chair.

"Don't worry," said Augustine. "I think they're so frustrated at the situation that the mere fact you are willing to fight for them is enough. Also I think they sense, as I do, that we have something here that we haven't had before." The waitress came to the table and Augustine ordered a bottle of Dos Equis for each of them and continued. "Now I want to know everything. What does this all mean? How did you strike upon it? Tell me everything!"

"It began with Geraldo," Alexander began after taking a long swallow of the cold beer. "I couldn't understand why he'd been beaten and I kept pestering him. Finally he told me it was because he was giving rides to workers who had been in the cantina and explained what turns out to be nothing less than a legal scam. When the workers walk back to the camp after having a few drinks the police charge them with being drunk in a public place. A friend or family member then posts a fifty-dollar bail so they can get to work the next day. Over the years it's become understood that if the person fights the charge he'll get a jail sentence and if he doesn't appear the bond will be forfeited to the city and that will be the end of it."

"Celia, did you know of this?" Augustine interrupted. Before she could answer the waitress came to take their order. Celia ordered the *tacos al carbon* and Augustine and Alexander ordered stacked red chili enchiladas. When she left Augustine looked at Celia for an answer.

"Yes, I've known it was going on. But I made a fundamental error. I challenged the constitutionality of the ordinance but it never occurred to me to research whether the defendant was entitled to a jury trial. When the Supreme Court upheld the ordinance I thought that was the end to any legal challenge. Since then I've considered it another abuse that could only be solved politically. It didn't occur to me that we could fight fire with fire in this way. It's brilliant."

Augustine turned to Alexander. "What does she mean fight fire with fire?"

"She means that this abuse is purely based on economics. If we can make it cost more to do than not do the towns will give it up."

The waitress brought the food. They were each hungry and the smell of the food proved irresistible. They occupied themselves with their plates for a minute. Then Augustine asked. "Now what will happen? How will this end the situation?"

"Think of it this way. In the valley there are ten towns and all of them have the same procedure. The result is thousands of dollars a year that they take from the workers and don't have to raise from the local people. If we're right they'll have to give all of these people a jury trial. That means establishing a system for selecting jurors, assembling enough of them to serve on the jury, paying them a small fee, or even finding enough people in the valley to fill all the panels. The cost will be far more than any money they receive from arresting the workers. We are going to make what they are doing cost them a lot of money."

"What made you think of this?" Augustine asked.

"It was the result of the conversation I had with Celia," he responded. "When we were talking about Ms. Sandoval's claim for a damage deposit she pointed out how futile it was to try and gain redress for these problems through the courts. Usually by the time it was resolved in the normal course of business it didn't matter. I decided that appeals to justice didn't work the solution was to hit them in the pocket book. This is it."

The next week Celia and Alexander visited each of the other courts in the valley. They entered their appearances on behalf of every migrant charged with being drunk in a public place. With each appearance the tension grew. By the time they attended court in the last town the judge merely asked them if they intended to ask for a jury trial for all the defendants. They answered yes and he said he would set the question down for hearing the following week.

In the course of the week Celia and Alexander had requested a total of over two hundred jury trials. If the towns decided to force the issue and hold trials for all these cases and jailed those that were found guilty, there weren't enough cells in the whole valley to house all of them and even if there were the cost to feed them and pay for the other incidentals of keeping them in jail would far outweigh the value of having them there. There was also the problem that if they put two hundred workers in jail it would cause a severe labor shortage just during the harvest.

On the day of the hearing in La Garita Alexander's emotions were on a roller coaster. He felt the outcome of the hearing could determine his future. It turned out to be anticlimactic and came and went with a whimper instead of a bang as he'd expected. He, Celia, and Augustine met Geraldo and the defendants at the court at the designated time but the door to the municipal building was locked. Alexander knocked loudly and soon the clerk emerged from her office carrying a piece of paper. She unlocked the door and allowed only Alexander to enter.

"Mr. Courage," she said. "The judge has entered an order in these cases and has asked me to deliver it." She handed him the single piece of paper. Alexander read it quickly. After the official heading it merely said "The following cases are hereby dismissed on the motion of the city attorney." This simple statement was followed by the names of all the defendants then signed and dated by the judge. Victory!

Alexander spoke to the clerk who stood by impatiently. "Does this mean the cases in the other towns are also being dismissed?"

"You'll have to find that out from each town. I'm not in a position to say." Her words carried a cold resentment that gave Alexander the chills. 'Let the battle begin,' he thought but only said 'thank you' and went outside to deliver the news to the waiting crowd.

After much cheering and congratulations Alexander, Celia and Augustine drove back to El Centro for supper. During the dinner there was a subdued air. The feeling that often comes after a hard won victory. They were pleased at the success but also realized this might unleash the full anger and vengeance of Richard and his cronies.

"Do you think there will be some retaliation?" Augustine inquired.

"I'm sure there will be," answered Alexander. "We'll have to wait and see."

"By the way," Augustine said. "Richard has invited me to cocktail party at the Hacienda on Saturday. He made a point of asking me to bring you along. In all the excitement I'd forgotten to mention it."

Alexander looked surprised. "What's the occasion?"

"It's being given for the governor of New Mexico who's here to help negotiate the sale of water to Albuquerque and Santa Fe. I suppose Richard would like to see the man who is upsetting the apple cart in the valley."

Alexander hesitated only a moment. This was what he'd been waiting for. How would he behave in the face of seeing his wife for the first time in four years and coming face to face with the man who was responsible for the agony and misery he'd suffered all these years?

Augustine took his hesitation for reluctance to go and said. "By the way," he looked at Celia and smiled. "Celia will also be there."

"Well then," said Alexander. "How can I refuse?"

CHAPTER 34

Alexander rode to the hacienda with Augustine and Celia. During the drive he found it impossible to carry on any meaningful conversation. Finally the two of them stopped trying and left him to his own thoughts. It was such a surrealistic world he found himself in. Sitting next to a childhood friend that had been like a brother and who didn't know him. Traveling across the land that his family had turned from flat, desolate wasteland into almost four million acres of irrigated land that he couldn't claim as his. Now he was going to his ancestral home to see his wife who he hoped wouldn't recognize him.

They drove along the flat surface past miles and miles of fields. At the end of the fields just as the road began the gradual climb to the Hacienda there were several ponds. Grebes, egrets, ducks and a few killdeer and other waders were still on the ponds but in the spring and fall they would be filled with many more kinds of birds including the sand hill cranes that he'd dreamed of at Los Altos prison. Then they turned towards the mountains and onto a road that led directly to the hacienda.

Augustine drove his car through the gates onto the cobble-stoned drive that led to the house. It appeared to Alexander that nothing had changed since he left. The lawn and trees and flowers that bordered the drive were well tended. The house itself, looming before them, was washed with the slanting evening light that gave it the warm glow of embers.

They were among the last to arrive and the party was in full swing. Many politicos from Denver and Santa Fe had flown in. There was no greeting line and the three of them walked in and began to circulate. After taking a glass of champagne from the tray of one of the waiters Alexander left Augustine and Celia and wandered on his own. Little had changed from the times he and his father occupied the house. If only he could speak once more to his father and share his present thoughts with him. There was so much he wanted to say.

When he returned to the main salon he joined Augustine and Celia.

"Quite a house isn't it?" Celia said. It was more of a statement than a question.

"You know, Alexander," Augustine said. "I grew up here. My father was Mr. Curran's valet and my mother was the cook. After Alfred Curran's mother died it fell to my mother to raise him and we grew up like brothers. Because Richard's father had so much responsibility for the daily operation of the valley he would be here often and Richard often spent the day. We were like the three musketeers."

"And when it was just Augustine and me it was more like the Cisco Kid and Pancho," a voice from behind them said. Alexander turned and was face to face with Richard Marquez. Happily Celia said something and he had time to collect himself.

"May we assume that in that situation you were always Cisco and Augustine was always Pancho?" she asked.

Richard gave her a look of superiority. "What do you think Celia?" he asked in a tone that suggested everyone knew the answer. He then turned to Alexander. "This must be Mr. Courage," he said not bothering to extend his hand. "I've heard about you. You're the one that's trying to ruin the treasury of every town in the valley with this idea of jury trials." Alexander looked at him carefully for any sign of recognition. All he could detect was a look of contempt.

"I understood that my job as a lawyer was to represent my clients." Alexander replied.

"Do you think it will benefit your clients in the long run if the towns are broke and the farmers can't afford to hire them, or clothe them, or feed them?"

"I believe that in America the constitution applies to everyone and if it's enforced it will benefit all of us in both the long run and in the short run." Alexander replied.

"An admirable and idealistic thought," Richard replied without much conviction. "But enough politics." He turned to Augustine and Celia. "May I borrow Mr. Courage for a moment? There are some people I would like to introduce him to?" It was a question in form only and when he finished he turned and walked away. It was obvious he assumed that Alexander would follow. He took a few steps and then turned slightly to allow Alexander to walk by his side.

"Mr. Courage, don't take offense at what I said back there. I admire anyone who'll fight for the rights of the down trodden. From what I'm told you're very resourceful and creative in your work for the legal services center." Just as Richard finished they arrived at a side room where several men were standing in front of couch talking to each other and to someone seated on the couch. Richard and Alexander approached and the men made room for them in the circle. As they moved aside Alexander saw a woman seated on the couch. Her beauty took Alexander's breath away as it always had. It was Patricia.

She was even more beautiful than he remembered. Her hair was perfect. Her make up was the product of great time and money. Her dress was a full-length royal blue taffeta. It was tight at the waist and bodice and emphasized her well-shaped breasts and small waist.

"Patricia," said Richard, "I want you to meet Alexander Courage. He's the new lawyer in the valley giving everyone such fits."

Patricia looked at him with eyes the color of a shallow sea and Alexander concentrated all his powers to see if there was any hint of recognition. Her eyes lingered on him with indifference before looking at Richard with obvious affection. Alexander was slightly taken aback. Suddenly he realized that he'd assumed

Patricia had married Richard out of grief and that he would find her unhappy and grieving. The opposite was obviously true. From the way she looked at Richard it was clear that in her heart he'd replaced Alfred.

Through a dry mouth Alexander managed to express pleasure at meeting her. She didn't respond in kind. "Mr. Courage you're here against my wishes. An enemy of the valley is an enemy of mine. I know Richard thought it best to invite you, and I hope you'll make the most of being here." She then turned and began a conversation with someone else. There was a brief embarrassed silence then Richard turned to Alexander.

"Mr. Courage please forgive my wife. She's very protective of the valley and sometimes she lets her emotions take the place of reasoned discourse. Here let me introduce you to these gentlemen." He then named the men who had been talking to Patricia. They were all from outside the valley and the last one to be introduced was Russell Farnsworth who Richard introduced as the senior partner in Denver's biggest law firm. Alexander shook hands with him.

"Mr. Courage," Farnsworth said. "Richard has told me about your rather brilliant use of the constitution to bring about a significant victory for your clients. I admire that in a lawyer."

"Thank you, Mr. Farnsworth. I hope it is the first of many."

"From what I've heard tonight that isn't a sentiment shared by everyone. You know someone with your talent could go a long way in our firm. I imagine you would want a couple of hundred thousand a year to come on board and I'm sure I could arrange that. What do you think? By now I would guess you've satisfied your need to represent the poor and oppressed for next to no salary. You've done a great job and proven yourself. Why not move on to bigger and better things?"

'So that's the pitch,' thought Alexander, 'two hundred thousand dollars to get me out of the valley. Not bad for a dead man with a false identity and a ticket to disbarment if the court ever found out how he'd gotten his license. And five minutes after I leave it will be business as usual in the valley.'

"That is a very kind offer Mr. Farnsworth," he said, "but I'm afraid I'll have to decline. Actually, instead of feeling I've accomplished what I set out to do I feel I've only just gotten started." He paused to be sure that Richard was listening. "I think the overthrow of the system of exploiting the workers by arresting them for being drunk is just the first step in gaining full rights for them. I think I'll stay and work a little more."

Farnsworth looked at Richard as if to say 'well I tried' and then to Alexander. "I can't say these offers last forever but if you change your mind in the next few weeks I think we'll be able to work something out."

"Mr. Courage, would you like to see my library?" Richard asked.

"Yes, very much," Alexander replied. He looked briefly at Patricia to say goodbye but she'd turned away from him.

When they were inside the library Richard turned on the lights and closed the doors behind them. Alexander could see that the room had not been changed since his father occupied it. On one side of the room was the large aerial map of the valley that his father had treasured. Richard led Alexander over to the map. They both stood in front of it for a moment with their own thoughts then Richard spoke.

"It's a remarkable thing isn't it? Almost four million acres of land. 100 miles long and almost sixty miles wide." His hand reached out and began to point out certain features. "The high mountains on each side of the valley help give it special growing qualities. In the ancient past it was a great lake that still exists just under the surface. That's why we can water all the fields so easily." He moved away from the map to a small bar and poured two snifters of cognac from a crystal decanter. Alexander could hear the ping of the glass as Richard flicked his finger against it. Even the decanter and glasses had been there when his father was alive. Richard and Patricia hadn't found it necessary to change much. Richard resumed speaking. "In many ways, Mr. Courage, the valley is like the human body. It's a unique organism that has evolved in a certain way. All the parts work in harmony with the others." Alexander remained silent.

"When the organism is threatened with a foreign virus it has its own way of using its immune system to eradicate the virus. It's quite remarkable how it works." He then changed the subject. "I couldn't help overhearing the offer Mr. Farnsworth made you. It sounded generous."

Alexander finally spoke. "Yes, almost too generous. So much money to an unknown quantity sounded unbelievable."

"Farnsworth is a very good judge of talent."

Alexander ignored the remark. "A moment ago when you spoke of a foreign virus did you mean me?" asked Alexander.

Richard didn't answer the question directly. "Mr. Courage, I'm only describing the world as I see it. It would be unfair of me not to share my understanding with someone who may be getting into a situation that results in harm."

"To borrow your analogy." Alexander continued. "Isn't it also true that the organism may be so infected that it must be injected with medicine to save it?"

"Now we are becoming philosophical." Richard replied. "I find philosophy works on the past and the future but not on the present."

"And what works on the present?" asked Alexander.

"Power." said Richard. "And I can assure you that the powers in the this valley can eradicate any foreign virus or medicine. Which ever it's called."

"Is that a threat?"

"I don't threaten." Richard's voice was filled with controlled anger. "I'm offering you my opinion. You should accept Farnsworth's job offer. There are forces in the valley that you don't understand because you don't come from the valley. These forces can sometimes become violent. I wouldn't want to see you hurt."

"Your concern for my welfare is thoughtful," said Alexander. "If I came from the valley would your advice be the same?"

"If you came from the valley it wouldn't be necessary," Richard responded. "Now I must rejoin my guests if you'll excuse me." He put his snifter on the bar and left. Alexander stayed for a moment. He decided that the next time he was in the library it would be his, and Patricia would be with him as his wife.

CHAPTER 35

In the weeks following the cocktail party the political storm erupted. The other towns in the valley followed the lead of La Garita and dismissed all the cases and stopped arresting the workers for public drunkenness. The towns now had to raise the money they had relied on from the workers by raising taxes. This enraged the permanent residents. Richard and his people made it clear to all of them that Alexander was the culprit.

There was open grumbling in the valley over the fact that the taxpayers were paying for the state rural services office just so some smart-ass lawyers could cost them money.

These complaints were made vocal at town council meetings. The more influential residents called their legislators to demand that the rural legal services office should be closed or that Alexander be fired.

All this uproar didn't bother Alexander. It was what he wanted. And if he was fired he could represent the workers on his own. He didn't need the money because of Don Francisco's legacy to him. What he found interesting was that his representation of the workers was taking on a life of its own within him.

He desperately wanted to clear his name in the murder of Chacon so he could reveal his identity and make Richard and his gang pay for what they had done. But he also realized that if that never happened he would continue to help the migrants gain their rights in the valley.

Several weeks after the party at the hacienda Alexander received a phone call at the legal services office.

"Mr. Courage," the caller said. "I'm the brother of Alberto Falcon. I've heard about the work you're doing in the valley and wonder if you would talk to me about my brother?" Alexander could hardly keep his heart from racing. If only he could convince Falcon's brother that Falcon should return to stand trial and let Alexander defend him. That would give Alexander the perfect chance to prove that Falcon and Alfred Curran had not committed the murder of Chacon.

"Yes! I'd like to do that very much. Where and when?"

"First, you must promise me that you won't tell anyone of the meeting. I don't know where my brother is and I don't want the cops hassling me because I spoke to you. If you convince me you can get him off I think I can get word to him."

"Of course I won't tell anyone."

"Then meet me at El Gato Negro restaurant in Conejos tonight. Be there at six and wait until ten. If everything is right I'll contact you. Do you know where Conejos is?"

"No," Alexander lied.

"It's about fifty miles south of the valley. Just across the New Mexico border. Take highway 417 South. You won't miss it. Remember you must be alone."

"Believe me I won't forget. I'll be there."

Alexander left El Centro with more than enough time to get to Conejos before six o'clock. Besides wanting to be absolutely sure that he would get there by six he also wanted the chance to think about what he might say to Falcon's brother. He was convinced the only to clear his own name was to clear that of Falcon, and to do that he would have to convince Falcon to come out of hiding.

On the way to Conejos Alexander reviewed the situation. The police said they had received an anonymous tip that there was drug dealing at the remote house where Chacon and Falcon lived. On the way to the house they passed Falcon driving away from the scene. Chacon had been shot once. They recovered a .38 caliber Smith and Wesson handgun that they traced to Alfred Curran. The only fingerprints on it were Alfred Curran's. There was also evidence of large amounts of cocaine being brought to the farmhouse and put into smaller packages for distribution.

They said that after the murder Curran had fled to Mexico. Falcon, they said, had driven towards New Mexico where the car broke down and he abandoned it and then disappeared. It was assumed he was hiding in Mexico.

After Curran's death in Mexico had been reported the case was put on hold until Falcon could be captured and returned for trial. Because the charge was first-degree murder there was no statute of limitations which meant they could try Falcon whenever they found him.

As the case stood now it was evident the district attorney could prove drugs as the motive and he could prove opportunity on the part of Falcon. Naturally Falcon's fingerprints were all over the farmhouse although not on the gun.

Alexander knew that he wouldn't be able to convince Falcon to return for trial with what he had so far. On the other hand he might be able to find out something from the brother that would give him a starting place to build a credible defense. And he hoped he could make him believe that he should be the person to defend Falcon when the time came, if it ever did.

The small town of Conejos was like most of the other small towns in the region. Its main street was only three blocks long and was a mix of businesses and homes. Each end of the town was guarded by gas stations and near the center was the El Gato Negro bar and cafe.

Alexander parked his blazer in front and went in. The bar was similar to the one in La Garita and was occupied by only a handful of people. He sat the bar and ordered a Bohemia beer and began his wait.

As the evening progressed more people entered the bar but he couldn't tell if any of them were Falcon. The bartender came over to him.

"You want to eat something?" There was something in the voice that suggested more than just a question about food.

"I guess so," Alexander replied. "What do you suggest?"

"There is a booth in the very back that is available. Why don't you take it? I'm sure you'll get what you want."

Alexander left a tip on the bar and carried his half finished beer to the booth. Just after he sat down the rear door opened and a man slipped through it and quickly sat in the seat opposite him.

"I'm Roberto Falcon the brother of Alberto." He said. He was of medium height with long raven black hair pulled back into a ponytail. His full beard was the color of his hair and his eyes were as dark as pools of black oil.

"I'm glad to meet you," Alexander responded.

Falcon didn't waste any time on preliminaries. "I've been watching what you're doing in the valley. There hasn't been so much progress since my brother was forced from the valley and Mike Chacon was murdered. You deserve a lot of credit."

"Thanks."

"Do you think you can beat the case against my brother?"

Alexander decided that it would serve no good purpose to mislead Falcon. "Right now I haven't found anything that will contradict what the police say. I was hoping that your brother might be able to help me in that respect."

"There's no way for you to talk to him. That's out of the question but I know all there is to know about the events. Maybe I can help."

"O.K. Let's try," Alexander said. "Right now the case would be the word of your brother against the police. But their case is very circumstantial. The hard evidence is that Curran killed Chacon. It was his gun. His prints were on it and he fled the country. But in your brother's case they can only say he was there because one of them says he saw him drive past him a short distance from the house as he was on his way to investigate. Was he there?"

"No. He was at an organizational meeting of the migrants in Arboles. He and Mike shared the car and he left it with Mike that night and caught a ride with one of the workers. The car was driven from the scene by someone working for the cops after it had been planted with the same drug wrappers that had been planted in the house."

"Are there witnesses to the fact he was at the Arboles camp that night?"

"They were all militant migrant workers. After what happened to Albert and Mike I think they all left the valley. It might be possible to find one or two. Even if you found them I don't think they'd be believed over the police."

"But it would be something. What about the allegations of drug dealing."

Falcon's nostrils flared. "Impossible! Mike and my brother didn't even smoke pot. Don't you get it, Courage? Mike and my brother were getting close to a full organization of the workers. They would have brought the fascists in the valley to their knees. The Curran's and their henchmen needed to get rid of them and they did."

Alexander held his anger in check. "If the Curran's were behind the murder and the frame up why was Alfred Curran included in the frame and then killed in Mexico?"

"That's a good question. He was no friend of Al and Mike. He didn't even know what was going on in the valley. He was too good for that. I figure there was some other reason to get rid of Curran and this was a good way to kill a lot of birds with one stone. But I can promise you there was no connection between Alberto and Alfred Curran."

Alexander thought for a moment. "Well we've made some progress. We have some evidence that contradicts what the police will say. The key is to find one strong piece of evidence that clearly makes one part of their case a lie and then the rest will fall of its own weight."

"I agree with you," said Falcon. "But until you come up with that piece of evidence you won't see my brother."

"If I do find the evidence will your brother let me defend him?"

"Yes, I think so."

"And if I find it how do I get word to you?"

"Tell Celia Chavez. She'll see that I hear." With that Roberto Falcon slipped from the booth and out the back door.

CHAPTER 36

After the meeting Alexander felt confident that he would eventually get Falcon to surrender. He just didn't know how. The fantasy gave him enough optimism to begin thinking about a trial. The first thing he needed to do was find witnesses that were with Falcon at the worker's meeting the night of the murder. Geraldo would be the man for that.

There was one other idea that had come to him since his battle over the question of jury trials. That had to do with making sure that the jury pool in the valley has as many Hispanics in it as possible. He thought Augustine would help him there.

He drove to La Garita the following day to enlist Geraldo's aid. Geraldo was more than willing to help.

"Geraldo," Alexander began, "I have information that on the night Michael Chacon was killed Alberto Chacon was attending a meeting in Alamosa."

"How did you learn that?" asked Geraldo.

"It's better that you don't know for the time being. I promise to tell you before this is all over. The important thing now is to find some workers who were at that meeting with Falcon."

"It might be pretty hard," said Geraldo. "It was over four years ago. I'm sure many of them left when Falcon ran and have been afraid to return to the valley."

"I guess that's true, but we have to try. Maybe we'll get lucky." Alexander said hopefully then changed the subject. "Geraldo, we must keep this quiet. I want it to be a secret as long as possible. If

Marquez and his men find out about it they'll do everything they can to stop us."

"I'll do what I can," said Geraldo. "When do you want me to start?"

"Would yesterday be too soon?" asked Alexander as he started for his vehicle. Geraldo only smiled and waved goodbye.

The next thing on Alexander's list was to return to El Centro to talk to Augustine about his plans for the jury pool. During his research for the use of jury trials to stop the abuses of the workers he'd learned a great deal about the history of the jury system. It had become clear to him that if citizens wanted to serve on a jury they had the right to. At least they had the right to be called for service. Whether they were selected for a jury depended upon the lawyers in any particular case. This led him to the idea that it was possible to increase the number of poor people, Hispanics, and working people in the jury pool. What was needed was someone with the ability to lead them to act. Clearly that person was Augustine.

When he got to El Centro he drove directly to Augustine's house. It was nearing the lunch hour and Augustine suggested they call Celia and have her join them for lunch. The idea appealed to Alexander. He found more and more that he sought every opportunity to be with her. He liked her in every way. There was no question in his mind that if everything was different he could easily fall head over heels in love with her. During the lunch Alexander brought up the subject of the juror rolls in the valley.

"I believe," he started, "that I'll be able to convince Alberto Falcon to return and stand trial. When that happens I want the cards to be stacked as much in his favor as possible."

"How do you intend to do that?" Augustine asked.

"One of the ways is to have as many jurors as we can that are Hispanic workers." He began. "Jurors that won't be just a rubber stamp for Marquez."

"That will be very difficult," Celia interjected. "The jury panels I've seen over the years are mostly made up of Anglos and usually owe their jobs one way or another to Marquez."

"I'm sure that's true," said Alexander. "It's probably because the information the jury commissioner uses for the names of potential jurors comes from property tax roles, voter registration lists, and vehicle registration. The result is that only people who pay property taxes, vote on a regular basis, and own vehicles end up on the list. People in the valley who fall into that category are permanent residents who are beholden to Marquez. That's what we have to change."

"But how do we do that?" asked Augustine.

"We must expand the lists so that people will be included who don't have cars or own their homes."

"But Alexander we can't make our own jury lists. That is left to the jury commissioner," Celia said.

"I know the jury commissioner in this district," Augustine interjected. "Her husband works for one of Richard's businesses. I'm sure she won't be on our side."

"Augustine," responded Alexander. "We learned during the fight for jury trials that while these people may work for Richard they won't go so far as to risk breaking the law for him, at least not over something as minor as this. I'm sure that if we can make it clear to her that if she refuses to do what we demand she'll be investigated by the state Attorney General or the Judicial department she'll do what the law requires."

"You may be right." Augustine replied. "What do you want me to do?"

"First you need to know how the system works." Alexander responded. "The law requires the commissioner to keep a list of people in the district who are qualified for jury service. Then for each term of court she's supposed to randomly pull names from this list and call them in for service during that term. Generally she uses a variety of sources for the names. Tax roles, vehicle registration, driver licenses, voter registration, and so forth. The problem with this is that a great many people in the valley who are poor but are qualified don't get on these lists."

Celia was beginning to see where this was leading. "Of course," she said. "The only qualification for service is that a person be 21 years or older, a citizen, and not have a felony conviction. They don't have to own property, or vehicles, or even vote."

"Exactly," Alexander said. "What we want to do is try and get as many of those on the list as possible. I've researched the law. If a qualified person goes to the jury commissioner's office and insists on being put on the rolls the commissioner must do it. The situation doesn't come up because most people are more interested in getting off the list instead of getting on it."

Celia looked at Alexander with admiration. "Alexander!" she exclaimed, "that's great! I'm sure that after your success at La Garita we will have no trouble getting people to volunteer."

Alexander smiled. Pleasing her made him feel very good. "Augustine, I want you to do everything you can to get people to go to the commissioner and have their names put on the list. If there are questions we'll say it's another of our techniques to bring equality to the valley. We won't say anything about Falcon. I don't want them alerted yet to the possibility of Falcon surrendering himself. Geraldo will help you."

Augustine couldn't contain his growing enthusiasm. "All right, I'll do it. It should be a good thing for the people whether or not Falcon surrenders."

"You're right about that," Alexander said. "But I'm sure Falcon will surrender. I just feel it." Based on the events of the past weeks and the enthusiasm of his two friends Alexander again tried to raise the issue of Alfred Curran.

"Augustine," he began, "is it possible to see the reports and files relating to the murder of Chacon?"

"Whenever I've asked to see them they've refused," Augustine replied. "There's a difficulty because the only court documents are the charges and an affidavit for the arrest of Falcon. I have a copy of them but they don't say much. All the rest of the documents are in the possession of Richard Marquez, and he refuses to let anyone see them. We have always supposed it was to protect Patricia and the estate. The only people at the scene were the police and Marquez."

Just then Celia interrupted. Are you sure they were the only people at the scene?"

"Yes, I think so. Why?" Augustine answered.

"Because it would seem logical that a medical examiner or coroner would have been involved. I've never known one to live in the valley. Every time something like this happens they have to bring one in from Pueblo so I was just curious."

"Now that you mention it I believe there was such a person. He was the coroner from Monte Alto. I don't know if he actually was at the scene and I don't remember who it was."

"Augustine!" said Alexander. "This is important. Whoever this person is, he may be the only person who isn't a part of the powers in the valley that knows anything about the case. He might know something helpful." Alexander couldn't contain his enthusiasm and both Celia and Augustine looked at him curiously as if wondering why he was so obsessed about this case that was four years old.

Alexander realized his mistake and tried to recover. "Now that we have begun to win some victories in the valley I think that if we could clear the name of Falcon for that murder we could show the extent of the corruption and also have Falcon back to lead the workers. "I would be a big help."

Both of them appeared to accept this explanation. Alexander went on. "Augustine, will you help me find this coroner. I'd like to talk to him."

"Of course," Augustine responded. "I'll ask friends at the bishop's office to look into it for me. If he's alive I think we can find him."

Augustine was quiet for a moment then said, "We already know that Richard and his people will stop at nothing to prevent change in the valley. We think they've already killed, and we know that many people have suffered terrible beatings. Next time they may attack you or even kill you. Is this all worth your death?"

"Augustine believe me it's not a question of my death." He paused. "It's a question of my life."

CHAPTER 37

For the next week Alexander's time was occupied handling everyday cases. On his regular workday at La Garita he found Geraldo helping fix a leaking roof on one of the worker's shacks. Geraldo was happy to see him and as soon as he finished his chore he climbed down and he and Alexander walked the short distance to the shade of the cottonwood trees.

"I'm excited!" Geraldo began, "I've finally gotten the key leaders of the various camps in the valley to meet with me and listen to my arguments for organizing into a union. Ever since the murder of Chacon the workers have refused to organize or hold meetings. Even before that it was hard to get cooperation because as soon as it was discovered that there was activity for organizing there would be raids on the meetings and several of us would be beaten. So the meeting must be a secret."

"Don't worry I won't say anything, but keeping it secret will be difficult."

"I'm sure the workers won't say anything. They don't want to be found out."

"Yes, but I'm sure the Marquez has an informant in the group."

"Of course!" exclaimed Geraldo. "I didn't think of that." He was quiet for a moment. "We must have the meeting anyway and take our chances. We'll be found out sooner or later. I hope that won't change your answer to my question."

"Which is?"

"I want you to come to the meeting tonight and tell the men that you'll fight for them as long as they fight for themselves. If they know that you'll sacrifice then it will be easier for them. Will you do that?"

"Just tell me where and when," Alexander said, "I'll be there."

"Tonight at seven at the Alamosa camp."

"Don't worry Geraldo. I'll be there at seven, and I'll be alone."

After work Alexander drove back to El Centro. He wanted to find out from Augustine if there was any news about the whereabouts of the coroner. He found Augustine at home where he'd just finished preparing for a mass for one of the residents that was to be buried the next day.

"Augustine," Alexander began. "Is there any news about the coroner in the Chacon murder case?"

Augustine invited Alexander into the house. When they were inside he said. "Yes, there is. I was able to find out that the name of the man is Harvey Rench. He retired several years ago and my friend isn't sure what happened to him, or indeed if he's still alive. But my friend believes he knows how to contact a sister who lives in Trinidad and says he has sent her a letter. He's waiting for an answer. We should know something soon."

"That's good news. I have a feeling this might be the break I've been waiting for."

Augustine looked at him curiously. "Alexander why are you so intent on reopening this old case. I know there was injustice but won't it just open old wounds? Wouldn't it be better to leave the past alone and go on to the future?"

"I thought you believed that Alfred Curran was innocent and wanted to see his name cleared?" asked Alexander.

"I do," Augustine answered. "What I don't completely understand is why you do." Alexander thought for a moment before answering.

"It's not the dead Curran I'm so concerned with," he lied. "It's Falcon. I believe that if we can clear his name and expose the frame up we will find out who was responsible and put them in jail. If it also happens to clear Curran that will just be a side benefit."

Augustine responded with concern. "There's a great deal of anger towards you by the permanent residents of the valley. You must be careful. We are very isolated here. We are in many ways like a foreign country. The people that have the power don't always leave their problems to civilized ways of solving them. Those who are believed to be troublemakers are beaten and shot. I'm afraid this will happen to you if you're not careful."

"What are you saying Augustine? That I should quit? That I should leave the valley?"

"No, of course I'm not saying that! But I think you should give everyone time to accept what you've done already before you do anything else. If things move too fast the reaction may be worse than if progress is made in small increments."

"Is that all? Do what I'm doing just take longer to do it?" he couldn't keep the sarcasm out of his voice.

"Please Alexander don't be angry. What I'm saying is that if we change things gradually, step by step, the chance of success will be greater and less dangerous. But I'm sure that if you continue to try and reopen the Chacon murder case your life will be in danger."

"Augustine I can't do what you ask. I would rather die than not try so there isn't any choice. In fact I'm beginning tonight to help organize the workers. There is a secret meeting at the Alamosa camp and I'll do everything I can to help the migrants organize a strike if necessary." When he paused he saw the anguish on Augustine's face. He went on. "Augustine I know you can't bear to see anyone hurt but if we don't take advantage of this opportunity there may never be one like it again."

There was resignation in Augustine's voice when he responded. All he could say was, "Please be careful."

Alexander left Augustine and returned to the office to finish some work before going to the Alamosa camp. The drive to the camp from El Centro would take an hour and he didn't want to be late.

When he arrived he found the meeting in a barn like structure where some farm equipment was stored and where several cars were parked. He parked his truck and went in. His entrance caused some stir among those present and Geraldo quickly came up to him.

"Alexander I'm glad you came. The men are very nervous. They believe that if the police know of this meeting they'll all suffer. Can you speak to them quickly and encourage them."

"Yes, of course." Alexander went to the front of the group and began to speak in Spanish. "Friends," he began, "you all know that you are treated as second class citizens in the valley. You must understand that without you the valley can't survive. They need your sweat, and toil, but they shouldn't have your blood or the blood of your women and children. You have the same rights as any American worker. You have the right to a decent wage, fair treatment, sanitary conditions, and education of your children. But you won't get these things if you're divided. You must form an organization and demand your rights with one voice. If you'll do this I'll use the law in every way I can to help you. But you must be strong and you must be willing sacrifice in the short run to achieve victory in the long run."

When he finished one of the men stood up. "It's easy to bear the misfortunes of someone else Mr. Courage. If we do as you say we'll lose our jobs, we'll be attacked, we'll be banished from the valley. We'll be the ones to suffer. But you will be unhurt. You have the law to protect you, we don't."

Just as Alexander began to answer the door burst open and four men entered. They were dressed in black and wore hoods. They quickly crossed the room and seized Alexander before he or the others could react. The men said nothing. Alexander demanded to know what was going on but there was no response. He was dragged outside and thrown face down on the trunk of one of the cars. He felt his hands being tied with rope at each wrist and the rope pulled tight and tied to the rear door handles of the car.

He'd been in this position before. Many times in the jungle they had tied him up and beaten him. He tried desperately to regain the mental state of those past times that would help him bear the pain and agony he knew was coming.

After he was tied and couldn't move the men moved away from him. He could tell from the movement around the car that the workers were being forced to watch.

The first bite of the whip seared his body and mind with unbearable pain. He knew from experience that any cries from his lips would only increase the number and viciousness of the blows. At least he wouldn't let them know they were hurting him.

Another and another followed the first blow. He began to feel the warm blood running down his ribs from the wounds opened by the ends of the whip. He could hear gasps from the workers, and he could hear what he thought were sounds of pleasure from behind him. He lost count of the blows and knew that blessed unconsciousness was near. The last thing he heard before passing out was someone say, "that's enough."

CHAPTER 38

Alexander regained consciousness slowly. The pain he felt was a dull throbbing sensation. It was substantially different from the pain he'd felt after the beatings at Los Altos prison. Somewhere in his unfocused conscious he knew the absence of pain was due to a painkiller. He was equally sure that when it wore off he would be brought back to the reality of the pain that such a beating produced. At the moment he was just floating with an incongruous sense of semi-euphoria.

He was sure the bed he was lying in wasn't his. It had a smell that could only come from a woman's touch. The light that came into the room through a small window had a slant to it that made him believe it was early morning or late afternoon. He lay still for a moment then made a tentative move. The pain shot through him like a crack in ice. He resumed his former position and decided he'd better wait before trying that again. He wondered how long he'd been here, and then his mind returned to the night of the beating. He hoped he was the only one that had been beaten.

The attack was obviously an attempt to drive him from the valley, and also to serve as a warning to the workers. Whoever had done it would be able to accomplish everything they needed to by just beating him and leaving the rest alone. The workers were already frightened and the example of a vicious beating to Alexander would be enough to keep them in line after he was gone.

Alexander floated in and out of consciousness for the next several hours. When he finally regained complete conscious the pain was more intense. Now he felt more like he did after the beatings in prison. He welcomed the pain because it meant there was no more narcotic to cloud his thinking, and he wanted to be able to think clearly.

The men who had dragged him from the meeting room had all been masked and he knew there was no possibility of identifying them. Presumably there might be some evidence such as tire tracks, or footprints, or fingerprints that could be gathered at the scene by trained forensics experts. Of course, there were no such experts in the valley and even if there were they wouldn't expend resources investigating the beating of Alexander Courage.

There was no doubt in his mind that the assailants were either members of one of the police forces or they acted with the sanction of the law enforcement authorities. With each throb in his back he thought of only one name as the person responsible for the beating, Richard Marquez. And with each throb he renewed his vow to bring Richard Marquez down no matter what the risk to himself.

He forced himself to let go of the dream of revenge and thought again about the events leading to the beating. The offer of a lucrative job in a prestigious law firm had been the carrot to lead him out of the valley peaceably. His refusal of the job offer and his failure to heed Richard's warning had made the beating inevitable. He'd misjudged Richard in several respects. He thought he would be given more time before Richard took such drastic action. Marquez must have decided that it would serve no good purpose to wait. After all, they felt they could act with impunity. Alexander's second miscalculation was in thinking they would wait to find him alone and beat him rather than do it in the front of witnesses.

While he was going over the matter in his mind the door opened and Celia came into the room.

"How do you feel?" she asked walking over to the bed. He realized then that he was in Celia's house.

"Fine," he said trying to turn his body to see her.

"Wait," she said. "I'll help you." She moved to the bed and helped him turnover. The movement caused him some pain but nothing unmanageable. He thought it wouldn't be long before he would be up and about.

"Why am I here?" he asked. She sat on a chair next to the bed where he could see her. Her eyes showed a combination of sympathy for his hurt and affection for him.

"After the beating Geraldo didn't know what to do with you. As soon as Richard and his thugs left you alone he had a couple of the workers put you in the back of your blazer and he drove you here."

"You have proof it was Richard?" Alexander asked excitedly.

"No real proof. No one saw the faces or recognized the cars. But who else could it be. It had to be Richard."

Alexander was disappointed. It would be nice to have firm evidence of Richard's involvement. Celia continued. "I've had some experience with these kind of things. When I saw you I decided you would be just as well off here as at the hospital. We got you into bed and I called our friend, Dr. Wilson. He agreed to come over and treat you. They beat you quite badly but he said you were in good condition and while it would be painful you should heal without complication."

"I already feel better," he answered, "but I assumed it was your tender loving care that made it possible." She blushed slightly and smiled and then just a quickly the smile vanished.

"Dr. Wilson also said there were scars on your back from previous beatings. What's that all about?"

Alexander thought for a moment. How he yearned to tell her everything, to take her into his confidence, to bare his soul to someone. He quickly checked his emotions. It would just have to wait.

"It happened to me in Mexico," he said. "There is nothing really to tell. Someday when all of this is over I'll tell you the whole story."

Celia seemed to accept the explanation and after a moment's

thought said. "Anyway the doctor cleaned the wounds and put a dressing on. He showed us how to change it and said all that was needed was time."

"You said us. Who helped you?" asked Alexander.

"Augustine's mother. You know it was very strange. She got here only minutes after Geraldo brought you in. It was uncanny, almost as if she knew it had happened without being told. But once she was here she wouldn't leave. She sat next to the bed all night and wouldn't let me or anyone else touch you. This morning she came downstairs and said you would be all right and she went back to Augustine's."

"I must thank her as soon as I can," was all Alexander could say. He hoped Celia couldn't see the tears in his eyes.

"I guess now you wish you had taken Farnsworth's job offer?" Celia asked.

"Not at all," he replied.

"Will you leave the valley now?"

With some effort Alexander sat up then swung he legs over the side of the bed and faced her. She began to protest but he waived her away. "I'm all right," he said. "They didn't hurt my legs. The sooner I get up the better. Believe me I know how these things work." He adjusted to the sitting position. "No," he said. "I'm not leaving the valley. All this beating has done is make me all the more determined to stay and do what I can to change what's going on."

"Alexander you can't," Celia said. "If you stay they'll find a way to kill you."

"Like Chacon?" he asked. Her eyes spoke the 'yes' her heart wouldn't allow her mouth to say. "That's a risk I have to take. Besides if I can get Falcon to surrender himself and let me prove he and Alfred Curran didn't kill Chacon I believe I can change everything in the valley."

"Alexander, if you did get Falcon to return to stand trial and he was acquitted how would that change things?" She went on before he could answer. "All it would do is prove that Falcon was innocent and we would have him back in the valley to organize workers." She sat for a moment and Alexander could see she was fighting back tears then she said, "I guess then they could kill both of you." She got up and walked to a dresser where she stood with her back to him.

"Celia, if I can prove that Falcon didn't kill Mike Chacon I might also be able to prove who did kill him. If we're right and Richard Marquez or his men killed him it will lead to their downfall. Once we have stopped the beatings and intimidations we will be able to organize the workers."

"You're forgetting one thing. Falcon has told people that he wasn't near the house when Chacon was killed."

"Exactly! Which means he couldn't have killed him."

"But it leaves Alfred Curran as the murderer. If Falcon is found not guilty the jury will just be convinced that Curran acted alone and we still won't have made any progress."

Alexander wished he could trust her with the truth. He wanted desperately to tell her that he was Alfred Curran. He just couldn't risk it. If his true identity was disclosed prematurely he would be arrested and put in jail without bail. Then he would be at the mercy of Marquez and unable to work to defend himself.

"That may be true," Alexander responded, "but if we can acquit Falcon and throw doubt on Curran's participation it'll make the people who really committed the murder hesitate about trying it again. It gives us leverage to get the reforms in the valley we need." He paused and Celia, seeing that he was going to stand up, came over to give him help. Other than being light headed from lying in bed so long Alexander felt all right. As long as he could bear the pain of the wounds on his back he could return to his normal life.

Alexander continued. "You said yourself that we needed to do more than put band aids on the wounds that existed in the valley. The victory over the jury question was a big step. But until we can put an end to the violence we'll never make the progress we need. I'm sure that after my beating the workers that were there will change their mind about organizing. We have to find a way to make it impossible for these thugs to go about whipping people into submission. If we can show that they murdered Chacon to get rid of organizers it will go a long way in ending the exploitation."

"But what if they kill you before you can expose them?" Alexander couldn't see the look of love on Celia's face.

"Don't worry Celia, I won't let that happen."

They were interrupted by Augustine's voice calling from downstairs.

"We're upstairs, Augustine. Come up." She cried. They heard his footsteps on the stairs and when he came into the room his look of concern turned to one of cheerfulness at seeing Alexander out of bed and standing.

"Alexander, look at you! Up already. A very fast recovery. One might think you were used to this sort of thing." Alexander was dressed only in pajama bottoms and the dressing on his back failed to conceal his physique. It was clear that the whip didn't penetrate any fat when it landed. All it found was solid muscle. Augustine had never seen a torso so perfectly formed. The muscles on the abdomen resembled the washboard his mother used to use, and the muscles of the arms and shoulders were all perfectly formed and delineated. He thought it was a good thing for the assailants that they had been able to grab him before he had a chance to fight.

With Celia's help Alexander very carefully put on a loose shirt. Once he had it on it added very little discomfort. He'd have to be careful about leaning against anything for the next few days.

The three of them went downstairs where Augustine resumed the conversation. "I've been afraid something like this would happen. These men have too much at stake in the valley to stand still while you threaten to bring down their empire. I'm only thankful that you have survived the ordeal so well."

Alexander didn't respond directly. "Augustine, have you spoken with Geraldo? Do you know what the workers will do?"

"I saw him yesterday. He wants to see you but worries that you may blame him for what happened to you. I told him you would think no such thing. He promised me he'd come here this morning. He said that the workers are very frightened. Each one had to show his card to the people that beat you. They even had a camera there, and took everyone's picture. They're afraid for their own safety and they know that without you they'll have no future in the valley."

"What do your mean without me?" Alexander asked.

Augustine looked abashed. "Won't you take that job in Denver?"

"No!" Alexander answered.

"I admire you for wanting to stay," Augustine said, "but next time they'll kill. Is it worth that?"

"There are different kinds of death. I'm staying." Alexander said this in a tone of voice that made any response superfluous. The door opened and Geraldo came in. He and Alexander faced each other for a moment then Alexander approached him and put his arms around him. Geraldo started to do the same but stopped when Celia spoke with alarm. "Don't touch his back!"

Alexander laughed. "I'm a little tender there. How are you my friend? Did they hurt you?"

"No," Geraldo answered. "Watching what they did to you was horrible enough to get the message across."

"All right," Alexander said, "let's get started figuring a way to get Falcon back here for a trial." He walked to the table and the rest followed. He looked at Augustine, "tell us what success you've had getting Hispanics on the jury rolls."

"I think I've done very well," Augustine said with obvious pride. "And I've learned a great deal. I've read about the jury system and how it works. It's strange to me that as citizens we consider voting in elections so important but see jury service as something to be avoided. Jury service is really just another vote that we have in a democracy, and it's much more powerful that any other. Just think of it! In a criminal case a single juror can prevent a conviction with their vote. In what other election can you be sure that your vote is the one that decides the outcome?" Augustine paused for a moment then continued.

"I found out something even more remarkable. I found out that a jury might even ignore the law. It may be convinced that a person has committed a crime and nevertheless find them not guilty, and there is nothing the government can do to them. Imagine! A jury can refuse to enforce a law they don't like. Or they can find that the police behaved so badly that in spite of a person's guilt they'll acquit him to give a message to the police. I'm convinced that in a free society such as ours the jury system is the greatest protection against government abuse. It's truly remarkable."

"Augustine, are you sure of this?" Celia asked. "I've never heard of such thing. The judge always makes the jury swear they'll follow the law whether they like it or not. That's a standard instruction."

"That's true. He does say that but what if the jury refuses? There's nothing he can do about it. It's an interesting paradox. On the one hand the jury is told it must follow the law but on the other there is nothing that can be done if they don't. Even the Supreme Court has recognized this fact. It's called jury nullification."

"Obviously I can always learn more about the law," Celia responded. "I can assure you that if we have a trial I'll know everything there is to know about this concept of jury nullification."

"Thank you," said Augustine, proud of his contribution. "Let me tell you what I've done. I went to the jury commissioner and had her tell me how she selected a panel. It was just as you described, Alexander. The result is that the only people on the panel are part of the establishment. So I asked her what would happen if someone who was qualified wanted to be on the panel. Her response was very simple. She said she wouldn't put them on. She also said her experience was with people wanting to get off the panel rather than getting on."

"So what has been the result?" asked Alexander.

"I'll tell you in good time." Augustine answered. "First, I want to finish my proud story. After learning all this I wrote a sermon about citizenship and responsibilities. I preach it in one form or another at every mass in every part of the valley. Many parishioners tell me they have signed up for the jury panel. But the most important news is that after mass last Sunday the jury commissioner herself informed me that she'd contacted the court administrator in Denver and he told her she had to put qualified people on the roles if they asked. Since then she said the jury panel had increased by fifty percent due to my efforts. Isn't that wonderful?"

"Yes," said Alexander. "It'll be a big help not only in this case but in every case. You've done a remarkable thing."

After congratulations to Augustine had gone around the table Celia turned to Geraldo. "Geraldo, earlier you said you were sure Falcon was nowhere near the house where Chacon was murdered. What are our chances of proving that?" she asked.

"I didn't think they were very good when I began," he answered. "It was so many years ago I thought most of the people had left the valley.

"That isn't the case?" Augustine asked.

"Most of them have." Geraldo responded. "But I've found four men who were there that night. They'll testify that Falcon was there the entire evening beginning about five o'clock. And that he didn't leave until the meeting broke up after they received the news that Michael had been killed."

"How did they find out?" Alexander asked.

"One of the police department employees at La Garita went to the cantina at the end of his shift and told everyone that Michael had been killed. He also told them that the police believed Alberto was involved. One of the men who heard this knew of the meeting so he drove to Alamosa and told them."

"What I don't understand," Alexander said, "is why Alberto ran away under these circumstances? He had an airtight alibi."

Celia answered. "To understand that you must understand everything that was going on in the valley. Alberto was young, and the people at the meeting wouldn't have any credibility. No one knew the exact details of when Michael had been killed or what evidence may have been planted against Alberto. It just seemed best to leave. As it turned out with the whole Curran thing and the workers scattering Falcon decided his chances were not very good."

Augustine turned to Geraldo. "Who are the four men? Will the jury believe them?"

"I can tell you who the four men are," Geraldo answered. "Whether the jury believes them depends a little bit on whether you have been successful in getting Hispanics on the jury rolls. Two of them are still migrant workers and only come to the valley during the season. But they are married with families and are responsible. The English of one is good. The other has poor English and may not go over so well with the jury."

"I was afraid of that," said Augustine.

"But listen to this," said Geraldo knowing he'd saved the best for last. "The other two are quite different. One is a car mechanic at the Ford dealership in Monte Alto. He has been certified in the Ford programs so he has good language skills. His work record is good. He should be a very good witness. The other one is Luis Padilla." He stopped and waited for Augustine's reaction.

"Do you mean the Luis Padilla that runs the Martinez Mercantile store here in El Centro?" Augustine was obviously surprised.

"The very same," answered Geraldo. "And he's very anxious to testify."

"Why are you so surprised?" Alexander asked Augustine.

"Because Luis is a very well respected person in El Centro. I guess I'm surprised he was a field worker such a short time ago. What's his story?"

"Luis had been coming to the valley with his family for three years the summer that Michael was murdered. While he was here he met Elena Martinez and they fell in love. She was the only child of the family and the family wasn't in favor of her marrying a migrant worker. On the other hand Luis is hard working and ambitious. Finally they said that if Luis agreed to get his high school diploma and attend the community college for two years they would consent to the marriage. It has turned out very well and Luis has prospered."

"Won't it hurt him to testify?" Celia asked.

"I don't think very much." Augustine responded. "The Martinez family is one of the original grant holders along with the Marquez family and my family. When the Currans first came here they treated those families very well and the Martinez family managed to buy the land the store is on. They are very secure and not so fearful of Marquez. Besides Luis feels very strongly that he must tell the truth about Falcon being at that meeting."

"This is terrific news!" Alexander exclaimed. "I think with all this we should be able to convince Falcon to come back and stand trial. Will you try and arrange a meeting?" he asked Celia.

"What are the chances of gaining an acquittal for Falcon?" Augustine asked.

"They're getting better and better," Alexander answered and then changed the subject. "What about the coroner? Have your friends been able to find him?"

"Yes!" Augustine exclaimed. "He's living in Trinidad and I have his address here somewhere," Augustine fumbled through his pockets. He finally produced a letter and handed it to Alexander.

"This is even better," said Alexander, reading the letter. "As soon as I can drive I'll go and see him."

CHAPTER 39

Several days after his discussion with Augustine Alexander felt well enough to make the three-hour drive to Trinidad to find Harvey Rench.

It was early afternoon when he got to Trinidad. He liked what he saw. It was a town that had retained its history and not replaced the buildings with modern steel and stucco. Its history was mining and the wealth that the mines had produced had been spent on beautiful old buildings that had intricate brick designs on the facades. The address he had for Rench turned out to be a rather run down hotel on a side street. Apparently Rench hadn't planned well for his retirement. He parked at the curb and went in. The desk manager told him he could find Rench at the bar next door.

The bar was in the same condition as the hotel and attracted the same clientele. It was dark and smelled of cigarettes, stale beer and stale bodies. He went over to the bartender and asked about Rench. The bartender pointed to a man at the end of the bar with a shot and a beer in front of him. Alexander walked over and sat on the stool next to him.

Alexander ordered a Tecate from the bartender and asked Rench if he wanted something. The answer was yes. The bartender didn't ask Rench what he wanted. He brought Alexander's beer and a shot of vodka and glass of beer for Rench. Rench dropped the shot into the glass of beer, and, nodding in the direction of Alexander, drank it all at once.

Rench was obviously a hardcore drinker. Alexander sipped from his beer and waited a moment. Rench went back to the beer he'd been nursing when Alexander joined him.

"You're Harvey Rench aren't you?" Alexander said.

"Yes, but everyone calls me Doc," he replied. "Who are you?" His voice started deep in his chest and filtered itself through a great many bouts with whiskey before rolling into the air.

"I'm Alexander Courage. I'm a lawyer over in the Sangre de Cristo Valley."

"Since this place isn't in any Michelin guide book I assume you are here to see me." Rench responded.

"Yes. I want to talk about a murder that happened in the Valley about four years ago. Do you remember?"

"Of course I remember. A Mexican boy. Name of Chacon. I was coroner for Costilla County at the time. What's your interest?"

"I've been asked by some people to look into it. They think one of the people involved is innocent."

"Well I'm sure whoever you're trying to help isn't the trigger man. His name was Curran. Crazy situation. When his father died he would have owned the whole valley. Must have had a loose circuit to get involved in drugs. I guess it was the thrill of it, or maybe the old man wouldn't give him any money. Who knows?" He stopped and finished his beer. Alexander signaled to the bartender for another round. When the drinks arrived Rench again dumped the shot into the beer and drank about half of it. Then he went on. "But Curran was killed in Mexico so you must be talking about the other guy. What was his name? Falcon?" Alexander nodded in agreement. Rench continued. "What do you want to know?"

"I'm not sure. The DA won't open any of the files and I'm just looking for something that might help."

"I don't know what that would be. I was the county coroner. I certified the cause of death but that was mostly ministerial. I went to the scene the night they found Chacon but the actual gathering of evidence and investigation was performed by Richard Marquez and his staff."

Alexander remembered what Don Francisco had told him. You can learn something from every person in the world if you're patient and willing to listen. He was sure that Rench could shed some light on the case but just didn't know it. Alexander ordered another round of drinks.

"How soon did you get to the scene?"

"A couple of hours after they called me. When I got there they were almost finished and were just waiting for me to examine the body. That's all I was expected to do."

"Was anything said that was out of the ordinary?"

"No. It was all pretty cut and dried. Chacon had been shot once with a .38 Smith and Wesson. He was sitting in a chair. I guess they found the pistol lying near the body."

"How long were you coroner for Costilla County?" Alexander asked.

"Twenty four years. But that was just a part time job. We didn't have many homicides. All the other deaths were pretty routine."

"What did you do besides being coroner?"

"I owned a drug store in Monte Alto, but I sold that a few years ago and retired here in Trinidad."

"Is that why they call you Doc? Because you were a pharmacist?"

"No, and it's not because I was the coroner. Although most people think coroners are doctors. It was because of my hobby. I was always interested in guns. I made a hobby of it. Even got qualified in court as an expert."

"In what way?"

"Ballistics. I was pretty good at telling whether a bullet came from one gun or another. I also got pretty good at telling the effect of a bullet fired into a human being. How a person would fall depending on how he was shot, whether the impact would knock him backwards or make him fall in place. That sort of thing."

"That's very interesting. How would you do that? I mean you couldn't experiment on people could you?"

"No, of course not. But you know pigs are a lot like people. If somebody were going to slaughter a pig I'd give them a few dollars to let me do it. Then I'd shoot it and cut it up to see the path of the bullet."

"Sounds like an interesting hobby," Alexander said encouragingly. Then went on. "Getting back to the murder of Chacon, why were they so sure that Curran killed him?"

"The gun they found at the scene was traced to Curran. The only prints on the gun were those of Curran. He fled just afterwards and the Mexican authorities confirmed he was involved with one of the drug lords. I think that's is about it."

"What about Falcon? What is the theory there?"

"As far as I remember the patrol car going to the scene passed him near the house. Then they found the car broken down and abandoned and there were plastic bags with cocaine residue on them that matched the bags in the house. And like Curran he fled the scene. All in all a pretty good circumstantial case. I don't know if they found his gun. They never told me and I never had occasion to ask. Considering the fact that any jury would come from the valley and owe something to Richard Marquez it shouldn't be difficult to get a conviction."

Alexander thought for a minute. He had to agree with Rench. It would be difficult to overcome the bias in the valley. He was sure everyone on the jury would be inclined to vote for anything the DA wanted, and if the case was at all plausible they could get a conviction. One thing Rench said puzzled him.

"You said something about Falcon's gun. What did you mean? I haven't heard anything about a second gun."

"I'm pretty sure there was a second gun involved. I'm just guessing it belonged to Falcon. It belonged to whoever fired the slug I found."

"What do you mean the slug you found?" Alexander was astonished.

"I mean the slug I found." Rench repeated and looked at Alexander as if he had a leaky roof. "After I examined Chacon I had to hang around while they finished up. Just in case there were any questions they wanted to ask me. I was just nosing around and I found a spent bullet near the base of the wall near Chacon."

"Did you tell the police about it."

"Sure. I turned it over to Marquez."

"So how do you know there were two guns involved?"

"I'm not sure I do. I never saw a report from the FBI so I don't know what they found out. But the slug I found didn't come from Curran's gun"

"What? You mean to say that the slug you found was from a different gun? How can you know that if you didn't examine Curran's gun?"

"It's pretty simple. Guns have a thing called rifling. It's either right handed or left handed. What that means is that when the slug travels down the barrel it spins from the left to the right or the other way. Curran's gun is Smith and Wesson and they all have right hand rifling. The slug I found came from a gun with left hand rifling."

"So that means two guns were used?"

"That or it means only one gun was used and it wasn't Curran's."

"You mean the gun may have been planted?"

"Maybe."

"What did the cops say when you told them?"

"I never told them. Curran was dead and they figured Falcon was in Mexico forever. I was selling the drug store and moving over here and the whole thing sort of slipped through the cracks."

Alexander could hardly control his excitement. If Curran's gun wasn't the murder weapon it would blow holes in the rest of the case.

"If there's a trial would you testify to what you've told me?"

"Sure. Why not?"

"Did you make any notes about this?" Alexander asked.

"I think I kept anything I had."

"Can you find them for me?"

"It might be difficult because it's all in storage and I owe the storage people some money."

"How much money?"

"A couple of hundred."

Alexander didn't say anything. Finally Rench said, "I think they'd let me get the stuff if I paid half. Then maybe I could pay the other half after I testified." Alexander ordered another drink for the two of them. When the drinks came Alexander put a hundred dollars on the bar. He and Rench raised their glasses to each other. "I hope I've helped you," Rench said.

"I think you've helped all of us." Alexander replied as they each emptied their glasses.

CHAPTER 40

It was late when Alexander got back to El Centro. He thought for a moment about stopping at Celia's. He wanted to spend more and more time with her. It was difficult to square those feelings with the fact that the whole reason for trying to clear his name was to win Patricia back.

One thing was certain; if he could prove his innocence and win back the Sangre he would make massive changes in the valley and if Celia wanted to she would play a big role. She was intelligent, she had a fine sense of social justice, he trusted her, respected her, and she had become a good friend. He decided to wait until morning to give her the news.

Celia was in the kitchen when Alexander arrived the next morning. She was putting things in a wicker basket and looked up as he came in.

"Celia," Alexander was barely inside the door when he started speaking. "I have good news."

Celia couldn't help smiling. "Not so fast. Sit down for a minute. I have to get just one more thing and then we're going for a short trip. You can tell me about it on the way."

"Where are we going?"

"It's a surprise. A special place I know about. It'll do wonders for your back and we both could use a day off." Alexander reluctantly stifled what he wanted to tell her. Celia handed him the basket and then picked up a backpack that was lying near the door and led the way to her Bronco. As Alexander watched her it was easy for him to forget all about Rench. She wore soft calfskin boots with a western heel that gave an Ingres line to the finely shaped legs that were covered by tight fitting jeans. The crimson blouse she wore tucked into the jeans accentuated her shoulders and breasts. Her raven black hair was pulled back into a ponytail that reached almost to her belt.

They drove through the town and turned east onto a road that led to the mountains. The crisp, cobalt blue sky was cloudless and formed a soft backdrop to the 14,000-foot peaks that capped the Sangre de Cristo Mountains. There was an occasional speck in the air pulling a long vapor trail behind it. The mountains were so massive they seemed close enough to touch but he knew from experience that this was deceptive.

They drove due east past irrigated fields and then at the edge of the valley the ground began an upward climb and the irrigated fertility gave way to the natural semiarid land of sage, wild grass, and yucca.

As the piñon pine and boulders gave way to spruce and fir the road became a narrow one-lane dirt road. The forest grew denser with each switch back as they climbed the side of the mountain.

The road had been built as an access road to the timber high in the national forest. After the logging was finished campers, hunters, and mountain climbers used it to get into the back country. Alexander recounted his meeting with Harvey Rench as they drove while Celia maneuvered the Bronco along the narrow winding road. He appreciated her ability to listen.

By the time he'd finished his narrative they were several miles along the dirt road and two thousand feet above the valley floor. When they came to another switch back Celia didn't turn but continued straight onto a track that was barely visible. After a hundred feet they were among the pines and invisible from the main road. Without saying anything Celia parked the truck and got out. She opened the tailgate and handed Alexander the wicker basket and took the backpack for herself, then she led him along a narrow path that wound through some boulders and traveled upwards and sideways along the mountain. After passing one large outcropping of rock she reversed direction. Taking a flashlight from the backpack she entered a small opening into the mountain.

When she turned on the light Alexander could see that they were in a natural tunnel not wide enough for two people to walk side by side and only high enough for him to walk in a semi-crouch. After thirty feet the tunnel grew even lower and Celia finally was on her hands and knees in front of him. They crawled this way a few feet and he became aware of the smell of sulphur. A few feet later the tunnel opened into a large cavern.

"Welcome to my special place," she said as she played the beam of the flashlight around the room. Stalactites on the ceiling reflected iridescent colors as the light struck them. In most places a complimentary stalagmite on the floor had formed to grow towards its counterpart above. "Here," Celia said, handing Alexander the flashlight. "Hold this while I light the candles." After they were lighted Alexander saw that the odor he smelled came from a mineral pool in the cave. It gave off a steady, gentle curtain of steam. Near the pool was a flat depression and Celia spread a fully opened sleeping bag over it and then a picnic cloth on that.

Alexander was mesmerized. In all the years of growing up in the valley he'd visited many of the hot mineral springs that laced these mountains, but he didn't know of this place. He sensed that Celia was sharing something with him that she'd not shared with many others. She took *empañadas* and cheese from the wicker basket and handed him a bottle of wine. Alexander uncorked the wine and poured each of them a glass. He held his glass towards her and said, "Here's to your special place and for sharing it with me."

"Now," said Celia taking a drink of wine and reaching for some cheese. "Let's discuss this information you have from Rench. It seems fairly simple. He recovered a spent slug from the scene that he believes was the bullet that killed Chacon. Because of the rifling he knows it couldn't have been fired by Curran's gun. He never heard of any tests being conducted on Curran's gun or whether another slug was even recovered."

"Exactly," said Alexander. "It raises several possibilities. It may mean Curran's gun didn't kill Chacon or that two guns were used."

"Doesn't it just mean that both Curran and Falcon could have had guns? Couldn't they just say that there were two guns involved and Falcon must have used the second one."

"Yes, but if I can surprise them with the information after they've rested their case it may throw them off enough to raise a good doubt in the minds of the jurors. I'm betting that they'll be nonchalant about the whole case. They figure that a jury in the valley will bring back any verdict they want."

"But we have a strong case now. We can show that Falcon was at the Alamosa camp meeting when Chacon was killed, and we have four witnesses to prove it. Why do we even need Rench's testimony? I don't see how it will help Falcon. If Curran was on trial it would be a different story. Sometimes I think you're trying to build a case for Curran instead of Falcon."

Alexander realized his mistake. He shouldn't have been so excited about his meeting with Rench. It did appear that he was defending Alfred instead of Falcon. "I guess it does seem that way," he finally answered. "I'm offended because this whole thing was set up to frame Curran. Falcon was just an added dividend and they haven't put a good case together against him. They just wanted him out of the valley and they accomplished that. If Falcon is acquitted it won't be any disaster for them. I think after all this time they'll be only half hearted in the prosecution."

"But why go to such lengths to get rid of Curran?"

"Think of it, Celia. Marquez has always believed the Currans stole the Sangre from his ancestors. His only chance to get it back was to get rid of Alfred. Old man Curran was eighty-four and wouldn't live much longer. He must have known that with Alfred out of the way he could marry Patricia, and when she inherited the Sangre, as Alfred's widow, Marquez would have it all. And it turned out just as he planned. Alfred is killed; the father dies not long after; Richard marries Patricia, and now he has the whole land grant."

Celia didn't say anything for sometime. She wasn't sure she understood all of Alexander's motives in doing what he was doing but she knew she was growing to love him and wanted to help. "What do you want me to do?"

"I want you to use your influence to get Falcon to return and stand trial." He paused a moment. "And I want you to help me try the case."

Celia didn't say anything in response. She stood up and began to unbutton her blouse. "Celia!" Alexander said. "What are you doing?" Celia continued undoing each button and then pulled the blouse from her jeans. As it fell open Alexander could see she wasn't wearing anything under the blouse. She slowly pulled it away from her shoulders and he gazed on breasts that were the color of honey.

"Why, Alexander," she said. "I'm going to soak in the pool. What did you think I was going to do? Take your clothes off and join me. It will do wonders for your back."

"I didn't bring a suit." Alexander said, fighting emotions and physical needs he'd long suppressed.

"Well in that case I won't look if you don't, " she said as she turned her back to him and began to remove her jeans.

Alexander wanted to join her in the pool but he couldn't control the physical evidence of the effect she was having on him. He got up and blew out the candle nearest the pool then quickly undressed and slipped into the pool. He hoped the water would drain some of the emotions from him. He turned to look just as Celia stepped into the pool and was sure he'd never seen a more perfectly formed, beautiful creature.

The pool was shallow and when they sat down their heads were just above the water. The water was hot and took some getting used to but felt wonderful on his wounded back. The effect was narcotizing and he realized how much tension he'd built up. The light from the candle played gently off the cavern walls and he sank deeper and deeper into a hypnotic trance.

With his eyes closed and his head resting against the edge of pool he felt Celia's hands on each side of his face. She was facing him with her legs on each side of his. She leaned forward and he felt her warm sensuous lips begin to slowly explore his. He put his arms around her and drew her closer. He could feel the contour of her breasts as she pressed against him. Her kiss became more intense and her tongue began to explore the inside of his mouth. She moved her hips so that his hardness found her sex and when all of him was in her she began to gently move her hips in a figure eight pattern. It wasn't long before they both sensed that this loving union would have its climax. She leaned into him and they held each other tightly as their bodies and hearts reached the ultimate physical display of love.

When it was over they rested in each other's arms. Neither had spoken a word. Words would have been superfluous to their actions. Finally Celia moved away and Alexander was left with his sense of euphoria. Alexander dozed off and was awakened by Celia's voice.

"Alexander," she said. "It's time to go." He opened his eyes and saw her standing at the edge of the pool fully clothed.

"Celia," he said, "that was wonderful. Thank you."

"I thought you would like it," she answered. "But now we must go. I've decided to see if I can get Falcon to come back and stand trial. I need to get started."

At the moment Alexander was too full of other thoughts to care about Falcon or the valley. "Celia," he said, not moving. "We may never be here again. Please get back in the pool. I would like to do what we just did only this time when I'm fully awake."

Celia looked at him with a shocked expression. "Obviously," she said, "you've had some kind of fantasy. The fumes and the water often do that. Believe me nothing happened between us. In fact nothing ever will happen between us in the present circumstances. I'm very old fashioned. When it happens it will be with my husband. Now please get out of the pool and let's go save Alberto Falcon."

CHAPTER 41

Celia came into the office at the Legal Services Center one morning with a big smile. "I have good news," she said. Alexander was sure he knew it was the news he'd been waiting for and stood up.

"Falcon?" he asked.

"Yes! He called last night and said he wants to meet you."

"Did he say where and when?"

"Tomorrow, and he said you would know where and when."

"This is good news Celia. I can't tell you how much it means to me. You'll understand if everything works out the way I hope it will."

"Where will you meet him?" Celia asked.

"If he didn't tell you I don't think I should. If his brother decides not to surrender it will be better that you haven't been involved in the discussions. I'm sure if Marquez finds out about my meetings he'll charge me with harboring a fugitive. If that happens I'll need you to defend me. I'll come by your house as soon as I get back and tell you everything that happened." Celia accepted this without comment but it was clear she was concerned about his safety.

That evening Alexander drove again to Conejos. When Alexander got to the cantina he went directly to the booth where he and Falcon had met before. He ordered a beer and a roasted habanero pepper and began to wait. He knew that Falcon wouldn't make his appearance until he was sure that Alexander had not been followed. Alexander was on his fourth beer and nearly half way through the habanero when Falcon appeared.

"I hear a lot about what you're doing in the valley," he said without preliminaries. "I like it."

"Thanks," Alexander replied. "Do you like it enough to ask your brother to return for trial?"

"It depends. Let me hear what your strategy will be if he does."

"The strongest point is the alibi. We've found four witnesses who'll testify that your brother was at a meeting when Chacon was murdered."

"My experience has been that the testimony of four migrant Mexican workers won't count for much in front of an Anglo jury picked by Richard Marquez." Falcon interjected.

"I agree that's been a problem," Alexander said. "But I think it's much less of a problem in this case. In the first place two of the witnesses are people that have been living in the valley full time since the murder and no longer work in the fields. One works as a mechanic at a car dealer in Monte Alto, the other operates a mercantile store in El Centro. They'll be very good witnesses."

"Why were they at a meeting to organize the workers?" Falcon asked.

"At the time they were field workers. Since then they've learned trades, and they live in the valley permanently with their families. Both of them feel secure enough to come forward to help you."

"That's better," Falcon replied, "but I still don't like the odds that an all white hand-picked jury will be convinced by two former migrants."

"But it won't be an all white hand picked jury. That's a thing of the past."

"Don't kid me," Falcon responded with skepticism. "Marquez has always protected himself by making sure the jury rolls were made up of well to do, property owning, Anglos who would do as he told them!"

"We've changed all that. The last time we counted the jury rolls were forty per cent Hispanic, and by the time your brother stands trial it will be over fifty per cent."

"How did that happen?"

"We made the jury commissioner aware of the fact that she had to enroll anyone that was qualified and asked to be enrolled. She didn't like it but wasn't going to go against the Supreme Court. Father Augustine Romero and Geraldo Guerrero have been organizing the workers to sign up.

"That's a good idea. Who thought of that?"

"I did."

Falcon looked at him with new respect. "First you use the jury system to bust the town treasuries, now you've come up with a way to load the jury system with Hispanics. Wonderful! Is there anything else?"

"I intend to show that the prosecution's case is so full of holes that even the most prejudiced jury won't believe it. We can show that a lot of evidence has been lost or misplaced. I think some of the people involved in the investigation have left the valley. I'm relying on the fact that the main target in this frame was Alfred Curran, and as long as he's dead and Marquez has his wife and the valley they won't care much whether your brother is convicted or not. I don't think they'll be very prepared."

Falcon looked at him a moment as if trying to look for an answer deep in his soul. Finally he said. "All right, I'll do it."

"You'll do what? Get hold of your brother?" Alexander asked.

"No," Falcon relied. "I'll surrender and let you be my lawyer."

Alexander was stunned. "You're Alberto Falcon?"

"Yes. I told you I was his brother because at first I didn't trust you. When I did trust you I didn't want to put you in a position of knowing who I was in case I decided not to surrender. That way you wouldn't be hiding a criminal if you believed I was someone else."

Alexander shook his head. All this time he'd been talking to the man that could save him without even knowing it. Then he said. "Now let me ask you something? You know the chances for an acquittal aren't a hundred percent. If you're convicted you'll go to jail for the rest of your life. You've managed to avoid capture this long. Why not just stay away?"

Falcon thought for a moment then said. "Mr. Courage, you can't know what it's like to live with a false identity. Before Michael was murdered, and I ran away, I was deeply committed to making things better for the workers in the valley. The moment I ran I couldn't do what I most wanted to. If there is any chance of beating the case I'm willing to take it. If I go to jail as the person I really am at least I'll have regained my voice. When I'm in jail I can at least fight for prison reform from inside. Now I'm nothing."

They sat for a moment each with their own thoughts; Falcon content with his decision to regain his identity and sure that Alexander couldn't understand the terrible need to do so; Alexander knowing what it meant to have your identity stripped and not able to tell Falcon the truth.

Finally Falcon broke the silence. "What happens now?"

"I'll tell the DA's office that you want to surrender and stand trial. I'll see if I can get them to agree to set bail so you can remain free until the trial. I don't think they'll agree to it. In that case you'll have to surrender and stay in jail until the trial is over and you're acquitted."

"How long will that take?"

"A few months."

"I noticed you didn't say if I'm acquitted. You said, "when I'm acquitted. You seem real sure."

Alexander responded in measured tones. "Believe me when I tell you we are in this together. If you win, I win. I intend to do everything I can to beat these charges."

The two men whose fate was now intertwined stood up. "How shall I get word to you about the details of the surrender?" Alexander asked.

"Leave a message for me here. Tell me where and when to meet you. Give me one day's notice. That's enough." The two men shook hands and Alexander left knowing that this case would seal his fate forever.

CHAPTER 42

It was dark when he left Conejos for the drive to El Centro. All the light of vespers had left the sky and had been replaced by patterns of stars that elbowed each other for room. The margins of the highway faded before him as he ate up the miles. Directly in the sky before him was the pole star, that constant guide of ancient mariners. He fixed on it as if it were the symbol of his dream of redemption and revenge, but he also remembered the words of Don Francisco telling him that ideals were like the stars; we can't reach them but they should always guide us.

Alexander's mind was spinning. Finally the reality of the situation set in. Falcon's agreement to stand trial caused serious doubts about himself. It was his hypocrisy that was troubling. He had to admit to himself that Falcon needed a lawyer with more experience. Was he looking after Falcon's interests or his own? The idea of winning back Patricia and the Land Grant made his head spin with joy. But was all this in the interest of Falcon? What if he had to choose between getting Falcon off and saving himself? If he turned the case over to a more experienced criminal lawyer he was sure that the vindication of Alfred Curran would never come into play. He'd tried to convince himself that he and Falcon had exactly the same interests and there would be no conflict. Was that just rationalization? The old Alfred wouldn't have considered morality in questions of his own interests. Was the new Alfred going to miss this opportunity at the expense of honesty? He could remember a time in his life when it was easy to make decisions without considering the moral consequences. Now the moral consequences seemed to be utmost in his thought process. Actually this realization pleased him. He liked the idea of living an idealistic life instead of one driven by greed. He decided that he would represent Falcon until he found himself in a situation he couldn't handle then he would reconsider.

The lights of El Centro brought him back to the reality of the moment. He drove directly to Celia's house to deliver the news she and Augustine had been waiting for. When he arrived he was happy to see that Geraldo was also there.

"Good news," he said as they settled at the dining room table. "The man I thought was Roberto Falcon is really Alberto Falcon. He's been hiding in northern New Mexico since the murder of Chacon. And he's willing to surrender himself and permit us to defend him."

Geraldo and Celia greeted the news with great enthusiasm but Augustine remained subdued. Alexander looked at him. "Why the long face Padre?" He asked.

Augustine took some time to answer as if searching for the exegesis of his thoughts. "I'm not convinced this is a good idea," he finally answered. "The valley is so corrupt that it will be a simple thing for Marquez to put on a case that convicts Falcon. Falcon will go to jail for his lifetime. We'll have lost a major battle, and Marquez will be stronger than ever. That's what worries me."

"Augustine," Alexander said gently. "If the worst that can happen does happen you may be right. I admit Marquez has corrupted the valley to such a degree that even the justice system can be manipulated. On the other hand this is our best chance to bring him down. If we can expose the corruption it will be the hole in the dam that will eventually destroy the dam altogether."

"Alexander is right." Celia injected. "For all these years we've been treating the cancer with bandages. This is our chance to use radiation and maybe get rid of it for good."

"But what of the risks to Falcon," Augustine responded. "If

he's convicted all of us go back to business as usual. He goes to jail for life."

"Don't worry about that," Alexander said. "He understands the risks very well. He doesn't want to live in hiding the rest of his life. He knows he's innocent and he believes now is his best chance of proving it. I agree with him. Now we must do everything we can to help him.

"All right," said Augustine. "I'll help in every way I can."

"Wonderful!" Celia exclaimed as she went around the table and gave Augustine a hug and a kiss.

"Geraldo spoke up. "What happens next?" he asked Alexander.

"I meet with Marquez and arrange Alberto's surrender. Then all hell should break loose."

CHAPTER 43

When Alexander walked into the office of Richard Marquez he was greeted politely. "Mr. Courage," Richard Marquez said as he rose from his desk chair. "Obviously you decided not to accept Mr. Farnsworth's generous offer of employment. I hope you won't live to regret that decision."

"I hope I'll live a long time whether I regret the decision or not," Alexander replied as he sat in one of the chairs facing the desk

"I suppose you're referring to that regrettable incident when you were beaten," Marquez said without any suggestion of regret.

"You have to admit it's a good example of something that can be dangerous to one's health," Alexander responded.

"Yes," said Richard. "I would imagine that if something like that's ignored it could lead to even greater discomfort, maybe even death."

"As it did with Michael Chacon?"

Marquez' eyes looked at Alexander with new attention. "Mr. Courage," he said, "I thought you made this appointment with me to see what progress had been made in finding out who beat you."

"I'm here for several reasons," Alexander responded. "That's certainly one of them. What progress have you made?"

Richard thought for a moment. "Unfortunately the police and sheriff tell me that they've made very little progress in identifying the individuals responsible. They believe that the group that beat you were members of the *Mano Negra*."

"What's the *Mano Negra*?"

"It's a secret society that has existed in this part of the world for many centuries. It was formed by citizens to act as vigilantes in the community. It's much like the Sicilian Costa Nostra or the Ku Klux Klan."

Alexander looked surprised. "Since I've been in the valley I've never heard of such a thing."

"I must remind you," said Richard, "that you haven't been in the valley very long. I should also remind you that it's a secret society. That being the case why should you know about it?"

"That would be particularly true if it were made up of the people sworn to enforce the laws."

Marquez's eyes flared. "As district attorney I'm the chief law enforcement officer in the valley. To suggest that the Black Hand is part of law enforcement impugns my integrity. I won't stand for that."

Alexander didn't take the bait and continued. "If it isn't made up of law enforcement and continues to exist that doesn't say much for the ability of the police in the valley."

"Mr. Courage I don't intend to sit here and listen to these complaints. We're investigating your beating. When we have sufficient evidence to charge someone we'll do it. Until then you must be careful. We can't guarantee your safety. Next time the results may be far worse."

"Very well," said Alexander ignoring the threat. "Let me get back to the murder of Michael Chacon."

"You mentioned that incident earlier. That was almost four years ago. What does it have to do with you?" Richard asked.

"When you mentioned this Black Hand society being responsible for my beating it occurred to me that perhaps it was also responsible for the murder of Chacon."

"Impossible!" exclaimed Richard. "We know exactly what happened in that case. The murder didn't involve anyone except Alfred Curran and Alberto Falcon."

"How can you be sure?" Alexander asked.

Instead of becoming indignant Richard's voice became

unnaturally calm. "This is what happened Mr. Courage. Michael
Chacon and Alberto Falcon were drug dealers. They claimed to
be labor organizers but that was merely a front for their drug
dealing. Their supplier was Alfred Curran. There was a falling
out among them. Apparently it was Falcon and Curran on one
side and Chacon on the other. On the night of the murder the
three met at Chacon's house. We suppose the situation grew nasty
and there was an argument. Then Curran shot and killed Chacon
and fled to Mexico where he was killed in a car accident. Falcon
took the cocaine that was in the house and also fled to Mexico.
That is what happened."

"You're telling me that Alfred Curran, the heir to this entire
valley was a drug dealer? And that he shot Michael Chacon several
times in cold blood then fled the country. That doesn't make
sense."

"Murder rarely does. We believe that Curran began using drugs
in College and was fascinated by the intrigue of international
drug cartels. Perhaps it was a combination of drug use, fantasy,
and boredom. Who can ever explain these kinds of things? But I
must correct you on one thing. You suggest that Chacon was
shot several times and therefore the possibility that this was some
sort of moment of passion. The fact is that Chacon was killed
execution style. He was sitting in a chair and was shot once in the
back of the head. It was a cold-blooded execution. And we
recovered Curran's gun from the scene."

"If it was so cold blooded why was the gun left behind? That
doesn't seem very well planned."

"We have speculated on that," said Richard. "Maybe he killed
Chacon while he was high on drugs and not thinking clearly.
After he'd done it the shock may have caused him to panic. You
must remember that Curran was a spineless person who had abused
his wife and had become an international drug dealer. None of
that is rational so why would he be expected to act rationally
when committing a murder. In any event we'll never know the
truth. He's dead and Falcon will never be found. I'm sure of
that."

"That brings us to the main reason for my asking for a meeting," Alexander said. "I've been contacted by Alberto Falcon. He wants to return and stand trial on the charges against him."

"What?" Richard was incredulous. "Falcon wants to return and stand trial. That's crazy. Why would he return just to serve a life sentence without possibility of parole?"

"He wants to clear his name."

"That's impossible. We have clear evidence of his guilt. Besides if he was innocent why did he run and why has he waited so long to return?"

"I'm sure all those questions will be answered in due course," Alexander replied. "Right now I want to arrange his surrender."

Richard had recovered from his initial shock. "That's very simple," he said. "Bring him in and we'll put him in jail, we'll have a trial, and we'll put him in the penitentiary for the rest of his life. And we'll do it with a great deal of pleasure."

"What about bail?"

"Bail!" Richard exclaimed. "There won't be any bail. He's charged with murder and has been a fugitive for four years."

"That's not the law," Alexander replied. "The state constitution provides that there will be bail in every case except in a murder case where the proof is evident and the presumption great."

"Which is precisely the situation here," Richard answered angrily. "His prints were in the house. He was seen driving away from the scene. The drugs found in the car matched those at the murder scene."

"The prints were there because he lived there" Alexander responded. "Falcon wasn't seen driving away from the scene. The car was seen. It would have been impossible for the police driver to make an absolute identification of the driver. With respect to the drugs let me remind you that this is a murder case not a drug case. I've researched the law and the judge can't refuse to set bail."

Richard's eyes were as cold as black ice. "Mr. Courage," he began in measured tones, "The judge will do exactly . . . ," then he caught himself.

"Do exactly what you tell him to do? Is that what you were going to say?" said Alexander. Richard had risen from his chair and stood with his back to Alexander. Alexander sensed that he was struggling to control his anger. After a moment he turned around. He smiled at Alexander. "You're right Mr. Courage. I want to be fair. There should be bail. We'll make a recommendation to the judge for bail in the amount of one million dollars. How do you expect Mr. Falcon to post that?" His lips curled into a vicious look. "Will it be cash or property," he laughed.

"You know very well that he doesn't have the resources to make that kind of bail," Alexander replied.

"You asked for bail," said Richard. "Now you have it. When will you surrender him? I hope it'll be soon. We wouldn't want to think that you're harboring a fugitive."

"Today is Monday," said Alexander. "I'll surrender him in court on Wednesday morning if that fits the courts' schedule."

Richard didn't answer. He pushed a button on his intercom and asked his secretary to come in. When the door opened he said. "Dolores, will you call Judge Celeste's clerk and see if we can have a time for an initial appearance on Wednesday at 10 am."

"Yes sir," she answered. "I'll have to give her the defendant's name."

"Tell her it's Alberto Falcon." Richard answered. Dolores stood in stunned silence. Finally she spoke.

"Alberto Falcon?"

"Yes," Richard said, "Alberto Falcon. I think we are about to have a very interesting time."

Dolores left to make the call and soon the intercom buzzed and she said the time was agreeable with the court. Alexander decided to see how far he could push Richard.

"You know, Richard, it seems strange to me that Curran and Falcon would commit this crime. They gained nothing by it and it's hard to see what they expected to gain."

"What conclusion do you draw from that?" Richard asked.

"It's not necessarily a conclusion," said Alexander. "It just seems that most crimes are committed with a motive. In this case neither Falcon nor Curran seemed to have benefited from the murder."

"They rid themselves of an accomplice that may have been prepared to expose them."

"But there were ways to do that without destroying themselves in the process."

"Well then," said Richard. "Who else benefited more than they did?"

"You did," said Alexander. "You managed to get almost four million acres of land, a beautiful wife, and a wonderful hacienda."

Richard looked at Alexander with murder in his eyes. "If circumstances were different I would beat you for those remarks. When this case is finished you will leave the valley. The only issue is whether you will be breathing when you go. Now get out."

CHAPTER 44

Wednesday morning the courtroom at El Centro was packed. The word had gotten out that Falcon was back in the valley to stand trial.

The two-story courthouse in El Centro had been built in the early part of the century using stone quarried on the west side of the valley. County offices were on the first floor, and the courtrooms were on the second floor. Alexander and Falcon sat at the defense counsel table with Celia. It was a beautiful courtroom. The ceilings were eighteen feet high. Along one wall were recessed windows that began at waist level and extended to the ceiling. The room was longer than wide and divided into two sections. One section took about a third of the room. It contained the judge's bench, the witness stand, a jury box and the tables and chairs for the defense and prosecution. There was a door behind the bench that led to the judge's chambers. Another door at one end of the jury box led into the jury deliberation room. The rest of the room contained benches for the spectators. The two sections were divided by a waist high railing called the bar. When a new lawyer was admitted to practice it was said he became a member of the bar and could pass through the railing for his business. People not members of the bar could pass the rail only with special permission or when ordered to do so.

All the furniture and the floors were solid wood. The ceiling was decorated with scenes from American history and with the two ornate chandeliers one was reminded of a temple.

Richard Marquez and his assistant, John Reed, arrived shortly after Alexander and Falcon. As soon as the bailiff knew they were ready he alerted the judge and then gaveled the court into session. The judge was Antonio Celeste. He was of French-Hispanic descent, and his family had lived in the valley for decades. He'd been hand picked by Marquez for the court, and no one doubted where his loyalties lay. He was known as an arrogant judge with a short temper. This is usually the case with judges who use their robe and power to shield their insecurities and ignorance.

The clerk began the proceedings. "Call the case of the People of the State of Colorado vs. Alberto Falcon."

Alexander rose from his chair. "Your honor," he said. "My name is Alexander Courage. I'm entering my appearance, and that of Ms. Celia Chavez, as attorneys for the defendant Falcon. Mr. Falcon is also present in person."

Celeste said nothing but only turned his head in the direction of Marquez who was now on his feet. "Your honor," Richard began. "Richard Marquez and John Reed appearing on behalf of the people."

"Very well," said Celeste. "This matter comes on for the first appearance by the defendant. Mr. Falcon please step to the podium with your counsel. Mr. Courage have you received a copy of the charges?"

"No, your honor."

"Very well, Mrs. Nieto will give you a copy." The clerk left her chair and handed a copy of the Information to Alexander.

"Mr. Falcon you are charged with first degree murder, and conspiracy to commit first degree murder. Do you want me to read the Information?"

"Your honor," Alexander responded. "We waive a formal reading of the Information and ask that the matter be set down for a preliminary hearing."

Marquez spoke for the first time. "Your honor, there is the matter of bail. The people request bail in the amount of one million dollars."

Before the judge could respond Alexander spoke. "We object

to that amount as being excessive. The law requires reasonable bail and says bail shouldn't be used to punish the defendant before he's found guilty."

"Mr. Courage," said Celeste, his voice developing an edge. "The law in Colorado arrived in this court well before your recent appearance. I don't need you to tell me what the constitution provides. This man has committed a murder and has been a fugitive for four years, I think the bail is low if anything." He paused for a moment and Alexander spoke.

"Your honor, I object to your saying that Mr. Falcon committed a murder. He's presumed innocent and for you to say otherwise is improper."

Celeste's face turned to icy anger. "Don't you dare interrupt me! If you want to get along in my court you better learn some manners. I said the defendant was charged with committing a murder. Perhaps you should listen more carefully. I've told you I think the bail is more than reasonable. It wouldn't take much to convince me that it should be higher. If you persist in your argument I may be convinced of just that. Now, do you want to continue?"

It was obvious to Alexander that Celeste had already made up his mind about the case. With him presiding it was going to be an uphill battle to receive even the semblance of a fair trial. A cashier's check for the million in bail had been arranged from Don Francisco's legacy to him. He intended to post the bail for Falcon in any case so it didn't seem a good tactic to fight Celeste on this issue. He didn't want to make Celeste increase the bail. He was sure that neither Marquez nor the Judge thought there was the remotest possibility that Falcon could post a million dollars. If they believed otherwise they might increase the bail and anything over the million would be difficult to meet.

"We'll accept the bail as presently set," Alexander responded.

"All right," said Celeste. "Bail will be set in the amount of one million dollars. Defendant will be remanded to the custody of the sheriff. What about a preliminary hearing? Do you have a date in mind?" The last question was directed to Marquez.

"Sometime at the end of next week."

"Next Thursday at 9 a.m.? Mr. Courage does that work for you?"

"Yes."

"Very well. Court is in recess." The gavel sounded once and Celeste was gone. Two sheriff's deputies came over to the counsel table and took Falcon to be booked. As he was led through the door Alexander turned to Celia. "This Celeste is going to be a lot of fun to try a case in front of. Is he like this with everyone?"

"Everyone on this side of the room," Celia answered. "The DA can do no wrong. It can get pretty ugly."

"Maybe we can get him thrown off the case. Let's look into grounds for a motion of recusal."

"Good idea," said Celia. "Shall I get started now?"

"I guess it's as good a time as any. You do that and I'll go down and bail Alberto out of jail."

"What?" Celia had just begun to walk away and turned back in surprise. "You are going to post a million dollars in bail?"

"I'm not going to," he lied, regretting it as he said it. "Remember I mentioned a foundation that was willing to pay the workers wages if they had to go to jail over the right to jury trial issue? It's agreed to put up a million in cash."

"What's the name of the foundation?" she asked not believing what she was hearing.

"I'm sorry I can't tell you. They agreed to do it on the condition they remain anonymous. It's a foreign foundation that helps political prisoners. I convinced them Alberto was a political prisoner."

"A political prisoner in America?" She thought for a moment. "Well, when it comes to this sort of thing the Sangre does seem like a foreign country. In any case it's wonderful news."

"Yes," Alexander replied, "and it will give me a great deal of pleasure to surprise Celeste and Marquez. In their wildest dreams they never imagined he would be able to make a million in bail. I can tell you one thing, if they'd thought he could make it they would have set it much higher. It would be a definite pleasure to see their faces when he's released. I guess I better get started. I'll see you back at your house when I'm finished."

"The people will be very pleased, Alexander. They already think you walk on water," she said as she walked away. He stood admiring her until the door closed.

Alexander went to the clerk's office and presented the cashiers check for a million dollars. It was drawn on the New York branch of the Royal Bank of Canada. The clerk at first expressed confusion over the fact the bank was headquartered in a foreign country. She disappeared for a few minutes. Alexander assumed she had a conference with Richard or the judge or both. He had no illusion that they'd let any ethical niceties stand in the way of how they conducted themselves. When she returned she was tight lipped but filled out the necessary papers and Falcon was released from the jail.

When they arrived at Celia's Augustine and Geraldo were also there waiting for them. This was the first time in four years that Alberto had been back in El Centro and Augustine and Geraldo welcomed him with open arms. "I never expected to be out of jail during the case," Alberto began. "Who posted the bail?" he asked Alexander.

"I can't tell you that," Alexander replied "But it will be a big problem if you do anything to jeopardize it."

"Don't worry about that," said Falcon. "When I decided to come back and stand trial I also decided that it might involve going to jail. I'm not going to run again. Besides with you handling my case I'm sure we will win."

"In that case we better get started," said Celia.

"What happens now?" Augustine asked.

"Next Thursday is the preliminary hearing," said Celia.

"What does that mean?" asked Geraldo.

Alexander answered the question. "Under the law the prosecution must show the court that there is good reason to believe that a crime has been committed and that Alberto and Curran committed it. It's called probable cause. They don't have to prove the case they only have to show that there is some evidence of it and some evidence that Alberto committed it. How much they have to present varies from court to court. From what I saw today it won't take much for Judge Celeste."

"What happens if he finds there's probable cause?"

"Then it will be set for a trial."

"Is there any chance he'll find there is no probable cause?" asked Augustine.

"Not at all," Alexander replied.

"Then why bother?"

"Because it can be very valuable in other ways. We get to see something of their case at an early stage and can begin preparing to meet it. Also the DA will have to commit to certain facts and if he tries to change them later at the trial we will have some basis for impeachment.

"While we're waiting for the trial," Alexander went on. "We can file motions. That's what I want to talk about now. I believe the most important motion is to have Judge Celeste disqualified. To do that we must show that he can't be impartial."

"What sort of things will help us?" asked Augustine.

Celia spoke up. "For instance, that he's related to Marquez, or that he has business dealings with him, or has a relationship with him that will make him prejudiced, or that he has made statements to people that mean he's already made up his mind against Alberto. Any of these things will help. I'll begin work on it tomorrow. I'll need the help of all of you."

"Of course," said Augustine, "we'll do what we can. But now I have another suggestion."

"What's that?" It was Alexander who took the bait.

"That we all go to Casa Melina for dinner and celebrate the return of Alberto Falcon." There were no dissenters.

CHAPTER 45

"Everyone please rise." The clerk banged the gavel twice. "The district court for the 22nd Judicial District is now in session." Judge Antonio Celeste entered the courtroom through the door just behind the bench. He stood for a moment and said, "Everyone please be seated," then he sat down.

"This is case number 3579 People vs. Falcon. The matter comes on for a preliminary hearing. Are the parties ready to proceed?"

"The people are ready your honor."

"Defendant Falcon is ready your honor."

"Very well Mr. Marquez. Call your first witness."

"The people call Detective Gaspar Ruiz." The detective was dressed in civilian clothes and carried a file folder in his hand.

Marquez began the questioning. "Please state your name."

"Gaspar Ruiz."

"How are you employed?"

"I'm a detective for the Costilla county sheriff's office."

"How long have you been so employed?"

"In June it will be 19 years."

"Directing your attention to september 11, 1966 and the murder of one Michael Chacon. Were you the chief investigating officer in that case?"

"Yes I was."

"Describe what happened."

"I received a call at my home about 7:30 pm telling me a

body had been discovered in a house outside La Garita. After getting the exact location I drove there immediately."

"What did you find when you arrived?"

"Deputy Johnson was there when I arrived. He'd called in the report. There were other deputies there as well. I was told there was a dead person in the house. I gave some directions about securing the scene outside the house then I went in. Oh, one other thing. Before I went in I asked that you come to the scene."

"What did you find in the house?"

"The house is a four room house. The front half of the house is one room consisting of a kitchen, dining area and living room. The rear half of the house is two bedrooms separated by a bathroom."

"What did you see?"

"Sitting in a chair near one of the windows was the body of Michael Chacon. It was slumped forward and I could see that he'd been shot once in the back of the head. I made a quick determination that he was dead."

"How did you know it was Michael Chacon?"

"I had had previous contacts with him and knew him personally. Also the body was later identified by finger prints."

"What happened next?"

"After making sure the person was dead I left the house and waited for you to arrive."

"Were you assigned as chief investigating officer?"

"Yes."

"What did that entail?"

"I coordinated all the investigation by the different departments. I assembled all the reports and directed the investigation."

"What did the investigation reveal?"

"On the night in question Deputy Johnson was on patrol in the La Garita area. He got a call from dispatch that there was a report of a disturbance at the house occupied by Michael Chacon and Alberto Falcon."

"I object your honor," said Alexander. "There is no evidence that Mr. Falcon lived in that house."

"Overruled," Celeste responded quickly.

"Deputy Johnson then drove to the house."

"Did he notice anything unusual on the way?"

"Yes. About a half mile before the house a car passed him going in the opposite direction. He recognized the car as one that Alberto Falcon was known to drive."

"Did he recognize the driver?"

"It was Alberto Falcon."

"Is that person in the courtroom?"

"Yes, he's sitting at the defense table. He's dressed in brown pants a white shirt. He has long black hair and a full beard."

"Let the record reflect that Detective Ruiz has identified the defendant."

"The record will so reflect."

"What else did the investigation reveal?"

"It was determined that Michael Chacon was killed by one shot to the back of the head. The murder weapon was a .38 caliber Smith and Wesson found at the scene. The gun was registered to Mr. Alfred Curran and the only fingerprints on the gun were those of Mr. Curran."

"What else did you find in the house?"

"We found quantities of cocaine."

"How was it packaged?"

"In one kilo packages with protective wrapping. Two kilos in all."

"Did you do anything to find Mr. Falcon?"

"Yes. We put out an all points bulletin for him and the car."

"What did that result in?"

"The car was found abandoned just across the New Mexico state line."

"Was Mr. Falcon found?"

"No, he disappeared. The car was searched and traces of cocaine were found in the trunk along with a wrapper that was the same as the wrappers on the cocaine at the Chacon house."

"Were the fingerprints of Mr. Falcon found at the house where the body was found?"

"Yes."

"Nothing further your honor," Marquez said as he sat down.

"Mr. Courage you may examine," Judge Celeste said.

"Thank you your honor," Alexander said as he approached the podium. "Detective Ruiz I would like to clarify a few points. You say the weapon used to kill Mr. Chacon was registered to Alfred Curran and that his fingerprints were on it?"

"Yes."

"Were any other prints found on it?"

"No."

"Were you able to determine the approximate time of death?"

"Yes. Based on rigor mortis and liver mortis tests the medical examiner guessed the death occurred one to two hours before the body was discovered. That would mean between 5 pm. and 6 pm."

"Where was Mr. Curran during this time?"

"Besides being at the Chacon house?"

"You didn't prove he was at the Chacon house did you? You found a gun there with his prints but you only assume he was there isn't that true?"

Marquez was on his feet. "I object your honor. This is improper. The question before the court is whether there is probable cause to bind the defendant Falcon over for trial. It has nothing to do Alfred Curran."

"Your honor," Alexander responded. "It has everything to do with Curran. One of the charges against Mr. Falcon is that of conspiracy to commit murder. In that case the issue of Mr. Curran's involvement becomes crucial."

"I'm going to overrule the objection for now," said Celeste. "However let me warn you Mr. Courage. Don't try to make this hearing into the trial. That will come later. Now move along."

Ruiz continued. "We were able to determine that Mr. Curran had left the hacienda at about 4:30. He arrived at the airport about 6:30 and left immediately for Mexico. We received notice from the Mexican authorities that he was later killed in a car accident in the state of Vera Cruz."

Alexander changed subject. "You indicated Chacon was killed with one shot to the back of the head."

"Yes. On first inspection it was believed there were two wounds but it turned out there was only one."

"Was the slug recovered from the body?"

"No"

"Was any slug recovered at the scene?"

"The coroner found a slug partially buried in the baseboard of the wall in front of the body."

"And you're sure the slug that killed him came from Curran's gun?"

"The ballistics tests matched the slug with the gun found at the scene."

Alexander was pleased with this turn of events. It didn't help the case of Alfred as much as it did Falcon. But now they were committed and they would have to prove that the slug found by Rench was different than the one Rench said he found. Once he had Rench's testimony he would be able to come forward and identify himself.

"I have no more questions."

"The people rest," said Marquez.

"Any witnesses Mr. Courage?" Celeste asked.

"No your honor."

"The court finds there are reasonable grounds to believe that a crime was committed and that the defendant Alberto Falcon is the responsible person. The matter will be set for trial. How long do you expect it to take?"

"The people's case will require no more than a week," Marquez replied.

"I believe about three days," said Alexander

"I'll give you two weeks altogether. Any suggestions as to a date?"

"We suggest September 22."

"Mr. Courage?"

"That's fine, your honor."

"Twenty days to file motions," said Celeste. As he started to raise his gavel Alexander spoke.

"Your honor, I have two motions to file at this time."

"Very well. Bring them here."

Alexander took the motions to Celeste and gave a copy to Marquez. By the time he got back to counsel table the explosion came.

"Counsel, how dare you file a motion demanding my recusal and for a change of venue. I can be absolutely impartial in this case and there's no doubt the defendant can get a fair trial in this district. If you expect me to just walk away from this case you have another think coming."

Alexander felt his own anger rising. "Your honor, the only thing I expect from the court is that it follows the law. I suggest you read the affidavits attached to the motion and the brief that accompanies it before you make a final decision."

Celeste had regained control by now. "We'll have a hearing on these motions, and any others you file, on August 12th at 9 am. Court's in recess."

CHAPTER 46

The preliminary hearing confirmed two important things for Alexander. His initial impression that Marquez didn't have a very strong case, and that Marquez was somewhat indifferent to the prosecution of Falcon was proving correct. The important target had been Alfred Curran and as far as Marquez was concerned he was dead and buried in Mexico. If Falcon was acquitted that wouldn't change. Apparently, the prosecution would put on its case but wouldn't go to any heroic efforts to get a conviction.

The important factor in the case against Curran was the admission by Ruiz that there had been only one shot fired into Chacon and the slug matched Curran's gun. Rench's testimony would contradict this.

This alone wouldn't be enough to get Curran acquitted but it was the key to him revealing himself. He felt he was halfway home and couldn't wait for the trial to get started.

His defense of Falcon would be simple and direct. Falcon had been at the workers meeting at the time of the shooting. He had four eyewitnesses to that fact. The testimony of deputy Johnson that he saw the car and assumed Falcon was driving it was suspect. Johnson was in a hurry, he was driving into the sun late in the afternoon, and it was doubtful he could have a clear view of the driver.

There was no other evidence except the fact that Falcon and Chacon shared the same house and drugs were found there. Alexander was sure the drugs had been planted in the car and the house to support the theory of Alfred's involvement in drugs. So far as the defense of Falcon was concerned they could concede that Chacon and Alfred might have been involved in drugs but that didn't prove Falcon was.

Alexander had several things going for him. The case against Falcon was a weak, circumstantial case. Falcon had an alibi that had become almost airtight. And the fact that Marquez having become the owner of the Sangre could afford to be lackadaisical in the prosecution of a four-year-old case.

Using the case to build a defense for himself at the same time fulfilling his obligation to Falcon could prove difficult. Judge Celeste wasn't going to permit Alexander to use Falcon to try the Curran case. He had to justify any evidence at all by arguing that it was relevant to Falcon's defense. The conspiracy charge gave him some latitude for bringing Curran into the trial, but he was sure Celeste would keep him on a tight reign.

In the days leading to the hearing on motions Celia thoroughly researched the law on the disqualification of the judge and for a change of venue. The conclusion was that they would be able to force Celeste off the case. Having a judge brought in from another district would help immensely.

They were less sure about getting the trial moved to another district, but they weren't disappointed with this result. Having a trial moved to a different location was always an iffy proposition because the defendant couldn't choose the new location for the trial. The change was often to a less favorable jurisdiction.

The day of the hearing on the motions was the kind of summer day in the valley that dawned hot and got hotter as it progressed. Crops were in full stride and a sense of abundance and success was in the air. Alexander and Celia walked to the courthouse with the confidence of knowledge and a naiveté about reality. The law was clear that Celeste had to recuse himself, and Celia had written a brilliant brief to prove it.

This was the first motion that was taken up by Celeste when court convened.

"Miss Chavez," he said addressing Celia. "Since you signed

the motion and the brief I suppose you'll argue it." Celia got up
and stood before him at the podium. He continued. "I've read
the brief and the affidavits submitted in support of the motion.
Do you have anything else you wish to present?"

"No your honor." Celia replied.

"Do you have any argument?"

"Yes. There are two fundamental grounds on why we have
asked the court to disqualify itself. The first is the economic
dependence and relationship between the court and the district
attorney. The house you live in is owned by the Sangre de Cristo
corporation and Mr. Marquez is president if that corporation. In
addition the same corporation owns your parents' house. Our
position is that such a relationship and dependency make it
impossible for you to make impartial decisions in this case with
Mr. Marquez as DA.

"Secondly, we have submitted three affidavits from residents
of the district that attest to the fact that shortly after the murder
of Mr. Chacon you expressed opinions about the guilt of Mr.
Falcon and Mr. Curran. These statements are evidence of the fact
you have already made up your mind about the guilt of the
defendant and therefore are incapable of being impartial. We rely
on the cases set forth in the brief and I won't repeat them. Thank
you."

Marquez started to stand up to reply to the argument but
was cut off by Judge Celeste. "Mr. Marquez I don't need to hear
argument from you. I'm prepared to rule. First, let me address
the economic relationship. It's true that the Sangre de Cristo
Corporation owns my home and that of my parents. What counsel
fails to point out is that this is true of 80% of the homes in the
valley. It's an historical fact. Therefore, since a vast majority of
the residents in the district have the same situation as I do I can't
see how it makes me incapable of hearing the case. Besides in the
16 years I've served as judge in this district no other attorney has
ever suggested a conflict. I might point out that unlike present
counsel most of the others have long experience in criminal
matters.

"With respect to the affidavits of bias. All of these relate to a time shortly after the incident. In other words almost four years ago. I've talked to each of the people that signed the affidavits in order to be sure my recollection is correct. They all confirm the fact that anything I said was said in the heat of the moment based on my outrage that my old friend Alfred Curran could even remotely be involved in such an incident. These were not utterances of prejudging the case but rather grew from the deep grief I felt."

Alexander sat in stunned disbelief. Celeste was literally standing the law on its head to meet his own needs. As for his long friendship with Alfred, Alexander had personal knowledge that the judge had never exchanged a word with him in his life.

"Therefore I'm denying the motion for disqualification," he concluded.

Celia was on her feet. "I object," she started. Celeste interrupted.

"Sit down Miss Chavez," he nearly shouted. "You had your say and I've ruled. If you don't like it you can appeal it at the end of the case."

Alexander stood up. "Does that mean the court has already determined that a conviction is to occur."

Now Celeste did blow up. "I just reminded your co-counsel of the law relating to appeals now I'll remind you of the law relating to contempt of court. One more remark like that and you'll find yourself in jail!" He paused for a moment and looked at some papers before him then he continued. "The motion for change of venue is denied. The motion to suppress evidence seized from the abandoned car is denied. That takes care of the motions. The trial will begin as scheduled on September 22. Court is in recess."

CHAPTER 47

September 22, the first day of the trial, was a beautiful autumn day in the Sangre de Cristo. The sky was like pure, clear blue ice. The colors of the landscape had been poured directly from the tube as if van Gogh had managed their selection. The cottonwood trees along the dry creek-beds were changing their opulent green leaves into electrifying yellows and oranges. Antelope, with their short horns and caramel coloring, grazed leisurely in the mowed fields. Cuneiforms of geese practiced their language against the mountains where new snow appeared in the highest places.

Alexander had been awake since dawn making last minute preparations for the opening of the trial. His anticipation had grown each day since the motions hearing, and he was as nervous as he'd ever been in his life. His doubts about what he was doing redoubled each day. He had no right to represent Falcon. He was a lawyer who had never tried a felony case, and here he was trying a murder case. His conscience kept telling him it was wrong to use Falcon's case to redeem Alfred Curran. If he failed it meant life in prison for Falcon. If he revealed himself and failed to prove his innocence it meant life in prison for him. But he knew he had come too far to change what he was doing. He could only pray it would turn out right.

By 10 a.m. on trial day the courtroom was full of people who had been summoned as potential jurors. Augustine's efforts to get poor workers on the roll of jurors had been successful.

Almost half of the jury panel was Hispanics who made their living in the fields. Alexander looked at them and tried to make as much eye contact as possible. No matter how the case turned out the jury system would have been changed for the best.

The jury selection took most of the first day and the final result pleased Celia and Alexander. More than half the jurors were working men and women who wouldn't be under the control of Marquez. Once the jury was selected and the spectator seats were no longer needed for prospective jurors they were quickly filled with curious onlookers. Alexander noticed that Patricia was in the first row behind Richard. Her beauty still took his breath away but he couldn't help but notice a harder edge to her than he remembered. He also found it curious that she wore dark glasses the entire time. He didn't have long to dwell on it however. As soon as the jury was sworn Celeste called for opening arguments.

Marquez made a brief almost causal one and Alexander reserved his for the beginning of the defense case. Richard's first witness was Deputy Johnson the officer who had discovered the body.

After some preliminary questions Richard asked him, "Where were you when you received the call from dispatch directing you to respond to the Chacon house?"

"I was patrolling county road 220 about three miles east of the house."

"What time did you receive the call?"

"6:57 pm."

"What did you do?"

"Turned on the emergency equipment and started towards the location."

"Did you pass any vehicles on the way?"

"Yes. Just after I turned on the emergency equipment I passed a white Chevrolet traveling in the opposite direction?"

"Did you recognize the car?"

"Yes. I'd seen the car on other occasions?"

"Did you see who was driving the car?"

"It was the defendant Alberto Falcon."

"How do you know it was the defendant?"

"I recognized him. I knew him."

"Did you have an opportunity to see the license plate?"

"Yes, it was Colorado MM 667."

"What happened when you arrived at the Chacon house?"

"I knocked on the door and got no answer. The door was unlocked. I used a handkerchief and two fingers to turn the knob and opened it. I could see Mr. Chacon seated at a chair with his back to the door. He was slumped forward. I called his name and got no response. I walked to the body, determined there was no pulse, and returned to my vehicle. I called dispatch and was told to secure the premises outside and wait for additional officers."

"Directing your attention to the vehicle you passed on the way to the Chacon house. Did you see the vehicle you've described after that night?"

"Yes sir. Two days later I traveled with Detective Ruiz to the New Mexico state line to inspect a car that had been abandoned. It was the same car I had seen fleeing from the scene."

"How did you determine it was the same car?"

"It was a white Chevrolet with the same license number."

"Did you assist in a search of the vehicle?"

"Yes. We found several personal items. In the trunk we found residue of a white substance and several pieces of wrapping paper that appeared to be waterproof. Everything was placed in evidence bags and marked."

"Thank you deputy. Your witness."

Alexander began his cross-examination. "When did you begin work on the date in question?"

"Twelve noon."

"Would the shift end at 8 pm?"

"Normally, but I worked the crime scene that evening so I didn't get off until later."

"You received the call from dispatch at 6:57 p.m. so you had been working about seven hours."

"Yes."

"What had you done for the first seven hours?"

"Patrol work. I'm assigned a sector of the county and I drive the roads and respond to calls for assistance. I also enforce traffic laws."

"So for the most part you drive your vehicle for eight hours on any given shift?"

"Driving is most of it."

"What percentage of the roads are paved?"

"Objection," said Marquez. "This is irrelevant."

"I expect to show its relevance," Alexander responded.

"All right," said Celeste. "I'll give you some latitude considering your inexperience in this court." That was the second time Celeste had made reference to his inexperience. "Objection overruled. But counsel I'll not let you waste this jury's time on trivia. They all have other things to do. You may answer the question deputy."

"Maybe ten percent."

"When you passed the white Chevrolet you were driving west?"

"Yes."

"It was approximately 7 pm. The sun was shining in your face?"

"I wouldn't say it was shining in my face."

"You could see it?"

"Yes, I could see it.

"The windshield was dusty from the seven hours of driving on unpaved roads."

"No more than usual."

"What kind of vehicle were you driving?"

"A sheriff's patrol wagon. A Chevy Blazer."

"Sits up higher than a Chevy sedan?"

"Yes."

"One more question. Did you see Alfred Curran that night?"

"No."

"No further questions," Alexander said as he took his seat. He'd made several important points with the deputy.

Johnson's windshield was dusty; the sun was shining in his face; and his high position made it difficult to see positively who was driving the car. Now it was five o'clock and the court recessed for the day.

The next day the prosecution called several technicians. These witnesses identified evidence collected from the house and car. One was a fiber and paper expert who testified that the wrapping of the cocaine packages found in the house was identical to what was found in the car. Alexander was able to make several points with each one concerning the fact that except on the gun there were none of Curran's prints anywhere at the scene. With respect to Falcon he was able to establish that while they found his prints all over the house they did not find any on the cocaine packages that were discovered in the house and in the car. After these foundation witnesses Marquez called the medical examiner to the stand.

"Please state your name and occupation."

"Dr. Richard St. John. I'm chief pathologist at Holy Names Hospital in Pueblo."

"On September 12, 1966 did you perform an autopsy on one Michael Chacon?"

St. John opened a folder in front of himself. "May I refer to my notes? It's been some time."

"Yes, please do."

"Mr. Chacon's remains were delivered to the hospital on that day and I performed an autopsy."

"Were you able to determine the cause of death?"

"Yes. Mr. Chacon had a gunshot wound that was the cause of death. The entry wound of the bullet was in the back of the neck just at the point where the spinal column meets the skull. The exit wound was at the front of the face. Mr. Chacon would have died immediately. There was only one wound. The bullet's entry point was surrounded by gunpowder residue. The weapon used was a large caliber. I would say .38 or larger."

"No further questions."

"No questions," Alexander said.

The doctor stepped down and Marquez called Detective Ruiz to the stand. Ruiz was sworn and taken through the same testimony he'd given at the preliminary hearing.

When Marquez finished he turned the witness over to Alexander for cross-examination.

"Detective Ruiz," Alexander began. "You have no witnesses to the fact that Mr. Falcon or Mr. Curran were actually in the Chacon house at the time he was murdered do you?"

"Yes we do."

Alexander was surprised. "Who?" he said leaving himself open.

"The people who murdered him. Mr. Falcon and Mr. Curran." This brought a smile to the lips of the jurors and the judge. It was a rookie mistake on the part of Alexander.

He recovered quickly. "I understand. But besides them are there any other witnesses?"

"I would say so."

"Who?"

"The fact that both ran away is a witness. The fact that Curran's gun was used is a witness."

Alexander became angry. "Your honor," he said. "The witness is being deliberately unresponsive and in so doing is attempting to prejudice the jury with his own opinions. I ask that he be directed to answer the question."

Judge Celeste was even more clever than Ruiz at hurting the defendant's case. "Mr. Courage the fact is your questions were not very clear. I think the detective understood you to mean was there any evidence that Mr. Falcon and Mr. Curran committed the murder. In so doing he was merely pointing out the fact they both fled the scene and the use of Curran's gun was evidence of the crime. Of course as you know I'll instruct the jury that they may consider flight of the accused as being evidence of guilt. And the use of Curran's gun in the murder seems undisputed at the moment. But I don't mind pointing out to the witness that you were referring to other living human beings as witnesses and ask him to confine his answer to that. Detective Ruiz," he said directing his attention to the witness, "do you know of anyone besides Mr. Curran and Mr. Falcon that witnessed the crime?"

"No your honor and in my experience as a police officer I've found that most murderers prefer to kill their victim in private." This caused the jury and the judge to laugh. Then Celeste said. "There Mr. Courage, you have your answer."

Alexander swallowed his humiliation and went on. "Detective Ruiz, in all your testimony there seems to be missing one piece of evidence. That is the slug that killed Mr. Chacon. Was one recovered?"

"Yes. The coroner who was called to prepare a certificate of death found the spent slug."

"What did he do with it?"

"He turned it over to us."

"Where is it?"

"I don't know."

"You don't know where it is?"

"No sir, it was lost. We have no idea how. There was a lot of evidence collected and somehow it was misplaced. I did look at it at the scene and based on my experience was able to tell it was a 38 caliber slug."

"Then there are no tests that say it came from the gun belonging to Mr. Curran?"

Marquez objected. "You honor it isn't Mr. Curran that is being tried here, it's Mr. Falcon. The facts before the jury are that the Curran gun was found at the scene and the bullet that was found was of the same caliber. So far as Mr. Falcon is concerned he's charged as co-conspirator in the murder and whether he participated is for the jury to determine. Unfortunately, the slug has disappeared and there may be an issue of whether it came from Curran's gun or another gun fired by Mr. Falcon but that is also for the jury to decide."

"Objection sustained."

Alexander had not made any progress with the witness and had hurt his case. It was time to get out except to try and cast some doubt on the information that came from Mexico regarding Alfred's death.

"You testified that you received information from Mexico about the death of Curran. What was that information?"

This time the judge intervened before Ruiz could answer. "This isn't a trial about the guilt of Mr. Curran. This court granted a petition filed by Mrs. Marquez to declare Mr. Curran dead. That ruling hasn't been challenged and I don't intend to re-litigate it here. It was a very painful experience for Mrs. Marquez and I won't allow you to put her through that again. Now I'll tell you for the last time. This is a trial to determine the guilt or innocence of Mr. Falcon not of Alfred Curran. I don't want to hear any more questions about Mr. Curran. Do you understand me?"

"Yes, your honor," Alexander responded. "I've no further questions of this witness."

"The people rest your honor."

"Mr. Courage you may begin your case tomorrow at 9 am. The court will be in recess until then."

CHAPTER 48

Alexander and Celia left the courthouse and walked the short distance to her house to review the trial so far and decide on the presentation of their case. The two of them were alone at the table and both felt good about the way the case stood. The problem was that each felt that way for different reasons. Celia saw the situation strictly in terms of getting Falcon acquitted; Alexander saw it in terms of giving him the chance to reveal his true identity. This difference would prove to be the basis for their first serious disagreement.

"You were right, Alexander," Celia said as she placed two cups of tea on the table. "Marquez isn't very interested in this case. He has gone through the motions, but I think we can win an acquittal the way things stand."

"I agree," Alexander replied. "He set this whole thing up to get rid of Curran. If Falcon is convicted well and good but his conviction isn't worth much expense or effort."

"What about our case?" Celia asked. "Have you decided on the order of the witnesses?"

"Since Reynaldo Herrera and Curtis Velarde are not permanent residents of the valley and have poor English language skills I think we should call them first. Then we'll put Ignacio Baca on the stand. His position at the car dealership will give him good credibility. After Baca we'll call Luis Padilla, he's definitely our best alibi witness. We'll finish up with Rench and Falcon. That should do it." Alexander mentioned these last two very quickly hoping Celia would agree and there would be no discussion. He was wrong.

"Rench?" she asked. "Why call Rench?"

Alexander had dreaded this moment. Rench had little bearing on Falcon's case and his testimony would only muddy the waters. He was sure that with the alibi witnesses they could get an acquittal for Falcon. But without Rench's testimony he couldn't reveal his own identity. He needed one piece of physical evidence that would support his story, and Rench was the one that could provide that evidence. Alexander was determined to put him on the stand.

Celia repeated her question. "Why do we need to call Rench? We have four solid witnesses who will testify that Alberto Falcon was with them at a meeting when Michael Chacon was murdered. And we have Alberto's testimony. That's enough to get him acquitted. Rench's testimony won't change that."

Alexander longed to tell her why the testimony was so important. But to do so meant disclosing who he was and he couldn't do that. He regarded her for a moment and decided he had to deceive her no matter how painful it was. "All right," he said, "we won't call Rench."

The rest of the evening was spent reviewing the expected testimony of the alibi witnesses and discussing the opening statement. After a supper at Casa Melina Alexander walked with Celia back to her house and then strolled around the town, his town, and watched as lights in the homes being turned off as the tired occupants put their daily struggles behind them and sought refuge in sleep. As the town grew darker the sky became brighter. The Pleiades hung like confetti just dropped from a hand, and Orion the hunter led his dog on a never ending chase of the sun. Alexander drew strength from the stars knowing that two thousand years ago great men like Aristotle reflected on exactly the same sky. It was like a connecting cord that bound him to the past.

At the trial the next day Alexander made a brief opening statement giving the jury a summary of what the testimony he was about to present would prove. He didn't name the witnesses thus concealing from Celia the fact that he would call Rench in spite of his promise.

The first two witnesses were the two field workers who each testified in broken English that they had attended the meeting on the night of the murder and that Falcon was there. Marquez conducted a brief and not enthusiastic cross-examination. He was able to establish that with their poor language skills their testimony wasn't as forceful as it might otherwise have been.

After them Alexander called Ignacio Baca. He testified that he also was at the meeting described by the other witnesses and that Falcon was there. He made a much better impression with the jury and Marquez made no headway in impeaching him.

The last alibi witness was Luis Padilla. Alexander conducted the questioning.

"Please state your name and occupation."

"My name is Luis Padilla. I'm the manager of Martinez Mercantile in El Centro."

"How long have you been so employed?"

"I've worked there for three years. I've been manager for the past year."

"Do you know the defendant Alberto Falcon?"

"Yes I do."

"Will you point him out?"

"He's the gentleman with the full beard seated next to Miss Chavez at the counsel table."

"How do you know him?"

"In 1966 I was employed with my father and three brothers as field workers near La Garita. I met him then. He and Michael Chacon were trying to organize the workers into a union."

"Were you aware of Mr. Falcon or Mr. Chacon dealing any drugs?"

"No. Absolutely not."

"Did you become aware of the fact that Michael Chacon had been murdered?"

"Yes. The evening he was murdered I was attending a meeting of the workers at Alamosa. There were about twenty of us there."

"Do you know Reynaldo Herrera, Curtis Velarde, and Ignacio Baca?"

"Only casually."

"Do you remember whether they were at the same meeting?"

"Yes, they were."

"Do you remember if Mr. Falcon was there?"

"Absolutely. He was conducting the meeting."

"What time did the meeting begin?"

"I arrived about five pm."

"Was Mr. Falcon there when you arrived?"

"Yes."

"What time did the meeting break up?"

"Between 7:30 and 8. I'm not sure of the exact time."

"Did something in particular cause the meeting to break up?"

"Yes. While we were having a discussion someone came into the room and said he'd heard that Michael Chacon had been killed."

"What was the reaction of the people at the meeting?"

"Disbelief that Michael could be dead. Also concern that it might have something to do with the fact that he was trying to organize the workers. I wondered if Mr. Falcon or any of us might be in danger."

"What happened then?"

"We all agreed that we should disappear for a while until we knew more about the situation. I heard one person offer to drive Mr. Falcon to New Mexico and then I left."

"So far as you know is there any way that the defendant could have been at La Garita between 4:30 and 7:30 the evening of September 11, 1966."

"No. He was in Alamosa at that time with twenty other people."

"Thank you. No further questions."

Marquez didn't bother to cross-examine Padilla and one could sense that the momentum of the case was definitely on the side of Falcon. Padilla was dismissed and the judge said. "Call your next witness."

Without consulting Celia Alexander took the plunge that he hoped would lead to his salvation.

"The defense calls Harvey Rench." Alexander heard a chair behind him scrape on the floor and then Celia addressing the court.

"Your honor," she said. "May we have a short recess? Something has come up that I must discuss with Mr. Courage."

Celeste looked at the clock on the wall. "This is probably as good a time as any for a break. The court will reconvene in fifteen minutes."

Celia took Alexander by the arm and led him into the room reserved for use by defense counsel. As soon as the door was closed behind them she began.

"I thought we agreed that we wouldn't call Rench!" Her eyes were flashing.

"I changed my mind," Alexander replied weakly.

Celia couldn't hide the shock in her voice. "But why? How will his testimony help Alberto? In fact it may hurt by raising the issue of a second gun being involved."

"I'm going to do it because it shows the DA has done sloppy work and it makes the case against Alberto even weaker."

Celia stared at him for a moment. "This is a mistake Alexander. Over the time I've known you I've come to," she almost said love but caught herself and said, "respect you. And I think you have done a masterful job in defending Alberto. But you're making a terrible mistake now. Please don't do it."

"I'm sorry Celia, but I think it's necessary." The look he received was anything but love.

Alexander was helpless to do anything but leave her and return to the courtroom. He saw Rench at end of the hall and was mildly surprised to see that he was talking to Detective Ruiz. Alexander went to the podium and busied himself reviewing his notes. He didn't want to face Celia again and it hurt him to know he'd deceived her. He could only hope that the bombshell he was about to explode would take her mind off the deceit. With the punctuality of the methodical Celeste reconvened the court exactly fifteen minutes after he'd declared the recess. Alexander once more said, "Call Harvey Rench."

Rench looked nervous and was visibly shaking as he took the witness chair. Obviously the lack of alcohol since Geraldo had picked him up the day before was taking its toll on his nervous system. Alexander could hardly contain his excitement. After all the years of suffering he was on the verge of giving up his charade and reclaiming his wife and his land.

"Please state your name."

"Harvey Rench."

"Where do you reside?"

"Trinidad, Colorado."

"I direct your attention to September 11, 1966. Where did you reside at that time?"

"El Monte, Colorado."

"How were you employed?"

"I owned a pharmacy."

"Did you hold any elected office?"

"Yes."

"What was that?"

"Coroner for Costilla County."

"I hand you People's exhibit 23 and ask you if you can identify it?"

"It's a certificate of death for one Michael Chacon and signed by me."

"Did you have occasion to go to the location where Mr. Chacon was found dead?"

"Yes. I arrived there about 8 pm."

"What did you do when you got there?"

"After I determined the identity of Mr. Chacon and that he was dead I filled out the certificate of death."

"Did you do anything else?"

"I examined the immediate area surrounding the chair where Mr. Chacon was sitting."

"Why?"

"I had observed an entry wound and an exit wound from the gunshot. I assumed there should be a spent bullet somewhere. I was looking for it "

"Did you find it?"

"I found a spent copper nosed thirty eight caliber bullet at the base of the wall."

"Mr. Rench let me back up for a minute. Do you have another occupation other than pharmacist?"

"I study ballistics but I guess technically it's a hobby."

"Tell the jury briefly what ballistics is."

"It's the science of matching bullets to the weapon from which they've been fired."

"How is that done?"

"Almost every gun has what is called rifling. This is a spiral groove cut into the inside of the barrel. When the gun is fired the bullet is propelled down the barrel and is given a spin that in turn gives it stability as it moves through the air. Much like a football thrown with a spiral. If the ball is thrown without a spiral it tumbles and doesn't fly straight; same thing with a bullet. This rifling is also called lands and grooves. The result is that the bullet receives marks from this spiraling and each gun produces a different set of marks. Because of this we can tell whether a bullet was fired by a particular gun.

"How is that done?"

"We take the bullet that is suspect. Then we fire another bullet from the gun in question. Then we put the two bullets under a magnifying glass and compare the markings. If they are the same we can conclude they came from the same gun."

"Is there anything about these markings that can be identified with the naked eye?"

"If the bullet is well preserved you can."

"What is it you can determine in that case?"

"As I testified earlier the spiral groove that is cut into the barrel is called rifling. It can be cut either in a clockwise or counter clockwise direction. We say a left hand twist or a right hand twist. It's easy to determine whether the spiral is right or left handed without a magnifying glass."

"Does each gun vary in the direction of this twist?"

"No. Each model will have the same twist direction. But it may vary from brand to brand and model to model."

"I hand you what has been marked as People's exhibit 32 and ask you if you can identify it?"

"Yes. It's a 38 caliber Smith and Wesson. The tag on it says it was the gun recovered at the Chacon house."

"Have you ever been qualified as an expert in the field of ballistics in a court of law?"

Judge Celeste interrupted. "Mr. Courage I'll accept Mr. Rench as an expert in the field of ballistics. He's testified in that capacity many times in this court."

"Thank you your honor. Mr. Rench do you know what spiraling the Smith and Wesson you have just identified has?"

"Yes. It has a clockwise or left to right spiral. We say a right hand twist."

"Now I direct your attention to the bullet you found in the Chacon house and ask you what spiraling it had."

Rench hesitated for a minute. He looked down at his hands then briefly at Richard Marquez. Fear was etched in his face. "It had exactly the same rifling marks. It had a right hand twist."

Alexander stood in stunned disbelief. He felt his stomach drop and thought for a moment he might be physically ill. He could only respond weakly. "Did you say the same marks?"

"Yes. The same marks. As far as I could tell the bullet I found came from the weapon that has been admitted into evidence."

"Mr. Rench. Didn't you tell me at a meeting we had in Trinidad last month that the slug you found couldn't have come from the Smith and Wesson because it's rifling was different."

"No sir! I told you the same thing I've said here today."

"You do remember the meeting?"

"Absolutely. You gave me $100 dollars to come and testify and promised me another $100 when the case was over." Alexander stood at the podium unable to speak. Finally Celeste asked him if he had any further questions.

"No your honor."

"Any cross-examination?"

Richard Marquez said "no" in a voice that barely contained his glee

"Very well," said Celeste. "It's close to the time for recess. This may be a good place to stop. We'll resume Monday at nine am. Court is in recess."

Alexander stood at the podium staring at the papers in front of him unable to say or do anything. Celia gathered her papers and put them in her briefcase.

"I'm afraid," she said as she passed him on the way out, "you have just snatched defeat from the jaws of victory."

CHAPTER 49

Alexander sat in a large overstuffed armchair looking out the window at El Centro and beyond it to the fields. The liquid evening light was shining on the highest peaks of the Sangre. As the sun grew ever lower the shadow on the mountains was like a theater curtain that began at the stage and closed upwards. Soon the sky gave up its daily contest with darkness and Capella rose above Crestone Peak.

His thoughts wandered in a desultory way from the beauty of the scene to his own sense of self-loathing. He'd botched everything in his stumbling attempt to play lawyer. He'd placed everything on the belief that Rench would tell the jury the truth. How could he be so stupid? He should have known better than to see a witness without someone there to verify the conversation. Any experienced lawyer would have known better. Now the only possibility he had to impeach Rench was to take the stand himself and that was out of the question.

Not only had he ruined his chances to reveal his identity he'd also seriously jeopardized Falcon's case. Before he put Rench on the stand Falcon had an airtight alibi and the jury was with him. He still had an alibi but surely the jury was offended by evidence that Curran had committed the murder and that Falcon's lawyer had bribed a witness.

It would take everything he could do to put his own disaster aside and concentrate on salvaging Falcon's case. One thing was certain. He couldn't divulge his true identity now and his best chance of ever doing it had slipped by on the thin ice he'd created through his own inexperience.

He poured himself another martini from the pitcher beside the chair. What would Don Francisco say? He would tell him not to dwell on the past. It didn't require a genius to recognize the terrible mistake he'd made in failing to interview Rench with a witness present. And it didn't take a genius to figure out that Marquez must have found out about Rench's testimony and done whatever was necessary to make Rench change his story. Alexander forced himself to put the past aside. He needed all his energy to find a way to save Falcon. Saving himself would have to wait for another day. He thought about the existential philosophy Don Francisco had explained to him. "No excuses," he'd said. "Everyone finds themselves in certain circumstances whether their own fault or not. Whatever those circumstances are must be dealt with and recrimination over how they occurred serves no purpose."

"All very easily said," Alexander thought, "but not so easily done." He tried desperately to take him mind of his own stupidity but kept coming back to the 'what ifs?'. No matter how he cut it and diced it and changed its shape it always came back to the fact that his desire to prove that Alfred Curran hadn't killed Chacon had seriously jeopardized the chance of an acquittal for Falcon. Finally, the anesthetic effect of the martinis and his tiredness helped him sleep and he welcomed it with closed eyes.

His dreams were the kind of troubled dreams he called frustration dreams. He kept finding himself in situations that required doing a simple task and at each try there arose an obstacle. He had no idea how long he had been asleep when he heard sharp knocking on the door. He first thought it was part of the dream. Another obstacle to frustrate him. As he managed to get closer to consciousness he realized it really was someone at the door.

Finally he answered. "Who is it?"

"Isabella Romero," it was the voice of Augustine's mother.

"I want to be alone señora," he replied. She answered him in Spanish.

"*Por favor. Abre la puerta. Estoy solo.*"

"*Señora, no quierro visitantes,*" he replied. She didn't respond for many moments. When she did her voice was very low.

"*Alfredo, soy su mama.*" Alexander couldn't believe his ears. She called him Alfred and said she was his mother. Maybe it was a dream or hallucination after all. He ran to the door and opened it. The mother of his youth stood there alone. He reached for her hand and pulled her gently inside and closed the door. It all proved too much for him and he put his arms around her and cried as he'd never cried before.

Isabella held him until the sobs subsided then led him to the bed where she made him lie down. She got a wet, cold towel from the bathroom and folded it into a compress for his face.

When he could talk he said. "Mama, how did you know?"

"I'm your mother Alfredo, mothers know these things."

"Does Augustine know?"

"No. He suspects nothing."

"How long have you known?"

"The first time I saw you I knew in my heart it was you. I knew it in my head when I nursed you after the beating. There cannot be another birthmark in the whole world like the one on your leg."

"Why didn't you say anything?"

"Because I knew you would tell me when it was time. I knew you were here for a purpose, and part of that purpose was to remain unknown.

"But why have you come now?" he asked.

"Because you are in trouble and you need me. I heard Celia and Augustine talking. They can't believe what happened. They fear you may have lost the case for Alberto Falcon and can't comprehend why. They are very hurt. But I know why. I had to come."

He sat up and kissed her on the cheek. "I'm glad you did. Does anyone else know you are here?"

"No," she paused then asked. "What will you do now?"

"I don't know. It's so horrible to see Richard have the Sangre. It's even worse knowing Patricia is forced to live and sleep with my murderer. When I was at the hacienda for the party it was if I had never left. Everything was exactly as I had left it. Richard took me to the library to warn me about staying in the valley and it was the same as the last time father and I had a conversation there. Nothing had been changed."

"I wasn't aware of that," said Isabella. "After you were declared dead, and your father suffered his stroke, Richard was at the house more and more. It soon became clear that Eduardo and I weren't welcome. We left as soon as your father died and we never went back. Then it was only a year before Eduardo died and I've lived with Augustine ever since."

"It must have been horrible for everyone."

"Especially for you Alfredo. Tell me what happened while I fix you come coffee." Alfred recounted the entire story from the time that he and Patricia returned to the Sangre to the present moment. When he was finished she only said.

"So that is where the scars came from, and how you learned to endure the whip."

For a moment Alexander could vividly remember those horrible days at Los Altos and all he'd suffered to return to the Sangre. Finally he said, "Yes, but that's all past. Now I must think of someway to prove Richard murdered Chacon."

Isabella thought for a moment as if trying to recover some forgotten moment. "I don't know if this will help. When you told me that the library had not been disturbed since you were there last it made me think of something Eduardo told me."

"What?"

"He told me that at one time your father had installed a secret recording machine in his desk. He said it only worked when someone was speaking. I'm sure that neither your father nor Eduardo told anyone of this. Your father had a very secretive side."

"You mean because nothing has been disturbed they may not even know of it."

"Yes. And because it had many hours capacity perhaps Richard has said something that will incriminate him."

"We can't be sure there's any thing there but it's worth a try," he said. "How do you think I should get in?" he asked Isabella.

"Do you remember that there is a jeep road from the foothills that travels along the back wall of the hacienda?" He nodded. "I don't think it's ever used and it will let you get near the wall without being seen. From there you are looking directly at the library on the second floor. There are many old ladders leaning against the house as decoration. Your father always thought it made it look like Taos pueblo. They are old but one might serve to get you to the balcony of the library. After that I don't know. Possibly a door will be open. They have nothing to fear there. Anyway I'm sure there is a panel in the center of the desk that is unlocked when one of the drawers is opened. I don't know which one."

Alexander thought for moment. "It will be dangerous," he said. "And if I'm caught it will really blow everything sky high. Well, at least that would cause a mistrial for Alberto. Next time whoever defends him won't ruin it the way I have."

"Chico," said Isabella putting her hand on his face, "don't blame yourself. You did what you thought was right. You've come all this way. Don't stop now."

"You're right mama. You always have been." He went to the closet and changed the red shirt he was wearing for a black turtleneck. With the jeans he was already wearing he decided he would be as unnoticeable as possible.

"Mama, please don't say anything about this. If I'm caught I suppose the fingerprint check they do will show that I'm Alfred. When that happens I'll defend myself as best I can. At least it'll be very interesting." He put his arms around her and held her tightly. "You better go now." They stood that way for a moment then she pulled the scarf over her head walked to the door.

"*Vaya con dios, Alfredo*," she said and was gone.

CHAPTER 50

Alexander slipped on a wind breaker to protect him against the cold night air and headed his truck north towards the Hacienda. It was two in the morning and there was no traffic. The road Isabella had mentioned began as a dirt road about five miles north of the Hacienda. It headed east towards the mountains. Several miles after turning off the main highway Alexander found the trail Isabella had described. It was little more than two tracks through the desert sage and cactus.

There was enough moonlight to drive by and Alexander turned off the lights. The track meandered over and around some low, sandy hills until he reached the top of one hill and he could see the Hacienda spread out below him. There were no lights on inside the house. The lights along the paths gave the garden a warm glow. He drove just past the crest of the hill and let the truck coast close to the wall of the hacienda.

The hacienda was surrounded by an adobe wall ten feet high with two small gates spaced along the back wall. Between the wall and the house was about fifty feet of landscaped gardens. The library was centered on the second floor. It had a balcony and a set of sliding glass doors.

The truck was close enough to the wall that anyone looking down from the house wouldn't be able to see it. When he got the truck in place he took some nylon rope from the rear storage space and tied it to the post between the front and rear windows of the truck. He then tied some knots in it at two-foot intervals and threw it over the fence. He climbed onto the top of the truck swung himself to the top of the wall and dropped down into the garden.

Using the shrubs and trees to hide his movement he worked his way to the wall just beneath the balcony of the library. He would need something to help him up the wall. He moved along the side until he found one of the ladders that Isabella had mentioned. It was old and some of the leather straps that held the cross pieces were coming loose. He tested several rungs with his weight. They held precariously but he decided he would have to chance it. He put the ladder against the wall and began to climb. He was nearly at the top when one of the cross pieces broke under his weight and the sound of the dry wood splintering was like a gunshot. He hurried the rest of the way and climbed over the balcony wall.

He tried the sliding door and found it was open. He moved directly to the massive desk. This would be the tricky part. He had no idea how the secret panel might open. He moved the large chair away and knelt facing the desk. He felt along the panels on each side of the leg well but couldn't find any indication that they opened. He then began to open each of the drawers in turn. Each time he opened one he would try and slide either side of the leg well panels. Nothing worked. Perhaps it was a combination of drawers, and he began to try that. He opened the top left drawer and the bottom right. Nothing. The light changed on the balcony and he realized a light had gone on somewhere in the hacienda. Someone may have heard the ladder rung breaking. He had to control his panic. Finding the way to open the panel would be possible only if he could be systematic in trying each combination. The doors of the library were closed and the fact it was sound proof made it impossible to hear anything in the rest of the house. He tried to concentrate on the job as if there was no chance of discovery but the sweat that dripped from his brow showed his body and mind couldn't believe it.

When he opened the lower left drawer and the middle right drawer he felt the panel on the left side move. He quickly pushed it all the way open and shined his small flashlight inside. There was a large reel-to-reel tape machine. One of the reels was full the other was empty. He quickly pulled the full reel out, closed the panel, and put the reel inside the front of his jeans against his shirt. He closed the panel that had concealed the tape machine. Just as he finished closing the drawers the library door opened. He couldn't see who it was but the silhouette made him believe it was Richard. Quickly he calculated the distance between himself and the sliding door. The beam from a flashlight played around the room. He quickly made his decision and sprang for the balcony door that he'd left open. By now Richard had reached the edge of the desk and just as Alexander got onto the balcony Richard grabbed him from behind.

Alexander swung his elbow as hard as he could against Richard's ribs. It was like striking granite. Richard had his forearm around Alexander's neck and began to choke him. Alexander managed to get his two hands slightly in between Richard's forearm and his own windpipe but the air was slowly being cut off. He struggled towards the balcony wall and was within two feet of it when the balcony was flooded with light and he heard Patricia say "Richard! What's going on?" Alexander felt just the slightest relaxing of the pressure against his throat. He suddenly used the leverage of Richard's arm to allow him to put both legs against the wall of the balcony and kick backwards as hard as possible. Richard had been pulling him in that direction and the sudden burst by Alexander sent them both sprawling. The fall stunned Richard and he lost his grip on Alexander. Alexander didn't hesitate. He jumped over the balcony and prayed the fall wouldn't injure him.

Alexander landed on the gravel path and the momentum caused his face to collide with his knees. He tasted blood but seemed otherwise all right. He could hear voices on the balcony as he ran through the shrubs to the wall. He found the rope and quickly pulled himself over the wall. Once in the truck and speeding over the dirt road he thought of the irony of the situation. Patricia had saved him so that he could return and save her.

Driving away from the Hacienda through the sand and sage he was confident that neither Richard nor Patricia could identify him or the truck. What he couldn't be sure of was whether they would call the sheriff and report the break in. When he reached the paved road he had to decide whether to turn north or south. South meant crossing most of the Sangre before being able to go to the nearest town that might have the equipment he needed. By turning north he would spend less time on the Sangre and have a shorter distance to Cañon City where he was sure he would find an electronics store. At the intersection he turned north towards Poncha Pass and then drove through Salida and into the Arkansas River Canyon. The road followed the river through the canyon that had been carved over the centuries. It was a tortuous route and required careful driving and slow speeds. He got to Canyon City without seeing a police car and at a motel threw himself on the bed for a few hours sleep.

In the morning he went to an electronics store and bought a machine that would play the large reel tape he'd taken from the Hacienda. The tape had a capacity of over sixty hours and he had no idea what, if anything, he might find. It meant a long weekend. He assumed that if there was any chance of something useful being on the tape it would be near the end. He set up the machine and began to listen from the beginning. The first conversation was between Eduardo and Sam Curran.

Eduardo: Sam, when you had this room made soundproof they did a great job. Today when the man was here installing the equipment in the desk I couldn't hear his electric drill even when I stood just outside the closed doors.

Sam: I'd forgotten he was coming today. How does it work?

Eduardo: It's very simple. He showed me everything. It's what they call voice activated. In other words, it turns on automatically when it hears voices and stops when the voices stop.

Sam: Did you learn how to change the tape?

Eduardo: Yes, but that won't happen very soon. He said the tape would record sixty hours of conversations before a change is necessary. That will take a long time.

Sam: I can't see anything. He did a good job. Where are the
          microphones? Does anyone else know about the
          recorder?

Eduardo: No. Just the man who installed them and the two of
          us. But he's from Denver. Probably won't have another
          job in the valley the rest of his life. In fact he'd never
          been to the valley before this.

Alejandro turned off the machine. Hearing his father and
Eduardo banter brought back a flood of memories. He fought
back the tears and forced himself to go on. It was clear from the
tape that it began the night of the birthday party at the hacienda.
That was months before the murder of Chacon. Alexander's heart
dropped. It seemed likely that the tape would have run out before
then. On the other hand if it had run out while his father was
alive he and Eduardo would have changed it.

This conversation was followed by business conversations
involving his father and others. Often he heard his own voice and
that of Patricia's. He soon realized that at the rate he was going he
would never finish in time to get back to court Monday. In any
event he knew there would be nothing that might incriminate Richard
until shortly before or after the murder of Chacon.

Alexander changed his approach. He skipped forward and
listened. If he appeared in a conversation he knew it was too early
and he would skip forward again. As it got closer to the time of
his disappearance he began to listen for Richard's voice as well.
Nothing. The tape was getting closer to the end and his hope of
finding anything was rapidly fading. He stopped the tape again
and ran it fast forward for a moment then stopped it. This time
the conversation he heard was between him and his father
discussing his departure the following day for Mexico. He let the
machine run and the next voiced her heard was Patricia's. He
listened from there to the end of the tape with a mixture of
disbelief and macabre fascination. When it was over he stared at
the machine with a nearly uncontrollable rage that slowly and
strangely turned to relief. He played the tape again.

Richard, I thought you would never get here. [It was Patricia's voice] What took so long?

Richard: Why are you in the library?
Patricia: Close the doors. You know it's sound proof. We can do as we wish and no one will hear.
Richard: Did you bring the brief case?
Patricia: Yes it's there on the chair.

(There was a pause and the only sound was that of a door being closed then the sounds of clasps of a briefcase being opened.)

Patricia: God it seems like a week. I'm dripping with excitement. It was just like you said it would be.
Richard: No Patricia that's not true. It wasn't just as I said it would be. You failed me.
Patricia: But Richard we did it together. Isn't that even better?
Richard: I admit it had a certain charm. But more importantly you disobeyed me. You know what happens when you disobey me.
Patricia: But Richard we both shot him. You stood behind me and put your hand on mine. We pulled the trigger together. I know it excited you. I could feel your hardness against me.
Richard: But that's not the way it was supposed to happen. You were supposed to shoot him with Alfred's gun. It caused me problems to have to use mine. The coroner found the slug from my gun and now I'll have to get rid of it and make it seem to have disappeared.
Patricia: Richard it will never be an issue. By this time tomorrow Alfred will be dead. There will never be any questions.
Richard: The issue is that you disobeyed me. For that you must be punished. (There is the sound of a slap.)
Patricia: Yes, Richard. I must be punished. (For a time there is only the sound of clothes rustling and moans.)

Richard: This use of the library was a good idea. No one will hear
             your sounds of joy. I like your position very much. The
             desk is a perfect size. Look, your legs just touch the floor
             and your wonderful ass is at a perfect height. (There are
             several slaps that sounded like leather against flesh.)

Patricia: Oh, Richard. You have no idea how alive you make me
             feel when you hurt me. Richard, I'll do anything for you.
             You own me. I've never felt so much intense pleasure.
             Oh! Oh! Richard when that gun went off in our hands I
             had an orgasm. It was like nothing I've ever felt before.
             (Her cries became louder. Then the tape was filled with
             sexual sounds but no discernible words. Then silence. After
             a few minutes the voices resumed.)

Patricia: It hasn't been that good since the first time. Do you
             remember? It was just after the old man's birthday party.
             It was the first time in my life I felt alive sexually.

Richard: This plan of yours is brilliant. We get rid of Alfred. We
             get rid of Chacon and Falcon. Soon the Sangre will be
             yours and then it will be mine.

Patricia: I won't feel complete until we confirm that Alfred is
             dead and with any luck the old man will be gone soon
             as well. Richard will you treat me like I've been naughty
             again?

Richard: Not tonight. But tomorrow night, who knows?

It was Sunday morning when Alexander finished listening to
the tape. He called Denver information and got the phone number
of a witness he wanted to have in El Centro the following
morning. He was lucky enough to reach him and made
arrangements for him to be in El Centro for the resumption of
the trial. He found an electronics store in Canyon City that did
high speed copying of tapes. He put one copy of the tape in a
large envelope and left it with the manager of the motel with a
small payment to keep it until he called for it.

CHAPTER 51

Monday morning the mood of Falcon's supporters was anything but jubilant. Celia and Augustine were already in the courtroom when Alexander arrived. Augustine came up to him.

"Alexander! Where have you been? We've been worried about you. I have news. Geraldo says that Rench told him that he'd been paid to change his story."

"We're almost ready to begin," Alexander answered. "Tell everyone that I've found something that will set everything right. I'll explain it when we are through. Go now, here comes the bailiff."

Augustine barely had time to convey Alexander's message before the bailiff called the court to order and Judge Celeste entered.

"Mr. Courage," he began. "Before I bring the jury in can you give me an idea of how long you expect your case to take."

Alexander stood up. "Your honor," he said. "I have no more than three witnesses to call."

"Three? All right. I hope they'll prove more helpful to your case than the last one. Bring in the jury." Alexander felt his face flush at this pointed reference to the debacle of Harvey Rench's testimony. It was heightened by the smirk on Richard's face.

After the jury was seated Celeste directed Alexander to call his next witness. Alexander took a deep breath. This was it he thought. All hell will break lose now. He looked around and saw that Patricia was in her usual seat in the first row behind Richard's table.

"Call Patricia Marquez to the stand," he said. Richard caught by surprise was slow to react. Finally he was on his feet.

"I object your honor," he nearly shouted. "There is no evidence in this case suggesting that Mrs. Marquez has any knowledge of the matter before the court. This is merely for the purpose of harassment. Mr. Courage is rightfully indignant at the turn of events that took place Friday. That was the result of his own incompetence. He shouldn't be allowed to injure Mrs. Marquez."

Celeste wasn't happy with what was happening. "Mr. Courage," he said, "what is your reason for calling Mrs. Marquez to the stand?"

"You honor, I believe that Mrs. Marquez has information that will aid this jury in rendering a decision in this case. Her testimony is needed only to make an identification of an exhibit. It shouldn't take long."

"Very well," Celeste said grudgingly. "I'll permit you to call her with that limited purpose in mind." Richard looked at Patricia helplessly as she walked to the witness stand.

Alexander began. "Please state your name."

"Patricia Marquez."

"You're the wife of Richard Marquez the district attorney in this case?"

Patricia eyes hardened. "You know very well I am."

Judge Celeste interrupted. "Mrs. Marquez I know this is difficult but we must make a record so please just answer the questions."

"Yes, I'm the wife of Richard Marquez."

"When were you married?"

"April 3, 1967."

"Were you married before that?"

"Yes."

"To whom."

"To Alfred Curran. Several months after Mr. Curran was declared dead I married Mr. Marquez."

"Mrs. Marquez do you have any personal knowledge about the death of Michael Chacon?" Alexander was merely seeking a 'no' answer as a foundation for his use of the tapes. The answer he got was surprising.

"Yes," she answered. Alexander was in a quandary about what she might say but he'd gone too far to stop now.

"And what is that?"

"Before the murder Alfred had been acting very strangely. Since then I've come to realize it had to do with his use of cocaine although I didn't know so at the time." Alexander looked at her in disbelief. She was obviously willing to perjure herself to bury Alfred even deeper than she believed him to be already. He didn't try to interrupt.

"On several occasions he mentioned Mr. Chacon and Mr. Falcon in a way that suggested he had some business with them. The night of the murder I went into our bedroom and saw him putting his pistol into his pocket. When I asked him what he was doing with it he said he needed it for rats."

"Mrs. Marquez what I meant to ask you was whether you have any knowledge of the actual shooting."

"There is one other thing. Alfred's father had cut Alfred of from any money and Alfred was . . ."

Alexander interrupted. "Your honor the answer is unresponsive. I ask it be stricken from the record and the witness be directed to answer the question."

"Mr. Courage you seem to have an amazing facility to present testimony that is helpful to the prosecution's case. But just because you don't like the answer doesn't mean it isn't helpful to the jury. I thought your handling of Mr. Rench set a new standard but you seem bent on going even further. Continue, Mrs. Marquez."

Alexander could sense more than see the smile on Richard's face. He looked at Celia who was shaking her head in wonderment at what Alexander was doing to ruin Alberto Falcon's case. Alexander turned back to Patricia. What he was going to do to her was becoming easier and easier.

Patricia continued. "What I was saying was that Alfred was desperate for money at the time."

"Thank you, Mrs. Marquez." Alexander placed a large reel-to-reel tape player on the table. "Mrs. Marquez I'm going to play part of this tape and ask you to identify the voices if you can." He turned on the machine.

"Richard, I thought you would never get here. What took so song?"

Marquez was on his feet. "I object your honor. There has been no proper foundation for playing this tape."

Celeste upheld the objection. "Mr. Marquez is absolutely correct." He turned to the bailiff. "Take the jury out while we determine the admissibility of this tape." After the door was closed behind the last juror he turned to Alexander. "I want an offer of proof, Mr. Courage. I want to know where this tape came from and how it was obtained, then I'll consider listening to it. Proceed."

"Your honor, information was provided to me that Mr. Samuel Curran had installed a secret voice activated tape recorder in his library desk. The installation took place only months before the murder of Mr. Chacon and the disappearance of Alfred Curran. Early Saturday morning I entered the Curran hacienda and removed this tape from the desk. The tape has sixty hours of recorded conversation. The conversation I was about to play occurs towards the end of it. The conversation incriminates Mr. And Mrs. Marquez in the murder of Mr. Chacon and in the disappearance of Alfred Curran." The spectators sat in stunned silence. Celeste may have been stunned but he was by no means silent.

"Mr. Courage," his voice was at the boiling point, "are you telling me as an officer of the court that during a trial you burglarized the home of the district attorney and stole this tape?" Alexander started to respond. "Never mind," Celeste continued, "the record speaks for itself. I'm declaring a recess while I listen to this tape in chambers, then I'll make a ruling. Court is in recess until further notice. The parties aren't to leave the courthouse." He slammed down his gavel and left the bench.

Alexander went into the hall and left Celia at counsel table surprised and bewildered at this turn of events. He stood by himself staring out the window at the land that he doubted would ever be his again. After a few minutes he sensed rather than felt some one standing behind him. He turned to face Patricia, the woman he'd loved and risked everything for.

"You'll regret this for as long as you live," her voice trembled with hate. "And if I have my way that won't be for very long."

"Is that a threat to kill me?" Alexander replied.

"Take it any way you want." As she finished the courtroom door opened and Richard said "Patricia!" Like a well-trained retriever she didn't hesitate and immediately went to him.

As she walked away Alexander said, "You mean again don't you?" There was nothing to indicate she heard him.

CHAPTER 52

Alexander returned to the courtroom just as the bailiff was intoning the ritual of "all rise, court is in session" and Celeste took his chair. He wasted no time.

"I've listened to the portions of the tape that counsel proposes to introduce and am prepared to make my ruling." He shuffled some papers on the bench in front of him and then continued. "The portions of the tape that Mr. Courage obtained as a result of his burglary deal only with the case of Alfred Curran who is dead. It has nothing to do with the case of Mr. Alberto Falcon." Alexander began to protest. "Sit down counsel. You'll have your say in a minute.

"That being the case it is unnecessary to inquire into its authenticity, its completeness, or circumstances of its origin. As I have reminded counsel throughout this case this is a trial regarding the guilt or innocence of Alberto Falcon. It has nothing to do with the guilt or innocence of Alfred Curran who is dead. If Mr. Curran was on trial it might be necessary to make further inquiry."

"With respect to the case against Mr. Falcon. Counsel failed to make a motion for dismissal at the end of the district attorney's case. An omission that would be surprising if counsel were anyone other than Mr. Courage. Nevertheless I have taken it upon myself to act as if a motion had in fact been made. Here are my findings. The facts as proven are that Alfred Curran murdered Michael Chacon. His gun was the murder weapon, his fingerprints were the only ones on it, and the slug found at the scene was identified as having the same markings as the murder weapon, and finally that Alfred Curran then fled the country. I must reiterate these are facts that relate to Mr. Curran who has been declared dead and therefore issues surrounding these facts have no relevance in this case.

"However, the case against Mr. Falcon has not been established and I am entering an order of dismissal. It is being prepared and when it is ready Mr. Falcon will be free to go." He paused as if gathering his thoughts and then continued. Alexander had been sitting at counsel table writing on a yellow legal pad. Celeste addressed him.

"Mr. Courage I now want to turn my attention to your conduct. During the trial I've prepared a long list of your actions that I intend to submit to the Supreme Court grievance committee. In my opinion they are sufficient to get you disbarred. But what has happened here today goes further than mere unprofessional conduct. Your admission in open court that you burglarized the home of the district attorney amounts to the admission of a felony. Therefore, I'm recommending that the district attorney file criminal charges against you and that the sheriff take you into custody.

Alexander turned quickly to Celia. "Now's your chance to show your stuff," he said. "Tell Celeste that you represent me and that you want to call a witness. I think he'll let you just to pretend he's fair. If he says yes do what I've written here for you." As he finished the sheriff was tapping him on the shoulder and telling him to get up. When Alexander stood up the deputy placed handcuffs on him.

"Your honor," Celia was at the podium.

"What is it Miss Chavez?" Celeste asked.

"I represent Mr. Courage in this matter and I would like to call a witness whose testimony is important."

"How long will this take?"

"Not very long."

"All right, but be quick about it."

"Call John Robert McGee." A tall, slim, distinguished, gray-haired man entered the courtroom carrying a manila envelope.

He was sworn in and took the witness chair. Celia was flying blind with only Alexander's written questions to guide her. She wondered if this would help or only serve to get her in the same mess as Alexander.

"Please state your name,"

"John Robert McGee."

"How are you employed?"

"I recently retired from the Denver Police Department after 35 years."

"What did you do there?"

"At the time I retired I was in charge of the police forensics laboratory."

"Do you have a specialty?"

"Fingerprints."

"Please tell the court your credentials."

"I've attended all the courses offered by the FBI at Quantico, Virginia. I've been qualified as an expert in court over six hundred times. And I've published over sixty articles on the subject."

"Your honor, we offer Mr. McGee as an expert in fingerprints."

Celeste looked at Marquez, "any objection?"

"No." Marquez answered. Celia turned back to the witness.

"Mr. McGee before coming to court today did you do anything at the request of Mr. Courage?"

"I went to the Denver police laboratory and obtained a copy of the official fingerprints of one Alfred Curran whose birth date is 11-7-34."

"What did you do subsequently?"

"I came to El Centro and obtained the fingerprints of another individual, then I came to the courthouse and compared the fingerprints from Denver with those entered into evidence in this case."

"Do you have those with you?"

McGee opened the manila envelope and removed two cards and handed them to Celia who in turn asked the clerk to mark them as exhibits, and then she gave them to McGee.

"Please tell the court what exhibits G and E are."

"G is the copy of the FBI prints of Alfred Curran, E is the set of prints obtained here in El Centro."

"Have you come to any conclusion based on the inspection of these exhibits and the exhibit containing the prints taken from the gun?"

"Yes. The prints on the exhibit taken from the gun alleged to be the murder weapon in the case against Mr. Falcon are identical to the fingerprints of the individual whose prints I took when I arrived in El Centro."

"Are you telling the court that the prints on the murder weapon did not match those of Alfred Curran?"

"I am not saying that. In fact the prints on the gun were also identical to those of Mr. Curran. What I concluded beyond any degree of doubt is that Alfred Curran and Alexander Courage are the same person.

The courtroom erupted. Celeste banged his gavel again and again. "Order! Order! If I don't have silence I'll clear the courtroom." The noise trickled to nothingness.

"Well," he said to Alexander. "You certainly know how to surprise us all. I think all of this will take a lot of sorting out. Sheriff take his cuffs off. Mr. and Mrs. Marquez," he turned his attention to them. "I'm ordering both of you to return to your home under police escort and to remain there. I'm appointing a special prosecutor in this case and we'll go from there. Mr. Courage, or should I say Curran, you have a lot of explaining to do. Don't leave the jurisdiction. Bailiff, clear the courtroom of all spectators. Court's in recess until further notice." And he left the bench.

In spite of the protests the bailiff made everyone leave the courtroom. Alfred and Celia were left alone at the council table. Celia put here arm around the shoulders of an emotionally drained Alfred. "You're some kind of guy," she said. "What happens now?"

"As the court said, I have a lot of things to explain. Committing fraud on the Supreme Court and practicing law without a license to name a couple."

"Under the circumstances I don't think you'll be treated too harshly. Then what?"

"I made a promise that I would build the best clinic in the world here in the valley. And as soon as my divorce is final I want to go back to the cave with you."

She reached around him and took his face in her hand. Turning it towards her she said. "Why wait? Let's go now."

"What about being old fashioned, and only going with a husband?"

She looked lovingly into his eyes and said. "For you, *hombre*, I'm going to make an exception."

THE END

BVG